The Case of the Cursed Candy

Witch Haven Cozy Mystery - book 12

K.E. O'Connor

K.E. O'Connor Books

ISBN: 978-1-915378-39-2

Written by: K.E. O'Connor

To my wonderful reader, Sherry, for all her positive messages and excitement over this series.

Is she the real witch in the family?

Chapter 1

The throbbing pain from the deep puncture wounds on my arm made me want to pass out. I gripped the injury, and the spell I was using to prevent Fire Fang from blasting through the bedroom door wavered as the pain grabbed me like a witch's clawed hand.

"I'm sorry. I didn't mean to bite you," his growling voice rumbled through the door.

I looked at my injury again, and my stomach flipped. When he'd grabbed my arm and sunk his enormous fangs into me, that had been exactly what he'd meant to do. Was my hellhound sick? It was possible. He'd been behaving weirdly for weeks.

"Storm, come out and we can talk. I haven't been myself since you revealed that secret. I'm struggling with this. You can't abandon me now."

"I'm not abandoning you, but I don't want my arm chewed off." I attempted a healing spell, but my thoughts were so scattered, the magic wouldn't focus. Was this my fault?

It had been four weeks since I'd told Fire Fang the truth about the test results from the vet. Things had been strained between us ever since he found out he was a mortal trapped in a hellhound's body.

But this was a new scale of strained. This was a murderous strained.

"Talk to me. I want to make this right. You're my witch. I'm bonded to you. I made a mistake. It can happen to anyone."

"Mistakes rarely end with bloody holes in my arm," I said. "What were you thinking by biting me so hard?"

"I wasn't thinking. You said something that made me snap."

"I asked if you wanted a biscuit."

"You did? Huh! I heard something else. Are you sure that's what you said?"

I unclenched my fist. I was still holding the dog biscuit I'd been planning on giving him. It was sticky from my sweaty palm. "Positive. I asked you, and you lunged. And that wasn't the first time you've gotten aggressive. I know you're angry with me for not revealing the test results straight away, but I needed time to figure things out."

There was silence for a moment. I crept closer to the door and pressed my ear against it. Fire Fang was out there, huffing angry sounding breaths.

"I understand," he finally said. "But those test results are wrong. It's impossible for someone with no magic to be turned into a hellhound. If such a spell was used on a mortal, it would kill them. And I'm definitely alive."

Something I was well aware of since he'd trapped me in my bedroom. "You're right. We'll get a second opinion. If that turns out the same, we'll get another one. It was the reason I didn't say anything. I knew that result had to be wrong. You're a hellhound. You breathe smoke through your nose, you levitate, and you growl all the time. But... you've not been yourself, and we need to fix that if we're going to keep living together."

"I know. We will. I've been struggling to process this. I don't know what's happening to me. I... I feel different. Broken, maybe?"

"Do you blame me?"

"For the results?"

I leaned my head against the door. "I figured you thought it was my fault."

"Did you cast a spell to turn me into a hellhound?"

"Well, no. But I knew something about you, and I didn't reveal it. Maybe if I had..." I had no clue how to end that sentence. What good would it have done either of us? If by some weird turn of events, Fire Fang wasn't truly a hellhound, what could I do? I didn't know the spell that had been cast to transform him. I'd do more harm than good if I tinkered with whatever had enchanted him. Weather magic was my forte, not transforming mortals into magical beasts.

There was a soft thump against the door, suggesting Fire Fang had a paw against it. "Come out and let's discuss this. I won't bite you again."

"Do you promise?" My arm throbbed along with my racing heart. I'd never feared Fire Fang. For all his growling, snarling, and stomping around, I'd always trusted him. But now I was trapped in my bedroom, shaking from head to toe, sweat dripping off me, and my insides a jumble of terrified butterflies. For the first time in my life, I saw what other people did when they looked at Fire Fang. He was a killing machine, and he'd put his kill focus on me.

"You can trust me. I protect you. I don't hurt you. I had a tiny lapse, but I've got things under control." He sounded genuinely sorry.

I took several deep breaths, giving my heart a chance to calm down. I used my uninjured forearm to wipe sweat off my forehead. If I didn't get control of my nerves, it could trigger Fire Fang again. "I'm coming out. Back away from the door."

There was a shuffling outside. "You don't have to fear me, Storm."

The trouble was, I did, but I had to brave this out. Fire Fang was hurting, and he needed my support. I'd be there for him while we figured out what to do about this situation.

I inched open the door. Fire Fang sat ten feet away. His head was down and his tail curled underneath him.

He glanced at me and looked away. "You see. I'm safe."

I pulled open the door and stepped into the corridor.

Fire Fang lunged. His eyes blazed red, his claws reaching for me, and his teeth exposed. He was aiming for my throat.

I staggered back, my hand raised to swipe down a spell, but then he was gone.

There was a howl and a blast of brilliant, multicolored magic. I dashed to the lounge door to see Binky on Fire Fang's head. Her teeth were dug into one ear, and her claws clamped around his muzzle. Her magic blazed out, covering Fire Fang as he roared and bucked to shake her loose.

She was an awesome little cat but no match for Fire Fang's ferocity.

I gritted my teeth, focused my magical energy into the palm of my hand, and blasted it into Fire Fang.

Binky shot off him just as he tipped back his head and howled. The noise reverberated down my spine, sending a shudder to the soles of my feet. Fire Fang fought my magic with every pound of muscle. This hellhound wasn't going down easily.

I kept blasting him with energy, and a second later, Binky joined in. She stood beside me, leaning against my leg as her sparkles of magic slammed into him, too.

He let out another unearthly howl before racing to the closed apartment door and smashing through it, leaving a gaping, hellhound sized hole behind.

I grabbed Binky and settled her on my shoulder. I ran to the window to see Fire Fang outside. He was staggering around and shaking his head, working off the magic blast he'd received.

Quickly, I cast a protective ward around my apartment to prevent him from getting back in. My magic wavered but eventually held. That would protect us for now, but I needed a permanent solution to the Fire Fang problem.

I rested my hot forehead against the glass as I watched him. He paced back and forth before slinking off. But I knew he'd be back. Fire Fang had unfinished business with me, and it didn't involve friendly chats while I rubbed his belly and talked about the day. He hated me, and I didn't know how to fix it.

My arm throbbed, and I grimaced. It was a reminder I had a more immediate problem to deal with. I stepped back from the window and tried another healing spell on the bite wounds. My magic was still so shaky it refused to hold.

Binky nudged me with her head. She looked at my arm and nodded at it.

"You think you could do better?" I said. "My magic is all over the place."

Binky clambered down my back and walked to the couch. She hopped up and gave a pointed look at the empty seat beside her.

I staggered over and gratefully flopped into it. I held out my arm for her to inspect.

She sniffed it several times, her small black nose wrinkling as if she smelled something bad. She gently brushed her rough tongue over each of the puncture wounds.

I bit my lip to stop from complaining as she continued to work on the injuries, but her healing magic slowly eased the throb. I'd only recently discovered Binky's healing powers, but I couldn't have been more grateful for them than I was now.

She licked my arm for five minutes before the pain vanished and the wounds closed.

I let out a relieved sigh and gently scratched Binky's head as she nestled beside me. "Thanks. I owe you a huge meaty treat for that."

She rubbed her face against my leg and gently purred.

"What shall we do about Fire Fang?" Ever since I'd revealed his mortal beginnings to him, he'd been meaner, sharper, and more likely to hurt someone than give them a second chance. And I wasn't the only one Fire Fang had issues with. He'd scared Odessa when he'd seen her in Witch Haven a week ago.

They'd always gotten on well, but he'd rushed over and knocked her off her feet. It had taken two of her scarecrows to chase him off. When I'd questioned him about it, Fire Fang simply said he thought she was someone else and had given him a funny look. But that made no sense. Fire Fang adored Odessa. He'd never get her muddled up with somebody else. And she never gave anyone funny looks. Her main purpose in life was to ensure other people were happy.

I stared at the window. "We have to get him back to his old self before he figures out a way around my magic. I can't keep that ward up forever, and we can't hide in this apartment for much longer." I absently stroked Binky's head as I mulled over the problem that had been haunting me for a month.

Binky rested her paws on my knee in a show of solidarity.

"He blames me for what happened to him. Maybe I was wrong to hide the results for so long, but I thought I'd figure out a way to get around it. I'd either find out the test was faulty or learn what magic was holding him. Then he'd have the option to reverse it and become a mortal again or stay as a hellhound." I tipped my head back until it hit the couch. "That was wishful thinking. I've never heard of anyone without magic being transformed like he was. All the books I've looked in and the online research has come up with nothing."

Binky hopped off my lap. She grabbed a piece of paper and brought it to the couch. Then she returned with a pen and climbed back up. She'd been doing this a lot lately, drawing squiggles and lines. Sometimes, she spent hours doing it and would get annoyed when I didn't understand her paw scrawls.

"It's an odd time to do one of your drawings," I said. "I need your brainpower to figure out what to do about Fire Fang, not another wonky flower or snake shape."

She ignored me, the pen stuck between her teeth and her head tilted at an angle as she drew something. She tried several times, her tail twitching faster and faster as she failed to create anything useful. After five minutes, she spat out the pen and flattened her ears.

I looked at the drawing, but it was just lines and circles. If it kept her happy, there was no harm in doing it. "I should sign you up for art class if you're serious about this."

She hissed softly and batted my leg with her paw. The claws were slightly out.

"Don't you get angry with me, too." I picked up my phone and sent a group message to my so-called friends, Odessa Grimsbane, Indigo Ash, and Luna Brimstone.

I have a problem with Fire Fang. He's lost control. Any ideas what I can do?

I sent it and waited a few minutes. The message went through, but if anyone read it, it was ignored. Just like the last thirty I'd sent. It had been this way since my three oldest friends had snubbed me.

At first, I'd given them time to cool off. Then I'd admitted to them I'd been a selfish jerk. I'd put my work before them, repeatedly turned down their offers of help, and pretended they couldn't be useful to me.

But those three witches were the most powerful magic users in Witch Haven, and I hadn't done it because I didn't believe in them. It was because I didn't want them getting hurt. My job as a private investigator sent me into shady situations. The last thing I wanted to do was put anyone I cared about at risk. But by doing that, I'd shoved them away too many times. Now, they were getting payback.

And I wasn't happy about it. Fine, give me the silent treatment for a couple of weeks, but it was time they grew up. We didn't exclude someone from the group because they didn't behave perfectly. None of them were perfect. Indigo had big issues. She was sharp, scary, and had been a dark magic enchanted, murderous teenager. Did I hold that against her?

And what about Odessa and those terrifying scarecrows she insists on churning out like pumpkin cream popsicles on a hot day? Those things were living nightmares, but did I call her out over them? Did I tell her to make them less powerful for fear they'll take over the magic community and destroy us? No, I kept quiet. Because she was my friend, and I trusted her to do the right thing.

And don't get me started on Luna. She was lousy with baking magic and had a hidden farmhouse containing chained magic users, which she drained so she could juice her power. Perfect? I think not.

None of us were flawless witches. So why was I excluded for doing my job well and keeping my friends safe? It was pathetic, and I was done with being worried. Now, I was angry. They used to pester to help, and the one time I needed it, they turned their backs.

We needed to have this out once and for all.

I sent another message.

Meet me at Albert's bakery in one hour. Payback is over. Either we're friends, or we're not, but you need to tell me face to face.

I let out a sigh as I set down my phone. This meeting would end in one of two ways. Either they wouldn't show up, which would confirm I no longer had friends in Witch Haven, or we'd work through this together as real friends should.

I looked at Binky, who was still glaring at the piece of paper she'd scrawled on. "Now, all we need to do is figure out how to leave this apartment without Fire Fang eating me."

Chapter 2

After checking outside for the tenth time, I could still see Fire Fang's tail poking out from behind a tree. He'd returned to lurking outside the apartment shortly after Binky and I had chased him out. It was the tree he'd been sleeping under ever since I told him about the test results.

"Are you sure you want to do this, Binky?" I turned to the cat, who was sitting on the windowsill, also watching Fire Fang.

She gave a single nod and a twitch of her tail.

"I could use a translocation spell to get to the bakery."

Binky shook her head. Even though she couldn't talk, she understood everything I said. And when I'd discussed the options of how to get out of the apartment and survive, we'd settled on her distracting Fire Fang while I crept out.

I could use a translocation spell, but every magic user left a signature trail. If Fire Fang sniffed me out, his nose would lead him to Fandango's bakery. And I didn't want him in contact with anyone else. He was too dangerous.

So Binky stepped up. She'd dashed around the apartment blasting out magic, dodging and weaving and hiding behind things to show me what she wanted to do. And, although I'd protested, I knew this little cat was powerful and fast.

When I'd first gotten to know her, she'd eluded me multiple times as I'd attempted to capture her and take her to a sanctuary. And the more I got to know her, the stronger I realized she was. Not only did Binky have healing magic, but she could tackle a hellhound head on and survive. This cat was awesome.

"If we're doing this, we need to go now. I'll lower the ward, and we'll sneak out together. You blast your magic and get Fire Fang to chase you. But if it gets too dangerous, back off. I don't want you getting hurt while keeping me safe."

She gave a nonchalant cat shrug, hopped off the windowsill, and walked to the door with the hellhound-made hole in it. When I got a moment, I'd have to get that fixed.

I checked I had my keys, wallet, and phone, and after a last look out the window, I lowered the magic ward. I dashed down the stairs with Binky, and we stopped by the exit. It was now or never.

I inched open the door so Binky could get out. She slipped through and crept closer to the tree on her belly.

I gripped my tongue between my teeth to stop from calling her back. She was so tiny compared to Fire Fang, but I'd underestimated this cat before, and she was more than capable.

Her multicolored sparkling magic shot out and slammed into Fire Fang. He leaped in the air, turned, and snarled at her.

Binky raced off, and Fire Fang shot after her, moving so fast, his legs were a blur.

Once they were far enough away, I hurried out and eased the door closed. I jogged in the opposite direction, looking over my shoulder every couple of seconds to make sure Binky was doing okay.

My last glance had my heart lodged in my throat. My eyes widened, and I stumbled over my feet. Fire Fang had changed direction and was heading toward me like a heat seeking magical missile.

I sped up and turned down the first alleyway I got to. If this fight was going down, I didn't need anyone else involved. I faced the entrance to the alleyway and backed away, magic primed on my fingers.

Fire Fang appeared, his head lowered and his fangs exposed.

Oh, boy. He was terrifying. "I guess you don't want to talk anymore, do you?"

He growled so loudly the ground shook. "I've always known there was something wrong with you, witch."

"I definitely know there's something wrong with you. Is it the magic keeping you in hellhound form that's malfunctioned? Could that be why you've turned so mean?"

"My magic is fine." He opened his mouth and blasted a jet of flames.

I ducked and thrust out a shield spell, the heat from Fire Fang's magic blasting around me.

"You tried to make me weak. You made me your pet. It's an embarrassment." Fire Fang slunk toward me, his claws scraping the ground.

"You chose to stay with me. I offered you a way out multiple times, but you never took it. You bonded to me. I was always looking for a new place for you, but you never wanted to leave. When I found out what you were—"

"Lies! I'm not a mortal. Look at me. Have you ever seen a non-magic user like this? It's not possible. You hate to admit when you've made a mistake, but you made a big one by messing with me. Was it a trick? You thought you'd weaken me and make me pliable by getting me to believe my magic wasn't real? Did you really think that would work?" Fire Fang kept stalking toward me.

I kept backing away. This alleyway was a dead end, but I wasn't planning on running from this fight. Not this time. I had to deal with Fire Fang. I didn't want to do it, but I had to take him down.

"I've only ever wanted to help you. I was as shocked as you when I discovered those results. I kept quiet because I didn't have a solution." I kept drawing him farther from the center of the village. No one else needed to be involved in this showdown.

"You kept quiet, so you could use the information against me. Typical, deceitful witch."

"Not deceitful. I'm your friend."

"I don't need goblin nobble friends like you," he growled out.

I spotted movement behind him. Binky was blocking the alleyway. I didn't draw attention to her, but she was building up to something. Her fur was bristled and her eyes glowing.

"Fire Fang, we can find a way around this. It doesn't have to be this way," I said.

"It is this way. Now, you're going to pay." He flew toward me.

I blasted the strongest restraining spell I could manage. It slammed into Fire Fang while he was in the air and wrapped around his legs. Just as my spell took hold, Binky also blasted him with magic. It rained over his body in tiny multicolored sparkles, seeming to burrow into his fur and latch onto him, making his skin glow.

Fire Fang howled and dropped to the ground, landing on a pile of trash bags. He writhed as he fought our magic, but whatever power Binky had, it complemented mine perfectly. Her magic enhanced my energy, and the restraining spell held. Fire Fang was going nowhere.

I moved toward him, magic still flickering on my fingers. "I'm sorry we had to do that, but there was no other way. You're out of control and a danger not only to me, but to anyone you meet." I blasted him with another spell and knocked him out.

Binky dashed over and sniffed Fire Fang.

I crouched and petted her as I checked him over. The magic holding him was strong. "Good work. Let's get him to my office. At least if he's in there, he can't hurt anyone."

He was too heavy to carry, so I cast another spell, and Fire Fang floated off the ground. I pushed him swiftly back to the office, unlocked the door, and shoved him inside. I lowered him to the ground then covered him with a blanket.

My heart hurt because of what I'd had to do to him, but until I figured out how to fix this problem between us, he'd have to stay this way. The restraining magic would prevent him from escaping, and he wouldn't be able to injure me or anyone else.

Binky had followed me into the office and sat quietly beside Fire Fang. She looked as sad as I felt. Binky and Fire Fang were friends, so this must be tough on her, too.

"Stay here. Watch over him. He shouldn't wake, but if he does, he won't be happy. Make sure not to get in his way if the worst happens," I said.

She nodded and settled beside Fire Fang. Usually, she'd snuggle against him, but even Binky was wary of Fire Fang's changes.

I stood over him for a moment then shook my head. I needed to talk options with someone. I pulled out my phone and called the vet, Doctor Hooper. She'd made the diagnosis about Fire Fang being more than he seemed. Or was that less than he seemed?

"Harvest Hill veterinary center. How may I help you?"

"I need to speak with Doctor Hooper. It's about a patient of hers. I'm worried about him."

"Doctor Hooper is out of the office today. I can put you through to her voicemail, or you can speak with another vet if it's an emergency."

"Do you have anyone who specializes in hellhounds?"

"Um... no. That would be Doctor Hooper."

"This is important. Is there any way I can reach her?"

"No. She's out all day, and she doesn't have her phone on her."

"Okay. Put me through to her voicemail." I hoped I hadn't sounded too sharp, but my anxiety was getting the better of me. I waited to be connected and listened to the recorded message. "Doctor

Hooper, this is Storm Winter. I need to talk to you about Fire Fang's test results. The last few weeks, he's not been himself. His mood is unstable, and I'm worried he could injure someone. I need to know if there's any way we can make him mortal again. If you have any suggestions, I'm open to them. Please, anything you've got that'll help him, I need it."

I didn't care I sounded desperate as I ended the message. I was. My gut told me something was horribly wrong with my hellhound, and I had to make it right. I couldn't lose him.

After giving Binky a pet on the head, I locked the office and headed to Fandango's. Maybe if I could get my friends to talk to me, they'd help, too. They knew all different magic. One of them could have come across a spell that would help or heard of a mortal who'd been turned into a magical creature and had the spell reversed. I'd try anything to get Fire Fang back.

When I got to the bakery, I was surprised to find it empty. That never happened. Fandango's was one of the most popular bakeries in a hundred miles, thanks to the desserts Albert Black conjured. He was a genius in the kitchen. The things he could do with a piping bag should be illegal. And the bakery had just had a grand reopening after a fire had decimated it. Albert had been running promotions all week, discounting desserts and offering deals to get his customers back.

But other than Albert standing behind the counter with a glum look on his face, there was no one inside.

I raised a hand as I walked in. "Hey. I figured I'd have to queue to get in."

He grunted. "Not likely. It's been like this for a while."

"Why? Your reopening was popular. I came to that."

"Only for half an hour." He sighed and prodded a tray of pink iced buns. "I'm wasting my time. No one wants cake anymore."

"They do! Everyone loves your cakes. It must be a slow day." I discreetly checked the tables at the back. Luna, Indigo, and Odessa were nowhere to be seen.

"More like a slow month. I don't understand it. Well, I do. I have a rival. A rival I have no idea how to beat."

"Another bakery has opened in Witch Haven?" It was the first I'd heard about it.

"No. It's that new candy store. It's stealing my customers. Ever since that place opened, I've seen a drop off in sales. It was a trickle at first, but now, barely anyone comes in. I have a few faithful regulars, and people who don't like sweet things, but most have swapped their allegiance."

"I'd forgotten about the new store. The novelty will soon wear off. People will come back, and when they do, make sure they buy double their usual order to make up for abandoning you." The candy store had opened a month ago, and I'd seen people fighting to get their hands on the treats. The chocolate they were selling must be amazing.

Albert grabbed something from behind the counter and stuffed it into his mouth. "Traitors, the lot of them. I should ban them. Then if they want to come back, they can't. That'll teach them a lesson. Hateful, shallow idiots."

I took a step back, startled by Albert's words. He was the sweetest guy I knew, and I'd never heard him say a bad word about anyone. "You don't mean that."

He jabbed a finger at the door. "I do. They're not welcome. If they'd rather stuff their faces with cheap confectionery than sample the unique desserts I create, they aren't worthy of stepping through the door. I'd rather go bankrupt than sell to those cretins." He grabbed more food and ate it.

Albert's mood was almost as bad as Fire Fang's. "What have you got behind there? One of your new creations? If you're looking for someone to taste test, I'd be happy to help."

He glared down at the counter. "Oh, no. I got a bag of peppermint snaps from the candy store. I can't stop eating them, even though I hate myself for doing so."

I arched an eyebrow. "You've been shopping at the new store, too?"

"To see what competition I'm up against. The awful woman who manages the place, Sherry something or other, was handing out free samples. I tried some snaps, and suddenly, I was buying an enormous bag. She has an excellent sales patter. I didn't even know what I was doing until I'd handed over my money and left." He popped more peppermint snaps into his mouth and chomped angrily.

Albert kept grumbling to himself and shooting angry looks out the window, while I stood there, not knowing what to say. Albert was Mr. Sunshine, not Mr. Sullen, so I didn't know how to handle him.

After a couple of awkward minutes of silence, I shuffled closer to the counter and tried to see through to the back of the store, but the door was closed.

"Is Luna here yet? I'm meeting her and the others soon." Hopefully, providing they didn't stand me up.

"She's gone somewhere with Cole. I don't know what that girl gets up to anymore. She's barely here and can't be bothered with me now she has that young man. Selfish creature."

"Albert! Luna isn't selfish. And she's getting married to Cole. They have a ton of planning to do."

"She barely speaks to me. Too busy, I suppose."

I shrugged. Maybe she was. Luna was marrying into a powerful werewolf family, managing A-Type parents, and running an animal sanctuary. "I'll have a black coffee while I'm waiting."

Albert ate more peppermint snaps then made my coffee.

I paid and settled in a seat facing the window, so I could see when the others arrived. My hands wouldn't settle, and my feet jiggled. I needed to make things right with my friends. We'd never gone this long without talking. And for once, I had a lot to tell them. It wasn't something I easily admitted, but I couldn't do this alone. My world felt like it was falling apart.

I repeatedly checked my phone, but no messages came in.

Ten minutes went by, then twenty. My coffee remained untouched. I was too nervous to stomach anything. While I waited, people kept hurrying by the bakery, and they were all going in the same direction.

I gave it another ten minutes then gritted out a frustrated sigh. They weren't showing up. I scowled at my phone. Was it broken? Maybe they'd sent me messages to say they couldn't make it, and I hadn't received them.

Who was I kidding? My phone was fine. Other people had sent me messages this morning. My grudge holding, childish friends just didn't want to be here. Their loss.

My scowl deepened. Honestly, I was surprised it had taken them this long to ditch me. I'd always been waiting for the day when they realized I was a trashy person and someone not to be relied on. But it stung like a possessed demon hornet that they'd done it this way. At least have the courage to tell me to my face.

I returned my mug to the counter. "Albert, where are all those people going? I've been watching them since I got here."

"One guess."

"Um... no clue. Is there some party I've not been invited to?"

He rolled his eyes. "The candy store, you idiot!"

"Really? Are they having a sale?"

"They don't need to discount what they sell. All people want is that dumb candy." He tossed his empty candy bag in the trash. "I need to re-stock."

"Maybe I should go look. What am I missing?"

He glowered at me. "You're a traitor, too. Everyone betrays me."

"Hey! I'm not. I'm just curious."

Albert grumbled some more. "Get me more peppermint snaps when you're there."

"If they have any in stock, I'll do that." I left the store and followed the crowd heading to the candy store.

I needed something to sweeten my mood after being ditched by my friends.

Whatever this new store was selling, it had better heal bitten arms and bruised hearts, or I wasn't buying.

Chapter 3

I followed a sizeable crowd to the candy store. There was a queue out the door that snaked halfway along the street. This candy must be incredible to make people wait for so long.

Several people hurried past me, talking about the store and what delivery would have arrived overnight.

People got so weird about dessert. I indulged now and again but had the least sweet tooth of all my friends. Of course, that was when I had friends.

"Hey! You pushed in front of me. Go to the back of the line and wait your turn like everyone else." A large guy wearing a padded checked jacket shoved a small gray-haired lady in front of him.

The woman staggered forward and righted herself. She turned slowly, adjusted her purse over her arm, and slammed a spell into the man's chest, sending him flying.

He hit the dirt and rolled several times, coming to a stop close to my feet. Before I could let him know it was never okay to shove old people, he'd jumped up and raced toward the lady, magic shimmering on his fingers.

She retaliated before he fired his spell. Sparks of red magic flew toward him.

He ducked, did a front roll, and grabbed the old woman around the knees, trying to knock her off her feet. But she was stronger than she looked. She wriggled one leg free and was about to kick him with a sensible brown court shoe, when I grabbed her shoulder.

"You don't want to do that. The Magic Council office is opposite this store, and if you're seen fighting, you'll be arrested for assault."

She glared at me, her watery blue eyes sparking with magic. "He started it. He said I pushed in front of him. Where are his manners? Women and children first."

"That only applies on sinking ships, not candy store queues," I said.

"She did push in," the man gasped out, one hand on his chest where she'd spell-slammed him. "She thought she'd sneak in and I wouldn't notice. I've been waiting half an hour to get into this store. I need my violet creams."

"Now you'll have to wait a bit longer," the lady said. "I'll have you arrested for attacking a defenseless old woman."

I arched my eyebrows at her. "Are you that defenseless? The spell you whacked him with was a zinger. You could have hurt him."

A small smile lifted her lips. "It's a shame he wasn't injured. More candy for me. Besides, he doesn't need more to eat. Look at the size of him."

"It's all muscle under this shirt." The guy clambered to his feet. "And you'll be the one who gets arrested."

"No one's getting arrested, and no one should fat shame anyone else." My glare settled on the woman. "Apologize for your behavior, both of you, and then wait your turn to get in. No one needs to die to get to the caramel bon bons."

"This isn't my fault. Why should I apologize?" the guy said.

"Because there are a hundred people watching to see if you'll be a dirtbag and keep attacking an old woman. Do the decent thing."

He glowered at me and then at the lady. "Fine. Whatever. Sorry. Push in front, you mean old bag."

"I didn't push in. I simply stepped out of the line for a few minutes."

"Is that your apology?" The woman got a stern look from me.

She frowned right back. "I'm his elder."

"But clearly not his better," I muttered. "No more arguing. It's just candy. Wait like everyone else for your sugar hit and tooth decay."

The man grumbled to himself as he brushed down his clothing. "It's not just candy. It's amazing candy."

"If it's so amazing, you won't mind waiting an extra few minutes. Anticipation is everything," I said.

The little old lady looked smug, suggesting she believed she'd won this fight.

"And how about, by way of a real apology, you buy this guy whatever he likes once you're inside?" I said to her.

Her smugness faded, but I continued to glare at her until she nodded. "I'll buy him one small bag. But that's not admitting this was my fault. A few years ago, people would happily let a doddering old lady in first."

I lifted a hand to stop the argument from starting again. "You're right. Modern life sucks. Enjoy the rest of your day." I stepped away from the queue but kept an eye on those two in case they continued their argument.

The queue moved slowly, few people coming out of the store to let others in. I didn't want to wait to get in, since I didn't have the greatest amount of patience.

My gaze ran over the store's cream and pink exterior. From what I could see through the window, there were shelves full of different candy. Hard-boiled sweets, chocolate, gold dusted truffles. Everything a sugar addict would love. And although it looked tasty, it didn't explain the huge queue. Maybe they were slow at serving.

"Storm! I'm glad I've seen you."

I turned at the sound of Olympus Duke's voice. He was hurrying toward me from his office, his forehead wrinkled and the bags under his eyes showing he hadn't slept well.

"What do you need?" I said in the way of a greeting.

That earned me a brief smile. "Nothing. I haven't seen you around lately. Is everything okay?"

His comment suggested Indigo hadn't spoken to him about our disagreement, and they shared everything, so he should know there was a problem between us. "I'm good. How about you? You look like you've been burning the midnight mugwort."

He huffed out a breath. "Busy. The new Head of the Magic Council, Jonas Notely, is being formally accepted at an inauguration ceremony in seven days' time. Everyone is insisting it goes off without a hitch. All the important members of the Magic Council will be there, and they've put me in charge of the security."

"Should I say congratulations? Is that a promotion?"

"Hardly. It's more like an obligation. I have to do that and keep up with the day job."

"Why the pomp and ceremony over another stuffed shirt rule follower taking up this post?"

Olympus's sharp look suggested he wasn't impressed with that description. "Jonas will have influence over every area of the Magic Council. It's not a ceremonial role. And from the rumors going around, he plans to shake things up. He'll be looking at every department across the organization. He wants to cut waste and revolutionize things. Those pledges got him the job."

"Isn't that what everyone who takes over the Magic Council says they'll do? I've yet to see any significant change."

Olympus rubbed his hands together. "Maybe not. But if things go wrong during the ceremony, it'll be on my head, and I don't want this guy's attention on my department. I'm glad there's been no crime to deal with recently in Witch Haven. It means I can give the ceremony my full attention."

"No crime?" I pointed a thumb over my shoulder. "I guess you missed the fight outside the candy store?"

"Oh, that. I heard a disturbance, but it was nothing. This new store has been causing excitement ever since it opened."

"Excitement! I had to stop two magic users from coming to blows. That little old lady over there has power. I don't know either of them, though. They must have traveled to Witch Haven just to buy candy. Seems extreme."

"It's great, isn't it? The store has been a boost to the village. We're getting people coming from over fifty miles away after hearing about the place."

"So far? It's really that good?"

"I haven't tried any yet. But everyone says it's amazing. Indigo's been going there every day. Haven't you been going with her? You two normally do everything together."

I stuffed my hands in my pockets, my heart giving an unhappy thud. "I've been busy, too. We haven't caught up recently."

"How about we go in now? I've got five minutes to spare."

"Sure. If we can get through the crowd. That guy involved in the fight said he'd been waiting half an hour, and I'm not waiting that long. I don't love shopping at the best of times, and this feels like the worst of times at the moment."

"The worst of times, huh? Let's see if I can change that." Olympus grinned and flashed his Magic Council credentials. "I've got us a shortcut. Follow me." He headed to the front of the line.

I tagged along behind him, not sure what he was planning.

"Make way. This is official Magic Council business." He flashed his badge, and after much muttering, people moved aside to let him in.

I couldn't help but grin as I heard the less than complimentary comments shooting his way as he used his influence to queue jump. I'd have been saying exactly the same thing if I hadn't been with him.

Once we were through the worst of the crowd, my nostrils flared at the overpowering smell of warm sugar and chocolate. The inside of the store was various shades of pink, brown, and yellow, like I'd just stepped inside a Neapolitan ice cream. There were floor to ceiling shelves loaded with candy, and a large, long, glass-fronted cabinet with even more treats on display by the cash register.

The place was crowded, with customers bustling around, full baskets over their arms. There were small tables set out, covered in trays of free samples of candy. And that candy was being grabbed up rapidly.

"So, this is what all the fuss is about." Olympus rocked back on his heels as he took in the scene. "It's something else."

"Yeah, like Willy Wonka." I wrinkled my nose, not impressed by the crowds, the noise, or the overpowering sweet smell. It was all giving me a headache.

"What would you like?" Olympus said. "On me."

I wasn't sure I wanted anything. I looked around but failed to be inspired. "What are you having?"

"I'm tempted to say one of everything. But I love pear drops and truffles."

"Then you've come to the right place." An apple-shaped woman in her early fifties with bright blonde hair and glossy pink lips appeared in front of us. "I'm Sherry Brown. Store owner extraordinaire. Welcome to my little paradise. Whatever your sweet need is, I'm here to meet it. And I can see you're someone important, so I'll take extra special care of you." She batted her long eyelashes at Olympus. Her pale blue eyes were framed by creamy, sparkling blue eyeshadow.

"It's nice to meet you, Sherry. I'm Olympus Duke. I run the local branch of the Magic Council in Witch Haven. My office is just over the road, and I've been watching all the customers come and go."

"Welcome, Olympus. I'm so glad you could visit. And yes, it has been busy since I opened." She turned to me and smiled.

"Storm Winter. I live around here." I got the same big smile and fluttering eyelashes as Olympus.

"You're both welcome. Take your time looking around and try as many free samples as you like. It's the best way to discover your new favorite treat."

"Thanks. We'll do that," Olympus said.

"Any questions, just call for me. If I'm not buried under chocolate, I'll be happy to help."

"You're working here on your own?" I said. That explained the huge queue.

"Yes. I love to help every customer. And there are self-service tills, so people can bag their own candy, weigh it, and make their purchase. Of course, for the extra special treats, I provide the personal touch." She turned as she heard her name called. "If you'll excuse me." Sherry bustled away, the petticoat of her pink and yellow dress scratching together as she moved.

"I've just spotted Indigo," Olympus said, a smile on his face. "Sneaky minx. She didn't tell me she was visiting again today. She can't keep away from the place."

I peered through the crowd and discovered not only Indigo but also Odessa and Luna. They had full baskets of candy and were chewing on free samples, expressions of rapt delight on their faces.

They'd come here, rather than meet me and figure out what was going on. At least I knew where their loyalties lay. It wasn't with me. It was with sugar-filled treats.

I hunched forward, the smell of candy making me queasy. "I'm done. I've seen enough."

"But you haven't tried anything. At least have some samples." Olympus wandered to a busy samples table.

All I wanted was to get out. I backed away a few steps to the door and trod on someone's foot.

"Watch where you're going," a woman snapped. "And keep away from the sherbet lemons. They're running low and I want them."

I raised a hand and stepped to one side. She could have all the sherbet lemons she wanted. I looked over to see Olympus filling his pockets with free candy.

My gaze went back to my friends. My heart was heavy and my stomach tight as I turned away. They were done with me, and I had to accept that and move on. I didn't want to, but if they wouldn't even talk to me, there was no way we could fix this situation. It was time to accept that I'd lost my friends for good.

A skinny man with a bright red face staggered into me. I was about to shove him away, but he wheezed out a breath, his hand going to his throat.

I caught hold of his shoulder. "Are you okay?"

He wheezed again as he sank to his knees.

"He's choking," a man standing next to me said. He popped a chocolate into his mouth, not looking at all concerned.

The guy on his knees kept wheezing and gasping.

I raced behind him and thumped him on the back. I did it several times, but whatever was lodged in his throat wouldn't move.

Several other people had stopped shopping and were watching with wide eyes, but none of them offered to help.

"Does anyone know the Heimlich maneuver?" I yelled.

No one stepped forward.

Sherry rushed over and joined me. "What's with all the shouting?"

"This man is choking. Probably on one of your candies."

Her mouth formed an O of surprise. She thumped the guy on the back several times.

I wasn't sure how to do it, but I had to attempt the Heimlich maneuver. The man's face was purple, and he was barely conscious. I heaved and pressed, taking the guy off his feet as I lifted and squeezed him. A huge globule of gooey orange candy shot out of his mouth and dropped onto the floor.

The watching crowd had grown, most of them still eating, as I lowered the man to the floor.

"Storm, what's happening? I heard you yelling." Olympus appeared, his pockets bulging with candy.

I didn't answer as I checked the guy's pulse. There was nothing there. I checked again. "Has anyone here got strong healing magic? If we're quick, we can still save him."

No one offered their magic. Most of them kept eating.

I growled out my frustration. Someone must be able to help, so why weren't they stepping up? Healing magic wasn't my specialty, but I tried several spells anyway. It had no effect. The candy was gone, so he should be able to breathe. But everything I tried failed to get him moving.

Olympus kneeled next to me and also tried a few healing spells, but we were too late. The man was dead.

Chapter 4

I sat back on my heels, defeat washing over me. "That shouldn't have happened. I dislodged the candy. He should have been able to breathe."

"Is there more stuck in his airways?" Olympus checked the man's mouth, tilting his head back. "I can't see anything."

"Bring him back to life," Sherry squeaked. "Why isn't he waking up?"

I shook my head, still staring at the dead guy. "I've got no clue."

"Try more magic. He can't die in my store." Sherry peered at the man, her hands trembling as she reached for him. "Are you sure he's not breathing?"

"He's dead," Olympus said. "Magic can't save him."

"Try! A resurrection spell would work, wouldn't it?" Sherry kept touching the dead man's cheek.

"Can you do that kind of magic?" I arched a brow at her. It took a powerful magic user to resurrect the dead safely.

"No! Candy is my specialty. But... what about you?"

"Even if I could, we're too late to bring him back whole. If he's resurrected incorrectly, you'll end up with a zombie in your store or a ghoul attached to you. Would you rather that than a dead body? At least a body can be taken away."

Her hands went to her mouth, and a muffled sob came out. "This can't be happening. People won't come here if they know someone died after eating my candies. What should we do?"

I glanced at Olympus. "Wait for backup?"

He nodded but kept checking the body. Maybe he was hoping to see signs of life, but this guy was toast.

Sherry shook her head, her blonde curls flying. "Shouldn't we take him outside? We could say he died out there. People don't need to know it happened in here."

"Nope." I studied the candy munching crowd, who looked more like they were enjoying a movie than staring at someone who'd dropped dead in front of them. "Even if we moved the body, which we won't be doing, it's too late. Witch Haven is gossip central. News of what happened will be all over the place within the hour."

Another sob came out of Sherry, and a tear trickled down her cheek. "He was such a lovely man. And an excellent customer. Why did this have to happen? It's so unfair."

"I expect the dead guy thinks so, too." I looked up at her. "You sound like you knew him."

"Well, I suppose I did. I always pay attention to my customers."

"How about you pay attention to the living ones for now? We need to shut this place while we figure out what happened to him," I said.

"You want me to close the candy store?" Sherry shook her head. "I can't. There are customers waiting outside to be served. They'll be so upset."

"They'll understand when they know what happened. Your candy isn't that addictive." I looked at Olympus for support, irritated he wasn't stepping into the role he was paid to do.

He shook himself and nodded, pulling his gaze from the body. "Storm is right. We need to close the store and deal with this gentleman. It won't be for long. I'll go to my office and put in a call. A team will be here shortly."

"Oh, I suppose you're right. But this is disappointing." Sherry's bottom lip wobbled.

She wasn't disappointed about the corpse, but losing out on the money being spent in her store.

"Everybody out," I said. "The store's shut."

Nobody moved. More candy got eaten.

Even my fiercest glare didn't get people moving, although several of them shuffled back. "Sherry, do me a favor. Take your free samples outside. It'll get rid of the corpse gawpers."

"Oh! Of course. Anything I can do to help. So long as this is handled quickly." After staring at the body for a few more seconds, she smoothed down her ruffled dress and gathered trays of samples. "Everyone follow me. We're going outside, and I'll tell you about the new pecan caramel truffles coming in next week's delivery."

That roused people to action. Like possessed mice after the pied piper, they followed the free sample trays, their eyes bright and noses twitching. It only took a few minutes until the store was empty, other than me, Olympus, and the corpse.

Olympus scowled at the body as if he had a personal grudge against it. "This is the last thing I need. A body means paperwork and questions. I don't have the time to deal with this."

The guy was all heart. "Make the time. I'm sure your new boss will understand if you're dealing with this death, rather than making sure the red carpet he'll walk along is crease free."

"Don't be so sure about that." Olympus ran a hand through his hair. "I don't recognize this guy. He's not from around here."

"Mind if I check for ID?"

"Go ahead."

I checked the dead man's pockets and discovered a wallet. His ID showed his license name was Galaan Foilmeister.

"Definitely not a local," I said. "I wonder if he came with anyone. No one seemed concerned when he died."

"I'll check outside with the crowd, see if anyone knew him," Olympus said.

"Once you've done that, send Sherry back in. I got the impression she knew Galaan as more than just a customer."

Olympus hurried out of the store. He seemed stunned by what was going on, which was weird, since this wasn't his first corpse.

I inhaled deeply and let the breath out slowly. My gaze ran over the body. Galaan was in his late forties, with receding hair. He was skinny, apart from a small pot belly, and dressed in practical clothing rather than the latest fashion. He'd dropped a basket of candy before he died, and a look through it showed mainly hard boiled orange candies, just like the lump he'd choked on.

There didn't seem anything remarkable about him. Perhaps he was just an unlucky guy who inhaled when he shouldn't and his candy went down the wrong way.

After a check of his pockets and finding nothing useful, I stepped back. Now the store was empty, I could look around. Gentle music played in the background, and there was a shimmer of magic in the air, but that could have come from all the magic users crammed into such a small space.

The store door opened, and Olympus returned with Sherry. Her hands kept worrying her dress frills, and her gaze flicked from the body to me several times, her tongue repeatedly licking her lips as if they were dry. Or she was nervous about something.

"No one outside knew Galaan," Olympus said. "But Sherry did."

"How did you know him?" I said to her.

Her quick moving hands shook. "I didn't know him well, but he's been staying in Witch Haven since I opened the store. He's got an extremely sweet tooth and came by twice a day."

"He's staying in the village just to eat your candy?" I said.

Her blue eyes widened as if I'd suggested something ridiculous. "Why not? My candy is exceptional. Have you tried any?"

I shook my head as she raised an almost empty samples tray toward me. "Not right now."

Sherry offered the tray to Olympus, and he took a truffle and put it in his already full pocket.

"Since Galaan has been coming here twice a day for a month, you must have gotten to know him," I said. "When we met, you said you take care of your customers. Did Galaan ever have any special requests you fulfilled?"

"He did. He loved the hard stuff." She giggled then clapped a hand over her mouth before lowering it. "Sorry, I didn't mean to laugh, but it's the first time I've seen a body. And in my store. All I meant was he liked hard candy."

"I noticed that from his basket. Did he always buy that much candy every day?"

"Not always, but he ate a lot of it. He'd come in whenever I had a delivery. I get them twice a day. First thing in the morning then mid-afternoon. I like to surprise my customers whenever I can by ordering something extra special. It's a great way to encourage people to come back. Galaan learned when the deliveries were due and would show up ten minutes after they arrived. He'd wait for them to be unloaded and try the new samples. He'd often buy a bag, even if they weren't his favorite."

"Did you chat with Galaan when he was waiting for the candy to be unloaded?" I said.

"I did. And he was a nice man. A little nervous, but a decent person. Softly spoken and polite. He'd always wait his turn to be served and would ask how my day was. Some customers aren't like that. They can be pushy. Nice but pushy." She giggled again. "I blame the candy. It's so popular."

"Was that the extent of your relationship with Galaan?"

Her cheeks mottled pink. "Well... this is a little embarrassing. We went on a date. Just one. I felt sorry for him. I think he was lonely. He was renting a room in a small lodging house, and his landlady was never around. Galaan didn't know anyone in the village. I know what it's like, being a newcomer. It can take time to find your feet. He asked me out, and I didn't want to hurt his feelings, so I said yes. And it was only coffee and cake, so I didn't see any harm in going."

"How did the date go?"

Sherry patted one hot looking cheek. "It got awkward. Galaan got the wrong impression. At the end of the date, he tried to kiss me, and he got a bit handsy. I had to be firm with him, but he backed off after that. He even apologized for reading the signals wrong."

I glanced at Olympus, but he was paying more attention to the store than the questions being asked and answered. "You're sure he was happy to take no for an answer? Some guys get mean when they don't like what they hear."

"As I said, he was a sweet man. Galaan seemed disappointed that I didn't want to take things further, but he respected me. He still came to the store twice a day. He was polite and stayed out of my personal space after that incident. And I was happy to keep him as a friend. I like to think of everyone who comes into the store as a friend."

"You're sure that's what happened?" I said.

Her eyes widened again, this time in alarm. "Yes. Why would I lie?"

I looked at Olympus again, but he was inspecting the candy in his pockets. I resisted the urge to roll my eyes. He was a messy distraction today and not worth having around. "It's a bit of a coincidence, don't you think? You go on a date with Galaan, you reject his advances after he comes on strong, and then he dies after eating candy you gave him."

The color drained from Sherry's face. "His death was an accident. Galaan simply didn't chew his candy properly, or it went down the wrong pipe. And... the man didn't have the best manners. When we were on our date, he ate a muffin with his mouth open most of the time. It made me feel unwell."

"Storm, what are you suggesting?" Olympus finally joined in the conversation after moving several pieces of candy into the top pocket of his jacket.

"I'm suggesting we look at all avenues when investigating this death. Sherry, what were you doing when Galaan started choking?"

"Filling the back shelf with chocolate lime bonbons. I was down to the last three boxes and didn't want there to be any arguments. I was on a step ladder, my arms full of candy. Everyone saw me."

"Look at the candy that killed him," I said. "What is it?"

Her nose wrinkled. "Do I have to? It's been chewed."

"Yes. It'll only take a minute."

She inched closer to the body and peered at the congealed lump of sugar near it. "It looks like an Orange Surprise. They were one of his favorites. And look, he had two bags in his basket."

"What's so surprising about them?" I said.

"You never know what flavor you'll get. They look like basic orange candy, but they can be mint, cherry, lemonade, lime, all kinds of flavors. Galaan said he liked the surprise."

"Do you have samples of Orange Surprise out today?"

"Oh, yes. I always enjoy seeing people's faces when they try them and get a different taste experience than the one they were expecting."

"And you put these Orange Surprises on the table today?"

"I did. I'm the only one who works here. I... I'm not sure what you're implying."

"Storm, have you got a minute?" Olympus inclined his head then moved to the door. I followed him. "Why the interrogation? Galaan choked to death. This was a tragic accident."

I nodded. It most likely was, but I didn't want to dismiss this man's death too quickly. Things were rarely what they seemed in Witch Haven.

Sherry planted her feet firmly and cleared her throat. "I'm not responsible for what happened to Galaan. I am sorry he's dead, but I had nothing to do with it. You're making me feel guilty for no reason."

"It was your candy that stopped him breathing." I turned to her.

"Which Galaan freely took. I can't control how a person eats their candy." She looked at the body again. "Although... if you really think his death wasn't an accident—"

"Yes. What do you know?" I headed back to Sherry.

"I'm not sure how this fits into Galaan choking to death, but he had an argument with that terrifying individual who runs the local library. They had a huge yelling match. Galaan even told me the unpleasant scaled man with the dead eyes threatened to kill him."

My eyebrows flashed up, and I got a ticklish sensation in my stomach. I'd stumbled into something bigger than a simple choking, if an angry, book obsessed half-dragon with a ferocious temper had just been thrown into the mix.

Chapter 5

I stood outside the candy store with Olympus as a small team from the Magic Council dealt with Galaan's body. While they were running tests and taking photographs, I looked for Indigo, Odessa, and Luna, but they were nowhere to be seen.

It was hard not to take that personally. They must have seen me helping Galaan, but they hadn't even bothered to ask how everything was going. They'd simply disappeared with their arms full of candy. Most likely, they were gossiping about me and laughing that I hadn't been able to save him.

I couldn't figure out how I'd gotten things so wrong with them. We'd had disputes in the past, mainly because I could be stubborn, and we'd even had days when I hadn't spoken to any of them, but we'd always worked things out.

Olympus gently nudged me with his elbow. "I'm certain this was an accident. It'll be recorded as death by choking when I file the paperwork."

I tilted my head, watching as the team took their final photographs and bagged Galaan's body. "What about Sherry's relationship with the victim? Shouldn't you look into that?"

"There's no need. Several customers confirmed she was stocking the shelves when Galaan choked. There was no way she could have shoved candy down his throat while balancing on a ladder. She was nowhere near him."

"Or the fight Galaan had with Nazan? He said he wanted Galaan dead, and here's the result."

Olympus shook his head. "Nazan would fight himself if there was no one else around. He probably caught Galaan stealing a library book and took him to task. He's even threatened me when I've been late returning books."

I grimaced. Nazan was fiercely protective of the books in the library. He called it his library, and he'd been the caretaker there for as long as I could remember. You never messed with Nazan's books. If you did, you lived to regret it. Maybe that was what happened to Galaan. He wouldn't have known about Nazan's temper and his bookish obsession.

My nose snitched. But why kill Galaan with candy? Why not thump him over the head with a hardback book? Given Nazan's strength, that would work and would have been easier than spiking candy and sneaking it into Sherry's store.

Olympus checked the time and looked at his office. "This case won't be any more complicated than a simple choking. It happens. There's no mystery here."

"I got the candy out of Galaan while he was still breathing. He should have been fine." I didn't like the vague look in Olympus's eyes. He was work dodging, so he could focus on his new boss's posh event. "You will get your people to analyze that candy before signing this off as an accident?"

"Of course. But don't be surprised if nothing shows up. Sometimes, these things happen. Life is a tragedy."

"You're hoping this is one of those times, because you're more interested in making sure your new boss is happy than checking into a suspicious death."

Olympus shifted his weight and clasped his hands behind his back. "I have to make a good first impression. I need to keep Indigo in the lifestyle she's accustomed to."

"We both know Indigo isn't into material things. She'd be happy if you quit working for the Magic Council."

"And do what? I've worked there most of my life."

I shrugged. It wasn't my place to tell Olympus how to tackle his career choices. And it was handy having an inside guy in the Magic Council when I worked on cases. He was usually helpful. Not so much today.

The crowd had thinned, but there were plenty of onlookers as Galaan's body was brought out and taken away. They muttered and pointed, still stuffing themselves with candy. Seeing a dead body had dampened no one's appetite.

"I'll wait for the coroner's results and then close the case," Olympus said. "But to be on the safe side, I do need a statement from Nazan."

At last, he was getting with the program. "That makes sense. You don't want to miss anything. If you do, your new boss won't think much of you. You could go to the library now and get it over with. The paperwork could be done by the end of the day if you hurry."

Olympus shuffled about. "I was wondering if you'd do it for me."

I groaned. "You're scared of Nazan, aren't you?"

"Of course not. That half-dragon is all bluster and no bite."

"It wouldn't feel like bluster if he blasted you with his flames."

"Storm, please. I've got fifty things on my to-do list today. I'll even pay you. It'll take a couple of hours tops to deal with this. Get Nazan's statement about the argument and see if he knows anything else. I'm sure he won't, though. And you know what Nazan is like. He won't trap you in the library talking for hours. You'll be in and out in ten minutes. That'll be the loose ends tidied, and I can close this case."

My gaze flickered over Olympus. The guy looked exhausted, so I cut him some slack. "I'll do it. But you owe me for dealing with Nazan. He's such a grouch."

"How about a bag of candy when the store re-opens?"

I glanced at the candy store. "That place makes my teeth ache. I won't be back soon."

"You're a lifesaver. Let me know how you get on with Nazan." Olympus dashed back to his office.

I had another look around for my friends, but when there was no sign of them, I turned up my collar and headed to the library. It was time to speak to a grumpy half-dragon, half-warlock and see what he knew about a potential murder.

It had gone midnight, and I was back at the library for the third time. My first visit had been just before closing time, in the hopes the place would be empty and it would be easier to speak to Nazan. But the doors had been bolted early, and that never happened. Nazan was reliable and kept to strict opening and closing times. As protective as he was of his books, he encouraged everyone to read and made sure the books were accessible.

But not today. Which was odd. And odd things made me suspicious.

After a quick check back at my office to make sure Fire Fang was still unconscious and not tearing the place apart, I'd returned to the library for a second time. Nazan often slept there when he was busy or was feeling particularly protective of his precious books. I'd knocked on the front door and walked all around the building, but there'd been no sign of him inside.

That made me more suspicious.

Now I was in stealth mode. I'd camped out opposite the library in a shadow on a bench and was watching for any signs of life.

The more Nazan hid from me, the more concerned I became. People hid when they had something to conceal. And with Galaan's death fresh in my thoughts, I was already linking them.

I rubbed my recently bitten arm, which throbbed slightly. I needed a top-up of Binky's healing magic.

As I waited on the bench, my thoughts turned to Fire Fang. I was deeply worried about him. Learning he was mortal had messed with his head, and I had no idea how to fix it. Maybe I couldn't and had to accept Fire Fang was a dangerous, out-of-control beast. I might have to let him go. But I wasn't ready to give up on him yet.

For now, I had the situation contained, and that was the best I could hope for until I figured out my next move.

A light flicked on inside the library. I leaned forward, my eyes narrowing. I knew Nazan was hiding in there. He always retreated to his books in times of trouble. And if he had anything to do with what happened to Galaan, he'd be feeling extra troubled.

After a quick look around to make sure no one was watching, I snuck around the side of the library. I'd already picked a window to get through, and it opened into one of the main corridors.

It took several tries before my unlock spell worked. Nazan knew how to keep people out of his library, but the window finally opened. I hoisted myself onto the ledge and was sliding through on my belly when my ankles were grabbed by two powerful hands.

My stomach flipped as I was yanked out. I came face-to-face with Nazan.

He huffed smoke in my face, his amber eyes glowing with a primal rage and the red scales on his arms flickering a warning. "Why are you breaking into my library?" His voice was a deep rumble in his broad chest.

"Err... hey, Nazan. Funnily enough, to get to you. And why did you close early? You must have heard me knocking this evening. Don't feel like talking?"

He lifted me off my feet. I knew better than to struggle, so I remained limp. "Some people know when to take a hint. If the doors are locked and no one answers, that means I don't want visitors. And what do you want with my library? You're not a big reader. You've been in three times this year."

"How do you know that?"

"I keep track of everyone who enters my sanctuary." Nazan lowered me to the ground but kept hold of me. "There can't be a book in there you need so badly it can't wait until the morning." His accusing gaze went to the window.

"It's not the books I'm interested in, although they're all amazing. It's you."

I got another face full of smoke. "You're as bad as your friend, Luna. I still haven't forgiven her for what she did to my book stacks."

I shrugged and tried to pull an innocent face. "I have no clue what you're talking about."

He grunted. "Of course you don't. You witches always stick together."

That was a kick in the gut. Not anymore, we didn't.

"Are you going to explain yourself, or should I have you arrested for trespassing?" Nazan growled out.

"No need. I'm here to talk to you about a suspicious death that happened in Witch Haven."

He jerked back a fraction. "A death? Who died?"

"Galaan Foilmeister. And just before he died, you were seen fighting with him. You even said you wanted to kill him."

Nazan's forehead wrinkled. "You're talking about the miscreant who smeared chocolate on the pages of one of my books?"

"That was what the fight was about?"

His nod was curt. He let me go, turned, and walked away. "I'll show you the damage he did. Then you'll see why I was so angry."

Nazan left me no choice but to follow him or be left outside. I hurried up the steps and through the door he'd unlocked. The library was an imposing gothic building with tall spires and small, dark, lead-lined windows. It reminded me of something out of a Victorian novel, with a vaulted ceiling in the foyer and lots of dark, polished wood.

Nazan marched to the main semi-circular desk. He lifted a book and placed it on the counter before flicking it open. "Look at this. It's a disgrace."

There were several chocolate smeared fingerprints on the pages.

"You wanted Galaan dead because of a few chocolate finger marks?"

"He destroyed a precious work of art. He was always sneaking in here with a bag of food. I even had to take a sack of candy off him one day. I threatened to ban him three times, but he didn't get the message. He'd creep in, hide in a corner, and stuff his face while he read my books. The man shouldn't be allowed near books if he doesn't respect them."

"He won't be near books anytime soon, since he's dead."

"I'm not sad to hear that." Nazan closed the book and pressed a hand on the cover. "I've already ordered a replacement, since I'm not sure I can save this one. But I hate to get rid of books."

"You could donate it to charity. There'll be someone out there who doesn't mind the stains on the pages."

He simply grunted at that comment.

"So, you thought little of Galaan?" I said.

"I despised him. Anyone who destroys books is not worthy of life."

"You wanted him dead?"

Nazan hesitated, his gaze settling over my head, his attention on something behind me. "So long as he kept out of my library, I didn't care what he did. But the man couldn't take a hint."

"So you threatened to kill him, and then he dies. Coincidence?"

A smoky snort shot out of Nazan. "There is a difference between a threat and the application of that threat. The man was a book menace, but I didn't kill him."

"You thought about it?"

"I think about killing many people." His gaze traveled over my face. "Especially those who interrupt my quiet time and bother me with pointless questions about pointless candy hogs who have no respect for creative works."

His growly threats had no impact on me. I'd tangled with Nazan before, and his behavior was driven by his passion for books and not a general desire to destroy. Books were the only thing he cared about. Providing I didn't hurt his books, I'd be fine.

"Have you visited the new candy store in Witch Haven?" I said.

He startled at the change of topic. "No. I don't like sweet things. Why do you ask?"

"Because that's where Galaan died."

Nazan smirked. "What a fitting end for such a greedy little man. Was it a heart attack?"

"He choked on a piece of candy."

He barked out a laugh. "Even more fitting. The very thing he got in trouble for in here killed him."

"I was there when it happened. Something doesn't add up about his death. I got the candy out, but Galaan still died. He stopped breathing."

"Why is that odd? His brain could have been starved of oxygen. He was simply a greedy grunt, not taking care of himself."

"Or there was something strange about the candy. Maybe someone planted it in the store, knowing it was his favorite. You took candy off him, so you knew what he liked."

Rather than growling at my veiled accusation, Nazan pondered the information. "You're thinking his death wasn't an accident?"

"That's why I'm here."

"And you think I snuck into a candy store, planted a piece of dragon poisoned candy where I knew he'd pick it up to get rid of him?"

When Nazan said it like that, his involvement didn't seem so likely. "I'll admit, it's a stretch."

"It's more than that. If I'd wanted Galaan dead, I'd have scorched him with my flames, not force-fed him candy."

"I was thinking you'd hit him with a book if you wanted him dead."

He sucked in a breath. "I'd never abuse my books in such a manner."

Was I seeing more in this case than there was because I'd failed to save Galaan? My guilt was digging for something more to make up for my error.

"You need to leave," Nazan said. "I had nothing to do with this greedy individual's death."

"Tell me your alibi, and I'll go. He died just after two o'clock this afternoon."

"You know what my alibi will be. I was here. I'm always here. This is my world."

"And who were you with?"

"As few people as possible. People don't come to my library to socialize. If anyone talks above a whisper, they know what happens to them."

"Someone must have seen you around that time."

"Take my word for it. They didn't. I'm a creature of habit. I was alone in the stacks, returning books to their rightful places. I do that every day between two and three. No one saw me." Nazan turned away from me. "If you're having trouble finding your way out, I'll take great pleasure in ejecting you."

I looked around the library and shrugged. This was a waste of time. It would have been impossible for Nazan to plant tainted candy in the store and be certain who would eat it. And if he'd hung around to see Galaan pick it up, he'd have been noticed.

After saying goodbye and being ignored, I headed outside. I hurried to my office, did another check to make sure Fire Fang was still there, and then headed up to my apartment.

I opened the door to find Binky half-asleep on the couch. She stretched, arched her back, then walked over to greet me.

I petted her head. "Any trouble with Fire Fang?"

She shook her head then trotted to her empty food bowl.

I filled it and made myself a coffee. Despite my reservations, this case seemed open and shut.

Olympus was right. It was an accidental choking. I'd do a few final fact checks then give up.

I snuggled in bed with my coffee, Binky, and my laptop warming my legs as I ran basic searches on Galaan. I was hoping I'd find nothing useful. My life was complicated enough with a missing sister, an out-of-control hellhound to deal with, and friends who hated me. I didn't need to make up problems in this case when there were none to find.

Chapter 6

My grumbling stomach woke me the next morning. I checked the time and groaned. I'd been sleeping for twelve hours. No wonder I was starving. I turned over and came nose to nose with Binky. She had something in her mouth.

I blinked the sleep out of my eyes. "Is that a collar?"

She spat it on the bed to reveal it was indeed another cat's collar.

"Where did you steal this from?" I picked up the purple and silver collar and turned it over a few times. There was a faint sting of magic on it, but I couldn't identify the spell, and it was weak, suggesting it hadn't been recharged for some time.

Binky jumped off the bed and returned with a piece of paper. She repeated the exercise and came back with a pen. She spent several minutes drawing on the paper. She dropped the pen and looked at me.

I sat up in bed and inspected her work. It was more scribbles. A few swirls this time but nothing I could make sense of.

She dabbed her paw on the paper then her nose on the collar.

"You're trying to tell me something, but I have no idea what it is."

She glared at me and thrashed her tail from side to side.

"I am trying. But I'm un-caffeinated and have a hangover from too much sleep." I turned the paper around, but it looked just as bad upside down.

She meowed her frustration and leaped to the floor.

I slid out of bed, used the bathroom, dressed, and headed into the kitchen. Once I had a coffee and a huge bowl of cereal in front of me, I grabbed the paper off the bed and looked at it again. I still wasn't any clearer about what Binky was telling me.

She hopped onto the kitchen counter and stared at the paper.

"I know this is important to you. I figured you just had a creative side and were doing some drawings, but now, I'm not so sure. Are these words? I suppose that first letter could be a B."

Binky bobbed her head and turned in a circle.

I scooped up cereal and ate it. "So here's my idea to make this communication thing easier. We could try a speech spell on you. It took a long time to get it right with Fire Fang, and he experienced a few side effects. I'll never forget the day he turned bright yellow after the spell went wrong."

Binky grumbled and wriggled her tail.

"But if we get it to work, it would help. You could tell me whatever you liked then, while you're still mastering your drawing skills."

She tilted her head from side to side several times as if considering the option but finally nodded.

I finished my coffee and cereal as I mulled over the spells to use. My former friends had helped perfect the speech spell, since it wasn't an area of magic I specialized in, but I knew the basics.

I grabbed several spell books and studied them at the counter, with Binky sitting beside me, reading along. I tapped a page. "This was the one we originally used on Fire Fang. We kept the base elements the same and tweaked or added one ingredient at a time. Of course, you're smaller than him, so the spell will need to be less powerful."

She wriggled her nose, suggesting she hated the idea of being less powerful than Fire Fang.

I scratched behind her ears. "You're both awesome. At least Fire Fang is when he's not wanting to eat me. You read through the spell and find the ingredients we need, and I'll go check on him. I expected to be woken by growls and howls, so his silence is bothering me."

After setting the book up so Binky could keep reading, I hurried down the stairs to my office. There was a chilly wind whistling under the door. I inched it open, and dread settled in my stomach as I saw the gaping hole in the window.

I stepped inside and looked around. There was a distinct lack of angry hellhound. I was surprised Fire Fang hadn't wrecked the place as revenge for being captured and knocked out.

He shouldn't have been able to get out of my restraining spell. I also found it odd he'd left the building, rather than charge up the stairs and attack me. It was all he wanted to do lately.

Leaving the office, I grabbed thick cardboard and strong tape from the storeroom at the back and sealed the broken window. I'd have to get that fixed later. I did the same to my apartment front door.

I went into the apartment. Binky had abandoned the spell book and was looking out the window. When I joined her, I discovered Fire Fang was lurking around his favorite tree and not looking happy.

She looked up at me and gave a soft sigh.

"As you can see, Fire Fang got free. He smashed the window in the office to get out. I didn't hear him last night, but then I was dead to the world."

She meowed softly and leaned against me.

"Yeah, maybe I needed the rest." We studied Fire Fang for several minutes as he paced and snarled. "From the look on his face, he's not done with me, but there's nothing we can do about him now. Let's see if we can get you talking."

Binky followed me back to the kitchen counter. She'd already gathered some ingredients for the spell. I got the heavier bottles and mixed distilled water, anise seed, and salt and dropped in a small piece of yellow agate.

Once the potion was mixed, I left it to brew for thirty minutes. I drank another coffee and checked over the information I'd discovered about Galaan on my laptop last night.

He had details of a girlfriend on his social media profiles. Her name was Juliet Lupin. She looked like a sweet lady, smiling in every picture, her round cheeks red and her blonde hair always windswept. There were also details of Galaan's brother, Nile. The two looked similar, although Nile was the younger brother and had more hair.

I wasn't planning to spend much more time on this investigation, but I figured I'd check in with these two to ensure Galaan had no concerns about his safety before his death. I was also curious to know why he'd moved to Witch Haven. It couldn't have been to go to the candy store twice a day. No one was that big a sugar addict.

"Meow."

Binky was sitting by the potion and sniffing it. I checked the time. "That should be ready to go. Are you sure you want to do this? I don't want to give you horns or white spots on your fur by accident."

She nodded and walked to her water bowl.

I left the couch, emptied the water from her bowl, dried it, and after giving the potion a final stir and a sniff, I emptied it into her bowl, making sure to remove the agate.

Binky stepped forward and gave it a thorough investigation before she began lapping. She'd only had a few mouthfuls before a huge spark flew out of the potion. It slammed into Binky then whacked into me, sending me to the floor and leaving my ears ringing.

The hair on my body felt like it was standing on end, and my spine shivered as the spell ran through me. I sat up, flattening my fluffy hair. Binky had vanished.

There was a scratching sound from the bedroom, followed by a thump.

"Binky! Are you okay?" It took a few minutes of searching, but I found Binky hidden under my bed, having kicked old magazines out of the way to hide at the back. Her fur was puffed out and her pupils dilated. She lay on her stomach with her ears down. "I'm guessing that didn't work? Try saying something."

She glared at me. "Meow."

I huffed out a breath. "Sorry. This magic isn't something I'm great at. We used the right ingredients, but it takes more than that to get a spell right. I could do with Odessa's help. She figured out how to get Fire Fang talking."

Binky gave another mournful meow then settled her chin on one paw and closed her eyes.

I hated to see her distressed. "I'll message Odessa and ask for help. She may hate me, but she won't turn you down." I slid off the floor and grabbed my phone. I sent Odessa a message letting her know about Binky but didn't get a reply or an acknowledgement.

After checking on Binky again and making sure she had her favorite food in her bowl, I looked up Juliet Lupin's location. She had a small business in Oakland. It was only an hour from here. While Binky was recovering, and I needed to stay out of Fire Fang's way, I'd pay her a visit.

"Binky, you good?" I whispered.

She meowed softly.

"You rest. I won't be long. Just visiting Galaan's family. Is there anything you need?" I peered under the bed at her.

Her eyes were closed, but she shook her head.

One quick translocation spell later, and I was outside Pets Paradise. It was a cute place, with a window display of dog bowls and pet food. I walked in to discover Juliet behind the counter, opening a box and taking out the contents.

She smiled at me. "Welcome to Pets Paradise. How can I help you?"

"I'm after information about Galaan Foilmeister. I'm Storm Winter, a private investigator." I walked over and showed her my credentials. "I believe you knew Galaan."

"Oh! Is he in trouble?" She set aside the box and studied my information.

"You haven't heard?"

"Heard what? I haven't seen Galaan for a while. We used to date but split up about a month ago. What's wrong with him?"

"I'm sorry to have to tell you, but he died yesterday."

Her hand went to her mouth. "The poor guy. What happened to him?"

"He choked to death on a candy."

Confusion wiped away the shock on her face. "Candy? Galaan didn't like sugary things. I'm the one with the sweet tooth. When we'd go to dinner, he'd order the entrée and main course, but I was always looking at the dessert menu."

"Well, I guess he changed. He was a regular at the candy store in Witch Haven. I was there when he choked, and he had a basket full of candy to purchase. Apparently, he went in twice a day."

"That makes no sense. But I know Witch Haven. We had our first date there. It's a nice place. It's strange now you mention it. Our last date was in Witch Haven, too. Galaan said he wanted to go back to see where things started for us. When I asked why, he simply said he wanted a change of scene."

"Why was that?"

She sorted through the bags of dog treats in front of her. "Things hadn't been going so well between us. I thought it was his way of being romantic. And I remember now, he saw a candy store. We even went in. I think it was the first day it opened."

"Why go in if he didn't like candy?"

"I told him to. Galaan was hungry and getting grouchy, so I suggested a sugar boost. He tried several candies." Her eyes were hazy with tears. "He really choked to death on a candy?"

"It seems like it. But there are a couple of things about his death that make little sense. It's why I'm looking into it." Juliet seemed shocked and sad by the news but not nervous. Perhaps she had nothing to hide. "How was your split with Galaan? Any bad feeling?"

"Not really. It's always awkward when a relationship ends. But things just faded between us. After that last date, I got in touch with Galaan several times to talk. We hadn't left things on a great note, but I was hoping we could be friends. We often went to the same social events, so I didn't want things to be uncomfortable, but he stopped replying to my messages. I wondered if there was bad feeling on his part."

"When did he stop replying?"

"About a month ago. I didn't hear from him after our visit to Witch Haven."

"Did you end things with him while you were there?"

"It was never really ended. Neither of us said it was over. It just faded away. I wasn't all that enthused about the relationship, so when Galaan stopped returning my messages and calls, I wasn't disappointed. I wanted closure though. Now, I'll never get it. I must admit, I'm stunned Galaan is dead. He was such a sensible guy. He never took any risks."

The door to the store opened. I turned and recognized the man who walked in, his arms full of boxes. It was Galaan's brother, Nile Foilmeister.

"Hey, babe. Sorry I took so long, but they didn't have the box of chunky pig-shaped dog bones you ordered. They're not coming in until next week. They had to make a few calls to see where they were." He smiled at me.

I glanced from Juliet to Nile. Why was Nile calling Galaan's ex-girlfriend babe?

"Oh, Nile, I've had terrible news about Galaan." Juliet hurried over. She took the boxes off him and set them on the floor before catching hold of his hand. "Something awful has happened."

The smile on Nile's face faded. "What is it?"

"Galaan is dead. He choked to death on a piece of candy. It's being investigated by this woman. Sorry, I've forgotten your name," Juliet said.

I walked over to join them. "Storm Winter. I'm a private investigator. I was there when your brother choked. I tried to save him, but nothing worked."

Nile's mouth hung open. "Is this one of his jokes? He's always doing dumb things like this and thinking they're funny. If it is, he's gone too far. It's not entertaining to make light of death."

"It's no joke. Galaan died yesterday. A team from the Magic Council is investigating, and I'm working with them to figure out how it happened. They should have been in touch with you."

"They haven't. And what do you mean, how it happened? You said he choked." Nile's expression was grim as he clutched Juliet's hand.

"Don't you think it's strange?" Juliet said. "Galaan didn't like candy. But he'd been visiting a store in Witch Haven and buying loads. Do you think he was sick? Can a medical condition give someone cravings for sugar?"

Nile's expression remained perplexed. "Not that I know of. Maybe. I don't know. Was he ill?" He looked at me for the answer.

"We'll know more about his health once the investigation is complete."

They nodded, both looking shellshocked.

"Had Galaan been behaving strangely recently? Or been worried about anything?" I said.

"I... I need a moment to process this," Nile said. "My idiot brother is gone?"

"Sit down." Juliet led him to the counter, and I followed them. "I'll get you a drink. Would you like anything?" She looked at me.

"I'm good." I stayed with Nile while Juliet disappeared into the back room. "Were you close to your brother?"

He puffed out a breath. "No, not that close. I mean, we were related by blood, but we didn't have much in common. I thought he was annoying, and he thought I was lazy."

"And since you're dating his former girlfriend, there must have been tension between you two."

Nile gulped. "How do you know we're dating?"

"Unless you call everyone babe, it was obvious when you showed up. Were you seeing each other before Galaan and Juliet split?"

"No! I thought little of the guy, but I wouldn't steal his girlfriend. Galaan and Juliet drifted apart. It got worse after he quit his job and moved to Witch Haven. If you're looking into odd behavior, that was a strange thing to do. He enjoyed his job at the farm. He did their accounting."

Juliet hurried back into the store with a glass of water and gave it to Nile. "How are you feeling?"

"Confused." He sipped the water.

"I'm the same." She placed her hand on his forehead, as if expecting him to have a fever.

"Did Galaan tell you why he quit his job?" I said to Nile.

"No. He just told me he wanted a change."

"He told me he was taking time out to enjoy himself." Juliet removed her hand from Nile's forehead.

"You knew he'd moved to Witch Haven?" I said.

"I did. I even asked him why he'd picked there. It's a cute place but doesn't have many opportunities if he was looking for a career change."

"What answer did he give you?"

"He said that was where he had to be. I couldn't get much sense out of him. It was after that he cut communication. I wondered..." Juliet placed a hand on Nile's shoulder.

"That he was angry about our relationship?" Nile shook his head. "He didn't care. I called him and told him I'd asked you out, but he wasn't bothered. He said he'd found a new focus and didn't have time for relationships, so I was free to date you if I wanted."

Juliet frowned. "You never told me that."

"Babe, I didn't want to upset you. He sounded so distant that I thought he might be on something or messing about with magic he shouldn't be using. You didn't need to worry about Galaan."

"How long were you and Galaan seeing each other?" I said to Juliet.

"Almost a year. At one point, I thought it was serious, but then it went wrong. And I've known Nile for as long as I've known Galaan. He started lending me a hand when my truck broke down and I couldn't pick up my deliveries." She squeezed his shoulder. "I'm not sure what I'd have done if he hadn't been here to help. Galaan wasn't half as practical."

Nile patted her hand. "I always thought you were gorgeous, and Galaan was punching above his weight. I know I am, now you're my girl."

"You're so sweet." Juliet kissed his cheek.

"I have a question. If Galaan choked to death on a piece of candy, what's there to investigate?" Nile said to me.

"Galaan shouldn't have died. I got the candy out, but he still stopped breathing. We're waiting on the results of the autopsy, but I need to make sure nothing was missed."

Nile straightened in his seat. "You think someone did this to Galaan?"

"I'm hoping it was an accident, but I need your alibis to rule you out of any involvement if we find foul play was involved."

"Alibis! I haven't seen Galaan in weeks," Juliet said. "And I wouldn't know the first thing about how to infect candy with something that would kill. My magic involves animal communication. It's why this store is so successful. The animals come in and tell me exactly what they need."

"That's a handy skill. I don't suppose you have any speech spells, do you?" I said.

"Oh, no. I don't need spells to talk to the animals. I form a temporary bond with them so we can communicate, just like a witch does with her familiar. Why do you ask?"

"I'm having trouble speaking to a cat. She's telling me something, but I can't figure out what it is."

"You're having trouble forming a bond with your familiar? If that's the case, I often find stress is the cause. I have spells to keep you and your animal relaxed while you create the bonding link."

"I have no plans to form a permanent bond with her, but I recently tried a speech spell, and it went wrong. I figured if you had something that could help, it would fix the problem."

"Why don't you want a familiar?" Juliet cocked her head. "They're fabulous company. I have a Great Dane, Minstrel, sleeping out back. She's the most adorable angel. And so helpful."

"I don't have room in my life for a familiar. Can you fix me up with something to get this cat talking or not?"

Juliet pursed her lips. "No, that's not something I can help with."

That was disappointing. "Then I'll take a pouch of your best catnip and your alibis. Galaan died just after two o'clock yesterday afternoon. Juliet, where were you?"

Her hand went to her stomach. "I was eating a late lunch out back, but I was on my own. Even Minstrel wasn't around. She was stretching her legs in the yard. I had nothing to do with what happened to Galaan, though."

That was hardly the most convincing alibi. "What about you, Nile?"

"I was in my van. I was picking up supplies for Juliet. I got there just before two. I was back here by three o'clock."

"Anyone with you?"

"No, I was alone."

Juliet nodded. "He's telling the truth. Nile got here at three, we unloaded the truck, and then stopped for coffee."

"Both of you were on your own when Galaan died?" I said.

"That doesn't make us guilty of murder," Nile said. "Juliet is right. Galaan withdrew once he decided to move to Witch Haven. He became a different person and wasn't interested in anyone or anything."

Were they being truthful or covering their guilt? I wasn't certain. "I'm just going to take your pictures."

"What for?" Nile said.

"To check with the candy store owner that neither of you were in Witch Haven at the time of Galaan's death. Any problem with that?"

Neither of them looked happy about the suggestion but let me take their photographs. When I got home, I'd ask Sherry if they'd been in her store or if she'd seen them arguing with Galaan.

"Do we need to come to Witch Haven to collect Galaan's body?" Nile said. "I'll make sure he gets a sendoff. He could be an idiot, but he was still my brother."

"Someone from the Magic Council will be in touch to arrange that with you. They won't be releasing his body for a few days, though."

"How certain are you his death wasn't an accident?" Nile said.

"I'm still gathering facts. We'll know more soon."

Juliet served me the catnip—a small peace offering to Binky after the speech spell shock—then led me to the door, and after saying our goodbyes, I headed out of the store.

They both had a motive for wanting Galaan dead and poor alibis. Maybe Galaan hated Juliet and Nile dating, and they'd fought about it. It wasn't the strongest of motives, though, but with their less than perfect alibis, I couldn't rule them out if this turned out to be more complicated than a simple choking by candy case.

I pulled out my phone. I wouldn't mind talking this over with friends, but I didn't have any of those.

Instead, I called Olympus. "Hey, I've got an update on Galaan. Let's get together and talk about our dead guy."

Chapter 7

Later that afternoon, I was in Olympus's office. Binky was with me, settled on my shoulder, having recovered from our attempt to get her talking, and after enjoying several manic moments rolling in the catnip I'd gotten her. We were friends again.

Olympus came out of his back office with two mugs of peppermint tea. I was disappointed not to get coffee. He loved to be caffeinated almost as much as I did.

I'd been filling him in on my conversations with Nazan, Juliet, and Nile. Not that he'd been paying much attention. Olympus had been fretting over some report about the la-de-da pointless inauguration ceremony for his boss. When he wasn't looking at that, he was eating candy from a box on his desk.

He settled in his seat and pushed candy my way. "You're sure you don't want some? I can't get enough of this stuff."

"So I can see. I'll pass. I ate earlier."

Olympus helped himself to a sugar dusted candy. "I must be stress eating. With everything going on for the upcoming ceremony, I've got too much to focus on."

"And of course, there's the dead guy to consider," I said.

"Which I plan to rule an accident. I just need the green light from the autopsy. But there's no evidence to show anyone had a reason to kill Galaan."

"Err... you have been listening to me for the last twenty minutes, haven't you? What about the fight Sherry saw Galaan have with Nazan? And when I questioned Nazan, he was open about despising the guy."

"But as you said, Nazan would have burned Galaan alive if he hated him that much. Why use candy?"

"Maybe so. But then we have Galaan's ex-girlfriend and his brother in the mix. There was no love lost there. Juliet could have played down the problems with the breakup. It could have been messy and there was bad feeling lingering. Add in the fact she's now dating Galaan's brother, who also thought little Galaan, and you've got a motive."

"They have alibis."

"Saying you were alone at the time of a murder—"

"Possible murder."

I held in a sigh. "Possible murder, isn't an alibi."

"Why would they lie?"

Was Olympus being serious, or had the sugar addled his brain? "Because that's what killers do when they want to get away with murder."

He grabbed a handful of candy and leaned back in his seat. "You're making too much of this. I can't think about an accidental death being anything more than that. I've got the Magic Council ceremony to focus on, and I've just had paperwork submitted for a public event in Witch Haven in five days' time."

"Put the social events on hold and focus on the murder. That's the most important thing." I thumped the desk, making Olympus's leopard familiar, Monty, jump in his plush bed in the corner. "It's no surprise people get frustrated with the Magic Council when you get your priorities so messed up."

"My priorities are fine." Olympus sucked in more candy, his cheeks looking hamster-like. "I understand now why Indigo is done with you."

My skin prickled, and I leaned forward in my seat. "What was that?"

He looked away, chewing on a mouthful of candy. "We were talking about Galaan choking and you trying to help him. Indigo told me she no longer considered you a friend. The same goes for Luna and Odessa. They've had enough of your stubbornness. So have I."

My insides tightened, and I found it hard to breathe. "Maybe I'm the one who's had enough of them."

Olympus shrugged. "If you say so. Are you sure you don't want any candy?"

I stood and swiped the box of candy onto the floor, sending it scattering. "This is a waste of time. You've made up your mind about this case. Even if there'd been a knife sticking out of Galaan's back and someone confessing to the crime, you'd still say it was an accident, just so you could get on with smarming up to your new boss and ensuring some pointless party happens. I don't operate like that. You're on your own." I marched to the door, yanked it open, and stepped out, making a point of slamming it behind me.

I hurried away, not looking where I was going as my eyes hazed with tears. Everyone was leaving me. Fire Fang, my friends, Eden, my parents giving up on me after Eden went missing. There was no one left. I was alone.

Binky, who'd used her claws to cling to me as I'd flounced out, rubbed her face against my cheek.

"I'm done with helping people. I'm focusing on myself from now on. I can hardly disappoint myself."

"Meow," Binky said, a hopeful note in her voice.

"You can go, too. If you stick around, you'll let me down. You'll leave me too, eventually." I tried to lift her off my shoulder, but she dug in her claws and hissed.

"I don't want you. Go away. Leave me alone."

Binky still clung on.

I heaved out a bubbly sigh and gave up on trying to lift her off. I stopped outside my apartment, and my gaze settled on a bright yellow poster. It was promoting a magic festival in five days' time, promising prizes, cash rewards, and a once-in-a-lifetime experience.

"This is what Olympus was so worried about. Maybe I'll invite all my friends, shall I? We'll have an amazing time."

Binky rubbed against my cheek again, her claws still latched on tight.

"Sorry, Binky. I didn't mean to be such a jerk to you, but Witch Haven can suck it." I dashed into my apartment and locked the door behind me. I was so done with this place.

I flipped over in bed and buried my nose in the pillow. I'd been here for two days, and my bedroom smelled funky.

Something warm landed on my feet and bit my toes through the covers.

"Go away, Binky. There's food in your bowl and toy mice on the floor. You'll have to entertain yourself. Go eat some more catnip."

She kept kicking and gnawing at my toes, and I was grateful for the thick covers so she didn't get through to flesh.

I eased my feet out from underneath her and turned over again. She was as restless as me. We were going stir crazy after days of barely moving from this bed. I'd have to get out of bed, eventually. The coffee mug on the bedside table was empty, and I was out of food.

Binky leaped on my thighs and grabbed them in a flying squirrel move, legs splayed and tail bushy.

"Quit it. I'm moving. See! I'm sitting up."

She looked at me and continued to attack my legs.

"If I promise to get you something tasty to eat, will you stop with the stealth attacks?"

Binky leaped off me and landed nimbly on the floor, her tail up.

"I take that as a yes. Give me five minutes." I dragged myself out of bed, grabbed the first clothes I could see, and headed to the door.

When I stepped outside, the wind felt strange on my skin, as if I'd been hibernating for months rather than had simply disappeared for a couple of days to sulk and scowl.

I breathed in the fresh air then hunched over and hurried along the street, Binky beside me. I didn't want to deal with people today. I was still smarting over the comments Olympus made about my former friends.

At least, since the truth was now out, I knew it was a waste of time getting them to help me or Binky. I was on my own. I always said I worked better alone, and I'd just gotten my wish. So why didn't it feel as good as I thought it should?

I turned the corner, and a menacing growl rumbled close by. I froze to the spot, an icicle of fear stabbing into my tail bone. I'd been so caught up in my troubles, I'd forgotten about Fire Fang.

But he hadn't forgotten me.

The ground rumbled beneath my feet, but I was already running, Binky at my heels. I didn't look around, since I knew exactly who was chasing me.

Rather than heading into the village and putting other people at risk, I diverted down a quiet residential street. I dodged into someone's garden and hid behind the hedge.

Fire Fang tore a hole through the hedge as he leaped through it. He hit the ground and swung toward me. His eyes glowed red, and flames flickered around his mouth.

"Binky, run! Get help," I yelled.

She sped away, her ears flat against her furry head.

"I knew I'd finally get you, you crazy buttoned witch. I just had to wait for you to screw up," Fire Fang said.

Magic sparked on my fingers as my fight-or-flight urges threatened to consume me. Run or fight? I didn't want to do either. "Fire Fang, I know you're angry, and I must have apologized a dozen times, but I've called the vet. I'm waiting to hear from her to see how we can fix this."

He took a step closer, his paw thudding down. "Fix this? How will you do that, goblin nobble?"

"I... I don't know. That's why I'm asking for help. Doctor Hooper may have heard of cases like this. It's worth a shot. I've been researching, too."

"All that sour slug, gooseberry bush, donkey helmet vet will do is stab me with needles and take more blood. This is all your fault."

Even though I hadn't turned him from a mortal into a hellhound, I felt guilty. Maybe if I'd revealed the secret sooner, we could have worked together to find a solution. Instead, I'd hidden it in the hopes I'd puzzle things out. Perhaps working alone on this hadn't been the right thing to do.

Fire Fang took another step, and I pinned myself against the hedge, sharp branches sticking into my back. "Hurting me won't fix anything. We can work this out together. We make a great team."

"The only thing I want to work out is which bit to bite off first." He threw himself at me, and his front paws slammed me against the hedge.

An overwhelming smell of warm honey flooded my nose. Fire Fang pulled his head back, his jaws open, about to take a bite.

I blasted him with a repelling spell. He staggered back but launched himself at me again. I ducked and threw out a shield spell, forging a protective barrier between us. "Stop! Think about what you're doing."

"I've been waiting too long to chomp you into donkey helmet tiny pieces." He smashed against my shield, and I got another waft of the odd honey scent.

"Where have you been?"

"Watching you."

"Why do you smell like that?" I crouched as he thudded into my shield spell several times and the magic wavered.

"You goblin nobble witch! Let me have you. You've done me wrong, and you have to pay."

"Pay for trying to help you?"

"Pay for lying. Pay for ruining my life. I was happy being your hellhound, and you opened your big gooseberry bush mouth and ruined things."

"That's the thing. You're not a hellhound. Not really." I cringed at the impact of his blow. "Something happened to you. Someone did this to you. They took away your memories and used powerful magic. You need to find out where you came from and who did this."

He slammed against my spell again. "Maybe you did it. All this time, you were lying. Did you find it amusing to turn me into a mutt and treat me like some whipped pet?"

"I'd never do that to you. When I took you in, it was only ever supposed to be temporary. You knew that. You were the one who bonded to me. I gave you plenty of chances to leave."

"I bonded with you because I thought you could be trusted, but you're just another sour slug, goblin nobble freak. I want it all gone."

"Then leave. If that's what you want. Get out of here and go figure out where you came from. Get your memories back and find out who you were before you came into my life." The words choked out of me. I didn't want him gone, but Fire Fang couldn't stay in Witch Haven. He was too dangerous.

"I'm not leaving. This is all because of you. And I want revenge." He reared back and blasted my spell with flames.

My magic was weakening, and cracks formed along the shield spell.

He pulled back again and was about to charge when Binky leaped on him, multi-colored sparks of magic flaring around her as she latched onto Fire Fang with tooth and claw.

And she wasn't alone. A thin ginger cat also leaped onto Fire Fang. Magic billowed out of the new arrival in a pale pink cloud, covering Fire Fang's head and making him choke and stagger.

I lowered my shield spell and thrust a hard knockback spell at Fire Fang, careful not to hit the cats.

They jumped off him as he rolled away but were on his back again the second he stood. This hadn't been the help I'd expected Binky to bring, but these fluffy ninjas were incredible as they slashed, howled, and growled.

"I'll eat you both for dinner if you don't get off me this second," Fire Fang snarled out, tossing his head and trying to dislodge them, but their claws were deeply buried in his skin. Those cats were going nowhere.

The skinny ginger cat adjusted her grip. Fire Fang took advantage. He grabbed her tail and flipped her in the air.

There was a horrifying screech as he bit the cat's back leg.

Thrusting out my hands, I threw all my magic at Fire Fang. He howled and flipped onto his back. Binky was blasting out so much magic, I could barely see what was going on. But those cats were in mortal danger, especially the ginger one, whose back leg no longer worked as she dragged herself from the fight.

I raced over, pulled Binky off Fire Fang, touched the ginger cat, and translocated them to my apartment. I sank to my knees, still clutching the cats to my chest. My magic was almost drained, and my eyes refused to focus.

I gently set Binky down. "Are you okay?"

She nodded as she flicked chunks of Fire Fang's fur off her claws, her attention on the wounded ginger cat.

I eased the cat carefully away from me. Her fur was bloody, and the cat was panting. She was a tiny slip of a female, no more than a year old.

"This looks bad. Thanks for helping, kitty, but now, it's my time to help you."

Chapter 8

After a call to Doctor Hooper, I was sitting in the waiting room at the veterinary clinic. Binky was beside me and the injured ginger cat on my lap. She was still panting and had barely opened her eyes since we arrived.

Doctor Hooper opened the door to her examination room and ushered us in. "Oh, the poor little thing. You said a hellhound bit her."

I nodded as I set the cat on the table and stepped back, so Doctor Hooper could work her magic. "Yes, you've met him. It was Fire Fang."

She didn't speak for several minutes as she inspected the cat. Waves of healing green magic flooded out as Doctor Hooper focused her energy on the deep bite wounds.

"Will the cat be okay?" I picked up Binky, more to reassure myself than her. I hated seeing any animal injured, and this cat got hurt helping me.

After not saying anything for thirty seconds, Doctor Hooper finally looked at me. "She'll recover. The bite marks are deep, but you got her here in time." She kept pulsing her healing magic over the cat, but it was slowing. "You said your own hellhound did this?"

"Yes. Have you listened to the message I left you about him?"

"I did. I'm sorry I haven't gotten back to you. We've had wall-to-wall patients for days, and one of my vets is off sick, so I've been covering for him."

"I'm not sure you'd be able to help, anyway. But this last month, Fire Fang's been losing control of his anger, and recently, he attacked me. He bit my arm, and I'm sure he wants me dead. He never used to be like this. Sure, he had a temper, and being a hellhound, he'll always be sketchy, but this is new. I'm actually scared of him."

"It sounds like you need to be. He must be contained if he's biting people. Where is he now? I can put in a call to animal control."

"Somewhere in Witch Haven. I'll find Fire Fang and contain him. I don't want animal control involved. They'll put him down when they see how unstable he is."

Doctor Hooper finally stopped using her magic and stroked the soft fur on the cat's head. "I never like to give up on an animal, but from all accounts, that could be the best thing for Fire Fang."

"There'll be another way. You discovered magic turned him into a hellhound. Perhaps, because he was once mortal, he's struggling to control his hellhound form. If we learn how it happened to him, we could reverse the magic. Stabilize it. Or if Fire Fang wants to remain a hellhound, we could find a way to get him better."

Doctor Hooper's expression was pensive. "I wish I had better news for you, but I have been doing some research in the evenings. There are so few cases of this ever happening before that there's little precedent. One case I learned about ended in failure. The person died. And any other information I've discovered is hearsay. There's been no scientific study of what such a powerful spell would do to a mortal. And it's no surprise. We all know it's illegal to use magic on those who have no powers."

"It's been done, though. Dark magic users are always prodding mortals to see how they can exploit them."

"I'm sure you're right, but the few times it has been attempted, it wouldn't have been documented for fear of reprisal by the Magic Council. I'm as much in the dark as you about what we should do with Fire Fang." Doctor Hooper gently pressed a warm hand against my arm. "Perhaps you should consider it more of a kindness to put him to sleep."

My gut spasmed. "No! It's not fair on him. Fire Fang wouldn't have asked for this to happen to him. He needs support and help. We have to figure this out."

"Let me get this little one settled, and then I'll see what I can do." Doctor Hooper's gaze went to the bite marks on the cat's leg. "She needs more treatment. That bite is already infected. Let me give her pain medication so she's comfortable, and we'll go from there."

Reluctantly, I went back to the waiting room with Binky and paced for ten minutes. The receptionist asked me several times if I'd like to take a seat, but my anxiety wouldn't let me remain still. Fire Fang wasn't a lost cause. There had to be a way to make this right for him.

After the longest half an hour of my life, Doctor Hooper finally asked us back into the examination room.

"How's the cat doing?" I said.

"She's sleeping. The wounds are healing, but I am worried. I've taken blood work, and there are high levels of toxicity in her system."

"From Fire Fang's bite?"

"It's possible. It's too early to say. You said he bit you, too? Have you had trouble with the wound healing?"

"No, thanks to Binky. Oh, Binky, can you heal the cat?" I looked down at her.

"Your familiar has healing magic?" Doctor Hooper said.

"She healed me. She licked my injuries. Although my arm still throbs occasionally. Should I worry about that?"

"No, familiar healing is powerful stuff. It's your bond. It joins with your strength and speeds up healing. Come through the back. The cat is in a cage."

We followed Doctor Hooper into a clean white room to discover several rows of cages. The lighting was low, and it was pleasantly warm.

She headed to a cage and opened the door. "Binky, if you wouldn't mind?"

Binky hopped into the cage, sniffed around the cat, and then licked her back leg.

Doctor Hooper watched, fascination in her eyes. "That's remarkable. Usually animals with healing magic attach to healers. Most of my colleagues have familiars with abilities to heal. I didn't know your magic involved healing."

"It doesn't. I'm a weather witch. And I'm as surprised as you about Binky's ability."

"Does healing run in your family? Perhaps a distant relative could heal and Binky identified that in you. Healing magic can skip generations if there are more dominant abilities in the family line. And weather trumps healing in ferocity."

I tilted my head. "I had a couple of great aunts who were healers. I didn't know them."

"That must be it. Look how quickly the wounds are healing. You have a powerful familiar."

I crouched in front of the cage and stroked the ginger cat's head. The wounds looked better, and the cat's breathing seemed easier. My attention turned to Binky. "Binky's not my familiar. If you know of a healer in need of a useful familiar though, she needs a permanent home. Somewhere stable and quiet."

Doctor Hooper arched an eyebrow. "That wouldn't work. You and that cat have a bond."

"We don't. We can't even communicate. She's managed a few written words and some bad drawings, but that's it."

Binky hopped out of the cage and glared at me.

I lifted a hand. "And you know why we're not forming a familiar bond."

Doctor Hooper hummed under her breath. "Not that I like to interfere in my client's business, but you should reconsider that. She's attached to you, and in your line of work, a familiar with healing abilities would be an asset."

"How do you know what I do for work?"

"There aren't many Storm Winters around here, and you have quite a reputation. One that shows you're excellent at helping people in need. And animals, by the looks of things."

"I take pride in my work." I flushed warmly under her praise. "You're the same."

"My love for animals trumps everything else. That's for sure."

I continued to pet the ginger cat. "Going back to Fire Fang, I don't know if this will help, but the last time I fought him, he smelled weird. It was sweet, a bit like honey."

"Honey! I can't think of any medical condition that would cause a familiar to smell like that," Doctor Hooper said. "Was it something he'd eaten?"

"It was coming off him, not just out of his mouth." And I'd been close enough to those teeth to be certain of that.

"I can look into it, see if anything comes up in the records, but it's not triggering anything for me." Doctor Hooper spent a minute checking over the cat before closing the cage door.

"You'll keep her here?" I said.

"Until she's better. She should be free to go in twenty-four hours, maybe sooner. I'll keep watch over her until then."

"I don't know who she belongs to. Her owner could be worried about her."

Binky tapped my leg with one paw and shook her head.

"Or maybe she doesn't have a home. I wondered if Binky had been looking after her. Not so long ago, she brought home ginger fur and a cat's collar. The collar could belong to this cat."

"Someone must love her if they gave her a collar."

"I don't know. It had an odd trace of magic on it. It made my skin tingle. It felt almost like a control spell or a tracking spell. I couldn't be certain."

"A tracking spell? Do you still have the collar?" Doctor Hooper asked.

"It's at my apartment."

"The owner could use the collar to find this cat. Send them my way if they turn up, and I'll reunite them."

Binky hurried to the cage and shoved her nose through the bars. The cats sniffed noses and chirruped to each other.

"Your familiar has made a friend," Doctor Hooper said. "That's sweet. If no owner shows up, do you have room for her?"

"I don't even have room for Binky."

Binky hissed at me but remained by the cage, sniffing and chirruping.

I held up a hand to placate her. "But we're adjusting, and we're useful to each other. She even helped me get away from Fire Fang the last time he attacked."

"I should still report Fire Fang to animal control." Doctor Hooper led us out, and we headed through to the examination room. "From what you've told me, he's a rogue familiar. We all know how dangerous they can be if they have no bond."

"Don't involve animal control. Not yet. Let me deal with him. I feel responsible for what he's going through."

"You don't know where he is. What if he attacks someone else?"

"He's only interested in me. He's leaving everybody else alone."

"For now. What if someone stumbles across him and he goes on the attack? You can defend yourself with magic, but someone else might not be so fortunate."

"I've got time to find him. I don't think he's a risk to anyone else."

"Just in case, let me give you something to help." Doctor Hooper walked to a locked cabinet and took out two small glass bottles. She mixed them together, put a lid on one, and handed it to me.

"What's this?"

"It's the strongest sedation spell I've got. It'll knock out anything and keep them unconscious for hours. There's also an added magic suppressor, just in case you get trapped by Fire Fang and need to minimize the damage he could do."

"Will it harm him?"

"It's not pleasant for whoever gets covered in it, but it'll slow Fire Fang down and make sure you don't get bitten again."

I tucked the potion in my pocket. "What do I owe you?"

"Settle up at the front desk. That potion is a freebie, though. My way of helping with your situation. I hope you get Fire Fang back under control."

"I'll make him see sense. He's angry with me because I didn't tell him about his test results until recently."

"He's blaming you for that?"

"There's no other reason he'd turn on me like this."

"Maybe, maybe not. You don't know his history, though. And those tests I ran on him show how unique he is, so there's no way of knowing what would trigger such an extreme reaction."

"I'm going for hatred. It always works for me. Thanks for the potion."

Doctor Hooper led me back into the reception area with Binky, where several patients were waiting to be seen. "Go home and get some rest. I'll keep an eye on the cat and let you know when she's ready to pick up."

"Pick up? I didn't agree to do that. Her owner could come looking for her."

"And if she doesn't? Binky won't be happy if you let her friend live on the streets." Doctor Hooper's smile was wicked as she looked at Binky.

Binky hopped up and down and nodded.

I groaned. I was about to argue the ginger cat had nothing to do with me, but I was too tired. So I simply nodded, paid the bill, and left the clinic with Binky beside me.

It looked like I had two cats and a killer hellhound in my life. How had that happened?

Chapter 9

My phone rang the next morning just as I got out of the shower. It was Doctor Hooper, so I answered it.

"Good morning, Storm. I'm happy to say your cat had a comfortable night. She slept through, and I've already examined her. She's ready to get out of the cage. Can you collect her?"

"I could, but she still doesn't belong to me."

"Ah! Binky didn't convince you to make room for one tiny, adorable ginger angel overnight, then?"

I glanced at Binky, who was snoozing on my pillow. "Not yet."

A soft sigh filtered down the line. "I know this is an imposition, but could you take her as a temporary foster? The shelters are full, and keeping an animal in a cage isn't fair to them. It'll only be for a couple of weeks until a space opens or we find her owner."

"Sure it will." Once I got that cat through the door, she wouldn't leave. Just like Binky.

"She's been no trouble. She's a friendly little thing, just nervous of new people. And she gets on well with your cat. They'll be good company for each other."

I rough dried my hair with vigor. "Okay, you don't have to keep selling her to me. I can collect her in an hour." I looked at Binky, whose ears had pricked up. If cats could smile, she'd be grinning from ear to ear. I said goodbye to Doctor Hooper. "Don't get excited. This is temporary. We'll ask around and see if we can find her a home. She could have an owner who's missing her for all we know. The ginger ninja isn't getting a bed of her own."

Binky shook her head. She seemed as determined as Doctor Hooper that the cat was moving in permanently.

Just over an hour and a half later, I was staggering through the damaged apartment door with the ginger cat in a carrier, a bag full of supplements for her, healing spells from Doctor Hooper, and a cat-sized shoebox.

I set down the carrier, and the ginger cat pawed to get out. I put her medications on the kitchen counter and placed down the shoebox. I lined it with paper and an old blanket and put it next to Binky's own fur covered box, then I unlocked the carrier.

The ginger cat poked her head out and sniffed for a few seconds. Binky chirped and trilled, encouraging her out. It took a few minutes, but the cat finally emerged. She remained low to the floor, skulking along and sniffing everything. Binky walked beside her, still making chirruping noises.

When I was certain the ginger cat wouldn't pee on the rug or in my shoes, I made a coffee then settled on the couch and watched them.

The ginger cat slowly grew in confidence, thanks to Binky's encouragement and my silence, and after half an hour of exploration, they settled in their shoeboxes and closed their eyes.

I got out the sedation potion Doctor Hooper had given me and placed it on the couch. This had to be a last resort for Fire Fang. My Plan Z. And even if I used it, it would be a temporary fix. I needed a permanent solution to this problem. I had to find the thing that triggered Fire Fang to turn violent.

If I didn't succeed, my time in Witch Haven would soon be over, since Fire Fang would eventually corner me, flambé me, and eat my charred remains.

Shouting in the street below had me off the couch and peering out the window. There were people running past. I couldn't hear what they were yelling about, so I cracked open the window.

"It's here! I saw the van drive through five minutes ago."

"What's arrived? Is it honeycomb creams?"

"I heard it was more candy canes. The peppermint kind."

"No, it's those dark chocolate truffles. I love those."

The voices were mixed, so I couldn't pick out who was yelling, but they were in a mad dash, heading to the candy store.

Why was everyone so into that place? It was all people cared about. Witch Haven could be sleepy, but one new store shouldn't cause so much commotion.

Something was off with that place. Could Sherry be using magic to persuade people to shop only there? She'd want to make her new store a success, but if she was using extreme measures and unfairly influencing people, it had to stop.

I finished my coffee and checked on the ginger cat. She was sound asleep, her little chest rising and falling in a regular rhythm. She was kind of cute.

Binky lifted her head from her shoebox and blinked at me.

"Don't think I'm won over by those cute toe beans and that little pink nose," I said. "The ginger ninja is only a guest."

Binky purred softly, a smug look on her fluffy face.

"You stay here and watch over her. I'm going to the candy store. I have a feeling Sherry Brown isn't the sweetheart she claims to be. And there's something about that place that leaves a bitter taste in my mouth."

Binky nodded and tucked herself back into the shoebox.

I put on my boots, grabbed my purse, and headed down the stairs. After a quick check to make sure Fire Fang wasn't nearby, I headed out. Several more people hurried past me.

"Hey, is there an event I don't know about at the candy store?" I said to one woman as she dashed past.

"It's another delivery. They arrive at the same time every morning. I overslept, otherwise I'd be there now."

"There's not a sale or giveaway or something like that?"

She was already ahead of me and had to look over her shoulder to reply. "No. I just need more candy. If I don't get there in the next ten minutes, I'll miss out."

"Or you could wait for the next delivery, like a sane person would."

She ignored me and hurried on.

As I approached the store, there was already a bustling, restless queue waiting. I glanced over people's heads to see the inside was bursting with customers.

Rather than joining the queue or attempting to force my way in, I grabbed a takeout coffee and set myself up on the bench opposite the candy store.

The queue grew increasingly fractious, and there was shoving and swear words flying around. People were jostling and complaining about how long everyone was taking inside. And when people finally emerged from the store, they came out with bulging bags of treats, and they were always eating what they'd purchased. Were they genuine sugar addicts, or had they gotten hooked on something in that candy?

A familiar voice had me looking around. My hands clenched on my takeout mug when I spotted Luna hurrying toward the store with Odessa and Indigo.

She carried two large, white bakery boxes, the same as the others. "I hope Sherry likes these. Uncle Albert made them to her strict instructions."

"They won't be half as good as what Sherry sells, but it gives us an excuse to get to the front of the queue," Odessa said. "I've been waking at six every morning to make sure I'm first in line. The scarecrows hate the early starts, but they'll have to put up with it. I'd do anything for Sherry's caramel deluxe swirls."

"We'll all have to get used to the early starts if we want Sherry's treats," Indigo said. "More and more people are hearing about this place and showing up. It shouldn't be allowed. Locals only."

"Sherry will have to open a second store," Luna said. "It's not fair we miss out on the candy because people buy more than their fair share."

I hunched in my seat, watching as they marched to the front of the queue and shoved past people to get in. Luna was using her uncle's bakery products to get what she wanted. It was sneaky but not surprising. She used that tactic to get people to talk to her when she needed information, so why not use her uncle's amazing desserts to get inside her new favorite store?

At least Albert had made use of his baked goods, even if it meant he had to partner with the candy store that was putting him out of business.

A fight broke out in the queue, and someone got shoved to the ground. Before I could get up to help, they were on their feet and shoving back just as hard. The skirmish ended as quickly as it started when Sherry emerged with a tray of free samples.

"Settle down, everyone. Your sugar fairy is here. Sorry for the long wait. I promise you'll get inside soon. Here's something to enjoy while you think about all the delicious treats you're about to buy."

The free samples calmed things, and the crowd was content to munch their treats and wait their turn. Sherry disappeared inside with an empty tray and a sickly smile on her glossy pink lips.

A quick glance around revealed no one from the Magic Council was paying attention to what was going on outside the store. No doubt Olympus was still caught up in making sure his new boss had a perfect ceremony, rather than dealing with anything important.

As more people came out of the store, the queue moved, but it wasn't getting shorter. More people were joining the end, waiting impatiently for their turn to get candy.

Twenty minutes later, Luna, Odessa, and Indigo emerged, minus the bakery boxes. They had full bags with them and chatted excitedly as they showed each other their purchases.

I crushed my takeout mug and put it in the recycling before marching over to them. I was done hiding. The least I deserved was an explanation for why they'd ditched me. I wanted to see the looks in their eyes when they told me we were no longer friends.

"Hey, I want a word with you."

Indigo rolled her eyes when she saw me. "What do you want?"

"Answers. Or are you all too cowardly to talk to me these days?"

"We're not cowards. We just can't be bothered with you," Indigo said.

Her words were like a gut punch, but I hid my pain with a grunt and a curl of my top lip.

"It's not that," Odessa said, "but we realized you're not a nice person. You're abrupt and blunt. Just like now. No hello or how are you? You stomp over and demand answers. Is it any surprise no one wants to be your friend?"

Luna nudged her. "Try these peppermint creams. They're out of this world delicious."

Anger lit a fire inside me, and I was tempted to rip the bag out of her sticky fingers. "Forget stuffing your faces. Why didn't any of you have the courtesy to tell me this friendship wasn't working? I had to hear it from Olympus. Although I'd figured it out a while ago when you stopped returning my messages."

"So you do have a brain," Indigo said. "It took you long enough to get the hint. All those messages and pretending you needed help with Fire Fang and Binky so we'd feel sorry for you. Kind of pathetic."

"These lemon and saffron creams are amazing," Luna said.

"Oooh, let me try." Odessa grabbed one, earning herself a scowl from Luna.

"You didn't answer my question." My hands curled into fists to stop me from slamming them with lightning for their cold indifference. "What went so wrong?"

"You went wrong," Indigo said. "We tried so hard with you, but it was like bashing on a brick wall. You wouldn't budge. Every time we offered to help, you turned us down and made it clear you didn't value our friendships."

It was my worst fears come true. "The cases I work on are dangerous. I didn't want anyone getting hurt."

"We can look after ourselves," Odessa said. "I have my army of scarecrows if I get in trouble. Luna has an alpha werewolf watching her back, and Indigo, well, she's Indigo. She could destroy the world if she wanted to."

"Not the world but probably a continent or two." Indigo shoved a hand into her candy bag.

I stepped forward and gripped her wrist. "I haven't always been the best friend to any of you, but I don't deserve this. We've known each other since we were kids. You don't just ditch someone like this."

"It's not our fault you didn't see the warning signs," Luna said. "Leave Indigo alone. Let her eat her candy."

"I'm good." Rage sparked in Indigo's eyes. "But I suggest you let go of my wrist, unless you want to regret ever meeting me."

I tightened my grip. What signs had I missed? They had to realize my intentions were good, even though I came at things with the blunt end of an instrument.

"Let. Go." Indigo spoke the words in a whisper laced with the threat of devastation if I didn't back off.

I stepped away, releasing my hold. "None of you are worth wasting time on. I don't know why we were ever friends."

"At least we agree on something," Indigo said. "You're a waste of space. You're not even helping Olympus with that murder case. You're no good to anyone."

I ignored the cutting insults. "Murder! Do you mean Galaan?"

"Yeah, the guy who died in the candy store."

"But he choked to death on a candy. I've looked into motives, but Olympus ruled it an accidental death. He was clear about that."

"There you go again, making assumptions. Olympus told me you'd fought, and you huffed out of his office before hearing the information. If you'd stuck around, you'd have learned Galaan's candy was cursed," Indigo said. "But you were too stubborn and angry with the world to find out all the facts. No wonder no one wants to spend time with you. Come on, ladies. We're done here." She turned and walked away.

Luna and Odessa glanced at me. They both shrugged and followed her, their mouths jammed full of sugary treats.

I stared after them, too stunned to react. Our friendships were over. There was nothing left for me to salvage. They hated me.

And because I'd gotten so angry with Olympus, I hadn't kept up-to-date on Galaan's case. From the start, I'd had a feeling there was more to his death than a simple accident, but I'd given up because I'd let my frustration get the better of me.

I should still stay away from the investigation. I had enough going on with Fire Fang.

But a murder in my village. There was no way I could ignore that.

Chapter 10

After my gut wrenching conversation with Indigo, Luna, and Odessa, I found myself sitting opposite Olympus in his office, trying to keep calm. It wasn't going well.

"You should have gotten in touch when you learned about the actual cause of death," I said.

Olympus shifted in his seat. "After the way we left things, I assumed you weren't interested in helping. You made it clear you were done with the case."

"Only because you made it clear you were ruling it an accidental death. Even after I'd looked into suspects and found motives for murder, you weren't interested."

His phone rang, and he grabbed it, seeming happy to have a reason not to talk to me. "Commissioner. I have the information you need. I was about to send it through, but I had an... issue to deal with." Olympus glanced at me, not hiding the irritation in his voice. "Of course. I understand how important this is. I'll send it immediately. Yes, we can't afford any delays." He ended his call and set down the phone.

"More ceremony business?"

"It's the key focus for the Magic Council. There are only a few days left to get everything together." He sighed and slumped in his seat. "I wish the results from that candy had come back clear. What a mess."

I dug my nails into my palms. "But they haven't. So surely, a murder caused by a piece of cursed candy needs to be your priority and not the ceremony table cloths and seating plans."

"And then there's the public event." Olympus kept talking like I hadn't spoken. "I need some of my people to attend that to make sure everything goes smoothly. Not an imposing presence, just enough to show the Magic Council cares about local issues."

"Like solving murders?"

"Public events are important. We have a reputation to maintain."

"One that shows your continued incompetence if you ignore this murder." I shook my head in despair. He was still focused on the wrong things.

Olympus opened his desk drawer and pulled out a bag of dark chocolate balls. He took one and sucked on it. "That's better. I need something to help me focus."

I stared at the bag of candy. "Let me guess, you got those from the store over the road?"

"Of course. I feel privileged my office is opposite the candy store. I get to see when the deliveries come in. And of course, Sherry knows me now and realizes what a busy man I am, so she lets me in first."

"Nothing like exploiting your position to get what you want."

Olympus slammed his drawer shut. "If you won't be helpful, you can leave."

I shoved down my irritation. I wanted to tell him to stick it, but if I didn't do something about solving this case, Galaan's murder would be forgotten. "I want to help. You know I can be useful. And an unsolved murder in Witch Haven is wrong. We need to figure out what happened."

"That's my plan." He tossed another ball into his mouth and smacked his lips together.

"So, what are you doing to find the person who cursed the candy?"

"I've looked at the results from the analysis."

"Do you know what curse was used?"

"There was no clear magic signature left behind. It was a generic death curse. Not that difficult to get, and many magic users could create it, even though it's illegal to use."

"It seems unlikely Nazan would have used a curse to kill," I said. "Have you spoken to him again to see how guilty he looks?"

Olympus lifted the bag of chocolate balls and took another. "Not yet."

"You're planning to, though?"

He set the bag down. "I'm considering my options."

"Olympus, you are looking into this murder, aren't you? The longer you leave it, the more likely it is that the killer will get away with it. And what about Juliet and Nile?"

"Who are they?"

I gripped the edge of the seat. "I already told you. Juliet dated Galaan, and Nile was Galaan's brother. Nile and Juliet are now dating."

"Oh, sure. Those two. I'll talk to them soon. After the event."

"Nile was asking about collecting his brother's body. Since the autopsy is done and the results are back, you need to work fast. What if he wants the burial done quickly to hide evidence?"

Olympus puffed out his chest. "Storm, I know how to run an investigation."

"Yet you're acting like you don't."

He tsked at me. "I have a full work schedule. Once I get things off my desk—"

"Like the dumb ceremony and this stupid public event you're so concerned about."

"Two crucially important events. The inauguration of—"

"I don't care about the ceremony. It'll happen whether or not the champagne has been chilled. But it sounds like you haven't even considered why Galaan was cursed. Who could have done it? Was it an isolated case? Are more people at risk? Could there be more cursed candy in that store and it hasn't been eaten yet? For all you know, there could be a dozen more deaths about to happen. Maybe the balls you've been gobbling down are laced with the curse."

He blinked rapidly, as if he hadn't considered any of this, then laughed. He actually laughed. "I trust Sherry. She wouldn't sell cursed candy. Galaan's death was a one-off. And no one else has died, which proves my theory."

"Yet! No one else has died yet."

He ate another ball, I'm sure out of spite or simply to show me he was the biggest bozo in the village.

I'd print him out a gold star and smack it on his forehead.

"Have you at least tested the rest of the Orange Surprises in the store?" I growled out through gritted teeth.

"Oh! I... I didn't think about doing that. Should I have?"

I clenched my hands and let out a long, slow breath. "If I was in your shoes, I'd have closed the candy store and searched it from head to toe. All the candy stock would have been cleared out and examined."

Olympus barked out a strained laugh. "That's the worst idea I've ever heard. The candy store can never close."

"Why not? You're too trusting of a woman who's only just moved to Witch Haven. What's Sherry's background? Where has she come from? What's her experience of running a candy store? Do you know anything about her magic? She could specialize in curses, not sugar. And she could be trying new curses on her customers. Her sweet and innocent veneer will crack like a candy cane if you prod her enough."

"Don't say things like that about Sherry. She's a wonderful addition to Witch Haven. She's generous with her candy, has time for everyone, and is always helpful. When she learned Fandango's was at risk of going out of business because of her, she set up a contract with Albert so he could sell his muffins in her store. She even donated sacks of candy to him to use in his recipes to sweeten the deal."

I still wasn't buying it. "She sounds like an angel, but even angels' halos slip. Don't you think it's weird how everyone is so obsessed with that place?"

Olympus shrugged. "Not really. Just because you're not into sweet things doesn't make everyone else wrong. Why shouldn't we enjoy a new store? I always support local businesses. Do you? How much candy have you purchased since Sherry opened?" He looked down his nose at me.

"I'm not saying there's anything wrong with shopping local, but just this morning people were literally running to the candy store because there'd been a new delivery. Big whoop."

"Oh, really! I couldn't make it over there this morning. What came in?"

I groaned and tipped back my head. "Olympus, you're not listening. That store has got everyone turned around, and you can't see the problem because you're focused on things that don't matter."

"A huge, free community event that'll unite everyone and bring happiness to this village is far from insignificant."

"Perhaps not, but why is it happening now? Why is it as interesting to you as the candy you're gorging on like a starving pig?"

"Oink, oink," Monty whispered from his basket.

"Monty, be quiet. I've warned you twice today about speaking when you shouldn't." Olympus's tone was so sharp it made me wince.

Monty whined and hid his head under one large fluffy paw.

After glaring at Monty, Olympus turned back to me. "I didn't say the event was of interest to me, but when I learned Sherry was involved and would hold demonstrations and give away samples and prizes, it seemed natural to support it. I rushed through the permit so it could happen smoothly."

I looked out the window at the heaving crowd outside the candy store. "We keep coming back to that sugar loaded place."

"You're so suspicious of something so perfect. There's always a buzz when a new store opens in the village. There's nothing wrong with that."

"Who is planning this big event? Is it Sherry?"

"I'm not sure. I'll have to check the permit. Is it important?"

"Yes. Check the permit."

Olympus shuffled in his seat but didn't move. "I don't have time for this. Besides, what does any of this have to do with Galaan's murder?"

"That's what I'm figuring out. Galaan died in that store, and Sherry went on a date with him. We should look at that connection again."

"Or you should stop looking for connections where there aren't any. You're always so mistrustful of people. Why can't Sherry simply be a nice lady who loves chocolate?"

"No one is that nice. Check the permits, Olympus. I insist. And I'm not moving from this seat until you do. I'm sure you want to get rid of me as much as Indigo does, so the sooner you do it, the sooner I leave you alone."

He grumbled for several seconds before going to a filing cabinet. He pulled out a file and flicked through it. "So much for your suspicious mind. Sherry is simply an exhibitor at the event, along with a host of other local businesses."

"Who applied for the permit?"

"Someone called Mary Smith."

I tilted my head. "We don't have a Mary Smith living in Witch Haven."

"Anyone can apply for a permit for an event. They don't need to live here."

"Sure, but that's got to be one of the most common names in the world. Don't you think that's odd?"

"No. Mary filled in the paperwork correctly, paid the fee, and even expressed the forms over, so I'd have time to process them."

"You didn't meet her?"

"If I met everyone who needed a permit, it would be my full-time job." Olympus turned from the cabinet. "The event is just what the village needs, especially after what happened to Galaan. People can move on and forget the troubles."

"You're moving on and forgetting the troubles even though you haven't solved the murder. Bit premature, don't you think?"

He shoved the file back into the cabinet and slammed it shut. "Enough! Storm, you're not helping. I know I asked you to assist with this case, but I've changed my mind. You're more trouble than you're worth."

"I found three suspects with no alibis in less than forty-eight hours. You're the one who can't be bothered to look into them. Too much like hard work, I guess?"

His glower was impressive, but the chocolate smeared on his chin detracted from his attempts at menace. "You shouldn't be allowed to chase criminals. You've probably intimidated dozens of innocent people into confessing to things they haven't done, just so you'd stop harassing them. When I have a moment, I'll be suggesting to the Magic Council we remove your license to practice as a private investigator."

I slid from my seat and stood slowly. "Try to take my permit, and you'll see how quickly I can shoot you in the head with a lightning bolt."

"That was a threat. Monty, you heard her. Storm threatened to kill me!"

Monty simply whimpered, his face still hidden under his paw.

It took all my control not to use Olympus as target practice for a weather spell. It was no less than he deserved. Instead, I took a breath. "This isn't about our mutual dislike for each other. That curse got into the candy somehow, and you don't even know if Galaan was the target. Anyone could have picked it up. You also don't know if there are more curses waiting to be consumed."

"None of that is factual. And that's all I care about. Facts."

"Once you've dealt with the ceremony and the public event where you'll get even more free candy to smear across your chin, you mean."

Olympus's lips thinned. "It's time you left."

"No. I'm staying and working on this case. Let me see the autopsy report and the results on the candy."

He planted both hands on the desk and leaned forward. "I don't need you here. I have everything covered."

"I can look into this myself. You can't stop me."

Olympus raised his palms to the ceiling. "Do that if you must, but stay out of my way. And stay out of my office. Monty, show Storm out and make sure she doesn't come back. Guard the door if you have to. You have my permission to bite her if she continues to be a nuisance."

Monty stood and stared at Olympus. "You want me to throw Storm out?"

"Yes. She's no longer welcome. See she doesn't come back in ever again." Olympus pointed at the door. "Leave."

I looked at Monty. He had an apologetic look on his furry face as he inclined his head at the door. "I really don't want to rough you up. Would you mind terribly leaving and not being too horrible to me?"

I glared at Olympus for several seconds. He was an idiot, just like my former friends. He had his priorities wrong, but nothing I could say would change his mind. "I will get to the bottom of this murder. It's wrong Galaan's death is such a low priority with the Magic Council."

"If you don't like the way I do things, file a complaint."

"Which you'd whisk away, never to be seen again. I wouldn't waste my time." I marched to the door, stopping to scratch Monty's head to show there were no hard feelings.

He whined. "Sorry, but please don't come back again. I don't like the taste of witch."

"I won't make trouble for you. You, on the other hand," I snarled at Olympus. "This isn't over." I opened the door, closed it, and stood outside.

I was on my own again. I'd never considered Olympus a great ally, but I could usually rely on him for information and to do the right thing, even if he took the scenic route to get there. And he'd wanted me involved. But the second I'd made things difficult, he'd baulked.

It didn't matter. This was my area of expertise. If Olympus didn't want me looking into Galaan's murder on behalf of the Magic Council, I'd take on the job myself. I'd work for free and figure out what happened. Then I'd rub Olympus's smug face into the solution. He wouldn't be able to ignore me when I revealed the truth about where that cursed candy came from.

But I needed to gather information and fast, and that meant queue jumping.

I marched to the candy store, and after much shoving and elbowing of disgruntled greedy guts, I'd made my way inside and was looking for Sherry. She was behind the counter, shoveling cocoa dusted truffles into a bag for an impatiently waiting customer.

After giving her a moment to get free, I stepped in front of the next person.

"Hey! Wait your turn." I got a shove in the back.

I turned and bared my teeth at the woman who'd put her hands on me. "Back off. I'm not in the mood for sugar induced hysterics. You'll get your fix of candy, but I need to talk to Sherry about a murder."

The woman's eyes widened. "But... I must have my candy."

"There's no need to argue." Sherry rushed around the counter. "There's plenty for everyone."

I ignored her and kept eyeballing the woman until she backed away. The mood I was in, I'd take on the entire underworld and win. I had some anger kinks to work out after my run-in with Olympus.

"Storm, is there a problem?" Sherry touched my arm.

I exhaled through my nose. "I need to talk to you. It's important."

"You mentioned murder. Is this about Galaan?"

"Yes. And there's something else, too."

"I'm happy to help in any way I can, but I can't leave the store. Too many customers, you see." She gestured to the anxious faces, their sweaty hands clasping money.

"And we're all waiting," the woman who shoved me muttered.

"I'm happy to talk about Galaan's murder in front of everyone if it doesn't bother you," I said.

Sherry's smile faltered a fraction as she went back behind the counter. "I have nothing to hide. Come join me. You can help if you like."

I wasn't serving customers, but if I was with Sherry, I wouldn't keep getting my toes trodden on as people inched closer to peer at the treats.

Once I was behind the counter, I could finally breathe, although there was an overpowering smell of warm sugar in the air and cocoa powder tickled my nose.

"Who's next?" Sherry said brightly.

The woman I'd barged in front of stepped up. "I'll have a pound of orange truffles, two pounds of dark chocolate covered mints, and a bag of honeycomb. Make that two bags. The last time I was here, you'd run out."

"Is that all for you?" I said.

"Of course. I'm not sharing with anyone." The woman's tone was sharp.

"People love their candy around here." Sherry swiftly gathered the order.

"I've got a picture to show you." I pulled up the photo I'd taken of Juliet and Nile on my phone and showed it to Sherry. "Have you seen these people in your store?"

She took a second to study the picture. "They don't look familiar. If someone visits once, they become a repeat customer, so I'd remember them."

"You're certain? One of them is Galaan's brother, Nile."

Sherry looked again. "I see the resemblance. No, he's not been in. I don't recognize the woman, either. Have a wonderfully sweet day." She handed the order to the woman, took the money, and moved on to her next customer.

"Are you serving, too?" A guy barged up to the counter and dumped his basket in front of me.

"No. Wait your turn, like everyone else," I said.

He glowered at me and slunk away.

"I won't be long, I promise," Sherry called after him. "They just keep coming, don't they? So, Galaan? How is the investigation going?"

"The Magic Council got the results back on the candy Galaan choked on," I said. "The Orange Surprise was cursed. That's what killed him."

Sherry dropped a metal scooper, and it clattered to the floor. "Cursed candy? In my store? But... but how?"

"That's what I wanted to ask you about. Since you don't recognize the other suspects in the investigation, it rules them out. Have you any experience with curses?"

"Never! My magic involves food. I'd never use anything dark. And I've never tried a curse. Give me a moment." Sherry cleared her throat and lifted her hands. "Everybody, it's just browsing for now. There's a problem with the register. I'm fixing it as fast as I can, and you'll get a ten percent discount off all purchases because of the wait."

Finally, someone was taking Galaan's murder seriously. "Is there something you need to tell me about cursed candy?"

Sherry moved me to the back of the counter, her grip tight on my arm. "Do you think anything else in the store could be cursed?" Her shock seemed genuine, as did her concern for the customers. It took me by surprise.

"That's what I suggested to Olympus, but he didn't seem worried."

She bit her bottom lip. "Oh, well, if the Magic Council isn't worried—"

"Olympus has other things on his mind and isn't thinking clearly. Has anyone complained of being ill after buying anything from here?"

"No! Everyone's been delighted with their purchases." Sherry clasped her hands together then pressed them to her mouth. "This is terrible news. What kind of curse was it?"

"Olympus was unhelpfully vague. He simply said a general death curse."

"To be on the safe side, I should remove the Orange Surprises. That was the candy Galaan loved."

"I suggest you close the store and empty the contents. Everything should be tested."

Her eyes flashed wide. "Is that necessary? Is that what I have to do?"

"Unfortunately, I can't order you to do anything. But get rid of the Orange Surprises, just in case Galaan wasn't the target and more people are at risk."

"Of course. If you think that's best." Sherry surveyed the sea of unsettled customers, all wanting to get their sticky fingers on the goodies behind the glass. "Would you mind collecting them? They're on the circular table in the middle of the room, with the lemon snaps. I keep the citrus flavors together."

I was happy to do that, since it would play to my advantage. I could take the candy and test it. Although, by now, the original batch of Orange Surprises would be long gone, maybe the killer had come back if they planned more deaths.

I left Sherry serving, grabbed a bag, and scooped the candy into it. I headed back behind the counter and tucked them away. "I also need to talk to you about this event happening in Witch Haven."

"Oh, isn't it exciting? This nice lady asked if I'd be the candy supplier. I wasn't sure I'd be able to handle it on my own, but she offered such a big fee, I couldn't refuse."

"Who is this nice lady?"

"Mary Smith. Everything is so organized. She showed me the plans for the event. It'll be a wonderful way to introduce the candy store to everyone in the village. I know there are some people who've been resisting the temptation."

I shook my head at the truffle she offered me. "Mary came into the store and told you about the event?"

"That's right. She said when she saw the queue outside, she knew this was the perfect business to make the day extra special. I'm the only candy supplier, so it's a big deal. Apparently, there'll be people attending from all the local villages."

"I know little about the event. Why has it been arranged?"

Sherry paused and tilted her head. "To give people a fun time. There'll be prizes, surprises, and treats. Mary asked me to supply a candy gift basket as a raffle prize. I was happy to oblige. And I'm going to make it the biggest basket I've ever put together. Candy for a whole year!"

"Have you got Mary's contact details?" I couldn't put my finger on it, but something didn't add up about this event. Why the rush to hold it so quickly? Who was the elusive Mary Smith? Why did she only want Sherry's candy served? What was her connection to Witch Haven?

"The paperwork is under the counter. Have a look. Her details will be on there."

I rifled around and discovered a single sheet of paper. It showed the eye watering fee Sherry was being paid, but other than the name Mary Smith printed at the bottom, there was no email, phone number, or social media presence. That was weird.

"How do you get in contact with Mary?" I asked.

"She comes by every couple of days to see how things are going. She's always in Witch Haven finalizing details. You've probably seen her around. She may even be in today if you have to speak to her. Why the interest? Do you want to host a stall for your business? I'm sure Mary could make room for you."

"Not my scene." Something felt wrong. Mary Smith could be hiding something. Maybe she was the one behind the cursed candy. I'd ruled out the other suspects, and Sherry was being her annoyingly sweet, obliging self and had seemed so shocked about the curse on the candy. It still didn't make me warm to her, though.

"You're welcome to wait here to see if Mary comes in," Sherry said, "but if you do, I'd appreciate it if you'd pick up a scoop and help. My lovely customers are getting agitated."

"You're good. I'll wait outside. The sweet smells play havoc with my sinuses."

"Oh, that's a shame. Take candy with you before you go. On the house. And grab whatever you want for your cute pup. I've been seeing him here a lot. He always causes a stir when he visits. Such an adorable dog."

"Fire Fang's been coming here?"

"Yes! And he loves the violet creams. Tell him I said hi. Please, take some candy."

I shook my head. I wasn't in the mood for anything sweet, especially not if it might come with a death curse attached. I grabbed the bag of Orange Surprises I'd confiscated and headed outside.

But I wasn't done with the candy store. I tucked myself into an alleyway opposite the store, opened the bag of candy, and tested each piece to see if there was rogue magic on it. While I did that, I watched the comings and goings from the store.

The crowd was relentless, almost verging on obsessive as they shoved their way in and emerged looking dazed with bags full of candy. That wasn't natural. Even if the candy was amazing, people couldn't get through that much candy every day and stay healthy.

It took me an hour to work through the Orange Surprises, and I didn't find any curse magic on a single piece. Galaan was either an unlucky guy and had picked up the only piece with a curse on it, or he'd been targeted for a reason. But I had no idea what that reason could be.

A movement caught my eye, and I tensed, my heart speeding up. Fire Fang was racing toward me.

I didn't have a chance to dodge out of the alley, so I turned and ran along it, drawing him away from the crowd.

A solid brick wall met me as I came to the end. There was no way out. With a thundering heart and a dry mouth, I drew on my magic and turned to meet Fire Fang. "Stay back. I don't want to hurt you." I swiped my hands through the air, conjuring a lightning bolt.

He snarled and kept running.

I slammed the lightning in front of Fire Fang, but he didn't slow. I slashed my hands through the air again and drew down more lightning. "It doesn't have to end this way." Did I have it in me to destroy him? Every nerve told me not to, but if I didn't stop Fire Fang, I'd die.

He lunged through the air, fangs aimed at my chest.

I pulled the sedation potion out of my pocket and slammed it over his head as his teeth brushed my throat.

I grabbed him and held him against my chest, his fangs snapping beside my ear and his claws raking down my chest, ripping my sweater. The potion drenched not only him, but me, and I staggered as my magic drained and my strength faded. But I couldn't pass out with a vicious hellhound on top of me. There'd be nothing to stop him from taking a big old bite if I blacked out.

Fire Fang was also feeling the effects of the potion. His struggling lessened, and his head slumped against my shoulder.

I tried to keep upright, but my vision was darkening. I sank to my knees, Fire Fang's weight taking me down too fast, and lost the battle to keep my eyes open.

Chapter 11

I don't know how long I'd been unconscious, but when my eyes reopened, the alleyway was dark.

The change in light was the last thing I was worrying about. There was a huge, naked man pinning me to the ground. And he was snoring!

Was this a dream? I shoved against the unconscious guy, but he didn't move. And he was solid. Definitely not a dream. More like a muscled nightmare.

Where had he come from? Why was he sprawled out on top of me, snoring? And where was Fire Fang? If he'd regained consciousness before me, he'd have finished me off. But there was no sign of him, other than the sting from the gouges on my chest where he'd attacked me.

I tried to squirm out from under the guy, but he was a large, unmoving dead weight. At least the gentle snores revealed he wasn't literally dead. I couldn't see his face because his long, dark hair covered it. He also had a beard that scratched the side of my face.

After much grunting and heaving, I wriggled out and rolled him away with my feet, so he landed on his back, revealing even more muscle and so much bare skin I wasn't sure where to look.

I stared at this stranger in disbelief. It made no sense he was here. I definitely didn't recognize him. And I could see every inch of his tattooed form.

I shifted until my back was against the opposite wall. Even that was an effort, and I was panting from that small exertion. The potion Doctor Hooper had given me to use on Fire Fang was crazy effective. I felt kitten weak and had to fight the desire to close my eyes again.

When I tried my magic, all I got was a faint flicker of a spell on my palm before it extinguished.

The guy groaned, and I tensed. He grumbled something that may have been a word.

I poked his tattooed bicep with my boot. "Hey, wake up. You have explaining to do."

He groaned again and slowly turned his head. He stared at me unblinking for several seconds.

"Who are you? Why did I wake to find you naked and unconscious on top of me? And where's my hellhound?"

He blinked once and slowly raised a large hand to swipe his hair off his face to reveal dark eyes with a red rim around the iris. "Storm."

I jerked back. "How do you know me?"

The guy went to move, but I forced out a trickle of magic and flared it in his face. "Watch it. I don't trust you. I don't know you."

The guy lifted one hand and inched back until he was sitting, his knees up to hide his crown jewels. "Storm, it's me." He looked down at himself. "Wow! It really is me. It's been a while."

"Who? Who are you?"

His smile was cautious. "I'm Fire Fang."

My hand dropped, along with my jaw. "You can't be."

He looked down at himself again and shook his head. "I don't know what happened, but it really is me. I'm back in my mortal body."

I narrowed my eyes. "I don't believe you. This has to be a trick." I used the wall to push myself upright. "How did you turn back?"

His forehead furrowed as he stared at his bare toes. "No idea. The last thing I remember, we were fighting."

"I didn't fight you. Fire Fang chased me along this alleyway and trapped me. I never saw you."

"That was me in hellhound form. I saw you hiding and felt this overwhelming urge to attack. It was like I had no control over my actions."

"Stop talking as if you're Fire Fang." I waved a hand at him. "And cover yourself. I can see everything."

He shrugged. "What's the problem? You've seen me naked for months."

"You're not Fire Fang! But even if you were, this is different. He's a hellhound with fur. You're a big, naked guy. A very naked guy."

He huffed out a laugh. "It's all the same to me. And I really am Fire Fang. Did you do something to get me to change?"

I hesitated, still in two minds about whether to whack him with a trash can or keep questioning him. "I hit Fire Fang with a sedation potion. It also came with a magic suppressor. But that wouldn't be enough to turn you, would it?"

"It must have been. Otherwise, I wouldn't be here." He lifted his hands and inspected them. "It's so strange being back in my old skin. I'd gotten used to the fur."

I struggled to get my head around this. It was all too much, and I needed a timeout. I also felt lousy after being hit with that suppression potion. And if this guy was Fire Fang, and that was a big if, and he suddenly changed back into a rabid hellhound intent on killing me, I had little magic to defend myself with. It felt too vulnerable being out here on my own with no magic and no familiar.

"I've got to go." I staggered a few steps along the alleyway, cold, shivering, and confused.

"Storm, wait. I'll come with you."

"No, you stay here. I need to figure this out on my own."

"We should work this out together. Something in that potion changed me, and we need to know what that is. I have to make sure I'm in control of this change."

"You can't be Fire Fang." I kept staggering, not making much progress with my jello-like knees and wobbling legs, and my eyes kept shutting when I didn't want them to.

"Why can't I be? I have no idea what turned me into a hellhound, and I don't know how the magic you used reversed the effects, but it has. I'm back. Trust me."

I still didn't believe him. This huge, muscled, and frankly gorgeous guy couldn't be Fire Fang. I didn't want him in my life. I wanted the hairy, fire breathing terror I'd been hanging out with for months. So long as he stopped trying to kill me.

It was all too intense, and I was close to a full-on freak out. When I'd thought Fire Fang was a hellhound with a few quirks, I'd let down my guard. I'd been myself around him. He'd seen me at my best and my worst. He'd slept beside me in bed, even hung out in the bathroom while I showered. But now, the mortal version of Fire Fang was naked behind me. This guy had seen it all. I was embarrassed and more than a little disturbed.

My cheeks flamed with heat, and I kept walking.

"Hey, you crazy buttoned witch. Stop. We have to talk about this."

I'd reached the end of the alleyway, but his words made me freeze. I turned back to face him. "You called me a crazy buttoned witch."

He tilted his head. "I actually swore at you, but it didn't come out right. I don't usually swear at a lady."

"If you were Fire Fang, you'd know I'm no lady. Say it again."

"You want me to cuss at you?"

"Yes, to prove you're Fire Fang. If you're him, you'll know why you can't cuss."

He shrugged. "Whatever it takes to show I'm being truthful. You're a crazy buttoned witch. A sour slug, a donkey helmet. You're a... goblin nobble."

I sucked in a breath. "It is you. The speech spell we used on you still works." My gaze flickered over him again, avoiding the x-rated bits. Almost. So this was Fire Fang in mortal form. Over six feet tall, broad shoulders, tattoos, ragged pirate hair, and a dark beard. A handsome face, if a little stern, and lines around his eyes suggesting he'd been through tough times.

He nodded, his gaze also roaming over me. "It's me. I look different, but I have all my memories of our time together."

That made my cheeks heat again. I had no idea what to say to that.

"Do you think this reversal is permanent?" he finally said.

I slid off my jacket and tossed it to him. "Cover yourself and follow me. We have a lot to talk about."

Fire Fang wrapped my jacket around his waist, and we left the alleyway.

I checked my phone and was shocked to see it had just gone eleven o'clock at night. I'd been unconscious in the alleyway for ten hours. I was cold, starving, and the wounds on my chest ached, but I wasn't focusing on any of that. I kept shooting glances at the mortal version of Fire Fang. This was strange, and I couldn't get my head around what I'd do now he was back in his non-magical form.

He seemed as equally stunned as me and kept flicking me glances as he strode along on bare feet.

We headed into my apartment, neither of us speaking, and up the stairs. I opened the damaged door and let him in.

Binky, who'd been sleeping in her shoebox next to the ginger cat, hopped up and chirped. She raced over and twirled herself around Fire Fang's bare legs.

"Hey, Binky. At least you recognize me, even though I've lost my fur." He picked up the cat and cuddled her against his chest.

"How does she know you?" I headed to the kitchen to grab snacks and strong coffee.

"Maybe I smell the same to her. And we've been hanging out together. She loves sleeping against my belly."

Binky was purring louder than I'd ever heard her purr before. She sniffed Fire Fang's cheek and licked him.

My eyebrows rose. "Huh! It looks like she's flirting with you."

He chuckled and tickled Binky's head. "I reckon she might be. Who's this?" He stood over the other shoebox that contained the ginger cat.

"Another stray I can't get rid of. You don't recognize her?"

Fire Fang kneeled beside the box. "Is this the cat that attacked me?"

"That's the one. And you bit her so badly I had to take her to the vet. That's where I got the sedation and suppression potion. Doctor Hooper was worried you were a threat and might need putting down."

"She wasn't wrong. I am so sorry I bit you." Fire Fang held one hand out to the ginger cat. She shied away at first but then sniffed his fingers. "I don't know what came over me."

"Rage, a desire to destroy, blood lust." I brought the snacks and coffee to the table and set everything down. "Take a seat. I'll find you something to wear." Although from the size of him, I had nothing that would fit.

After a hunt through my closet, I found a baggy pair of sweatpants and a stretched out gray sweater with a hole in the armpit. I returned to the living room and passed the clothes to him, turning my back when he went to put them on.

"You don't need to be embarrassed. It's not as if you haven't seen all of this before."

"I definitely haven't seen all of that before." I kept my back turned as I waved a hand behind me.

He chuckled, and it had the same grumbling tone as Fire Fang's laugh, which made sense, since he was almost certainly the same person. Or hellhound. Or person hound. This mess would take some unravelling.

"You kind of have, although it all looked different. But seeing me like this is the same as me seeing you when you've strolled out of the shower with nothing on," Fire Fang said.

I groaned. "Let's forget that ever happened. And you're mortal now, so things have to be different."

"Different how?"

I had no answer for that, but we couldn't go back to how things used to be. If Fire Fang was mortal, he had no place in my world. Magic killed mortals. They were too weak to handle it, and they weren't allowed to know about it.

After an awkward few minutes of silence, Fire Fang let out a sigh. "Storm, are you okay?"

"Not completely."

"Is there anything I can do to help?"

"Give me a minute. I'm coming up with a plan." I dashed to the bathroom and pulled out my phone. Even though Indigo, Odessa, and Luna were no longer my friends, they'd have to help with this. They wouldn't ignore the fact there was a mortal in Witch Haven who knew the truth about magic. It had ramifications beyond our no longer liking each other problem.

I opened the group chat we had and was about to start a message. I'd been blocked. There was no way I could contact them.

I set down my phone and let out a slow breath. I had to face this problem alone, but I had no idea how.

Chapter 12

It was gone midnight, and I was on my third mug of coffee, sitting as far away from Fire Fang as I could on the couch. We'd gone in circles several times, trying to figure out why he'd turned back into a mortal. The only conclusion we'd come to was the magic used in the sedation and suppression potion had caused the change. But how long that would last was anyone's guess. And that had me worried.

Fire Fang shuffled around on the couch, moving Binky from his lap, where she'd curled up the second he'd sat down. That cat adored him and wasn't fazed by his lack of fur.

"What'll happen if I turn back?" He glanced at me, his expression serious. "Will I be back to normal, or will I keep attacking you?"

I lifted my shoulders. "Your guess is as good as mine. Why did you attack me in the first place?"

He scrubbed his fingers through his beard. "I can't tell you, but I just kept getting waves of rage hitting me. All I wanted to do was destroy you. I kept seeing red and feeling so angry with you."

"Because I hid the results? You were angry because I didn't tell you about you being a mortal?"

"That didn't bother me. I mean, I was stunned by the mortal revelation. I didn't feel mortal. I still don't, but I wasn't angry you kept it a secret from me."

"You had a general feeling of hatred toward me for no reason?"

He mulled over the question. "I guess I did."

"And do you feel that now?"

"No. I mainly feel confused. I want to know how I became a hellhound in the first place and if this change back is permanent. And if it isn't, what do I do next? How long have I got before I sprout fur and start growling again?"

I rolled my mug between my hands. "Do you want to stay as a mortal?"

His mouth twisted to the side. "I'm not sure. I had fun being a hellhound."

"What about your memories? Do you remember what your life was like before you turned into a hellhound?"

Fire Fang shook his head. "It's still a blank. I get the occasional flash, but it's nothing I can cling to."

"You said before you had memories of a red brick house. It could have been your home. Maybe you have a family living there. A wife and kids wondering where you went."

"If I do, I have no clue how I'll explain any of this to them. Magic, hellhounds, potions." He huffed out a breath. "It's too surreal. Although I always knew it was real. I remember that much. Before I turned into a hound, I believed so strongly there was something else out there. Something more than my mortal life. I just couldn't prove it."

"You can't talk about any of this." I leaned forward. "No mortal can know about magic."

"I was kidding. Kind of. I'm still wrapping my head around this mess. I won't blurt it out to anyone. Besides, who would I tell?"

"The woman you married?"

"Whoa! We're jumping ahead about a thousand steps. I don't think I'm married."

"How can you be sure?"

His dark eyes flickered over me. "Why are you so interested?"

I scowled at him. "To make sure Witch Haven remains a safe place for magic users and non-magicals don't poke around and get nosy. They're not welcome here, no matter their connection to you."

"You sure that's the only reason?"

I didn't know what he was getting at. "Why else would I care?"

"It doesn't matter." He rubbed his forehead as if trying to dig out memories. "My past is a blur. Being a mortal hasn't returned my memories of life before I was a hellhound. But... there is one thing that's different."

"What's that?"

"I'm sure if I was simply a mortal before my transformation, I'm not now."

"What makes you say that?"

Fire Fang lifted his hand and a jet of flame shot out. It caught the edge of the cushion on the couch and set it alight.

Binky leaped up, gave a startled yowl, and hid under the table.

"Donkey helmet! Sorry. I didn't know the flame would be that big." Fire Fang patted the flame out with his hand. "I'll get you a new cushion."

I was too stunned by the revelation he still had magic to care about my second-hand cushion getting charred. "Is that ability new?"

"Maybe. Or it could be left over from being a hellhound. Or the magic that turned me into Fire Fang in the first place has given me permanent powers."

I blew out a breath. A mortal changed into a magic user. It was unheard of. "To answer that, we need to find the person who turned you from mortal to hellhound. Any idea who that was?"

"It's a blank. They could have wiped my memory, so I wouldn't be able to go after them and demand answers. Just like you did with Chance Starlight to stop him from being killed."

"That makes sense, but they took lots of other information you need." I felt more relaxed knowing Fire Fang still had some magic. It meant I wouldn't need to evict him from the village and take every memory he had of us together. "I was thinking, if you were back to being a mortal for good, you wouldn't be able to stay in Witch Haven. It's illegal for non-magicals to live here."

"And now you know there's more to me than that, you're happy to keep me around?" Those dark eyes got all intense again, and I didn't know where to look.

"It's something we need to figure out." I downed the last of my coffee. "How will you explain your sudden appearance to other people? You can hardly go around calling yourself Fire Fang."

"Is it so weird? I can't have been the first mortal changed by magic, can I?"

"Err... you pretty much are. We don't cast powerful spells over mortals because it usually kills them. You're a rarity, that's for sure. Doctor Hooper's been looking into cases to see if there was anything we could do for you, but she drew a blank. Well, almost. There were a few cases, but things didn't end well."

"You mean the changed mortals died?"

"Let's just say it wasn't a happy ending."

Fire Fang surprised me by leaning over and grabbing my hand. I winced, and my free hand went to the wounds on my chest.

He instantly tensed. "What's the matter?"

"You, or rather, you in your hellhound form, got in a few good scratches before we passed out in the alleyway. I haven't been able to heal them with magic. I'm all sparked out."

Horror crossed his face, along with a heavy dose of shame. "You've been sitting here all this time, injured?"

"It's nothing serious. But they sting when I move. I'll have to heal myself the old-fashioned way, at least until I get my magical mojo back."

"Take your top off. I'll look at the injuries." He was already reaching for the bottom of my sweater.

I batted away his hands. "I'm not getting naked in front of you."

"Storm, this isn't the time to be a prude. You wear those shorts with a hole in the butt most nights. They leave little to the imagination."

"You shouldn't have been looking at that hole. Or my butt." I pulled my hand away from his. "I can fix my own injuries. If you want to be useful, go make more drinks."

His hand still hovered. "Are you certain you don't need my help?"

"If I need help, I'll ask for it."

He grunted a laugh. "We both know that's not true."

I left him in the lounge and headed to the bathroom, my cheeks hot with embarrassment. It was irritating this guy/hellhound/part mortal, whatever he was now, knew me so well. It left me feeling vulnerable, and who enjoyed that?

It took effort, but I peeled off my sweater, grimacing at the deep scratches running from my breast bone to my waist.

I tried a spell to heal the wounds but barely got a tickle of magic on my skin. Doctor Hooper's potion was still working at full force. I washed the wounds with soap and water, then applied antiseptic healing cream and several large plasters over the deepest gouges. They'd started bleeding after I'd cleaned them.

A thump and a startled meow from the lounge had me turning my head. "Is everything all right out there?"

There was no reply, so I opened the door and stuck my head out. Fire Fang the mortal had turned into Fire Fang the hellhound. I squeaked and slammed the door shut.

I slashed my hands through the air, attempting to conjure a lightning bolt, but all I got was a faint crackle and then nothing. I grabbed the only weapon available, a blunt pair of nail scissors.

Rather than the door crashing in and Fire Fang lunging, there was a gentle tap on the wood. "Sorry, I didn't mean to scare you."

"Who says I'm scared?" I glowered at my shaking knees and swiped the sweat off my top lip.

"I'm in control of myself. I wanted to see if I could change form. And what do you know? I only had to think about it and I was back on four paws and covered in fur, wagging my tail," Fire Fang said.

I lowered the nail scissors. "And how did you feel? Still want to rip my throat out?"

"The urge has gone. I felt the same as I've always done when I'm with you."

I inched closer to the door. Fire Fang had fooled me once this way before, so I wasn't getting tricked again. "Binky and... ginger cat. Restrain Fire Fang."

"There's no need for that. I... Ouch! Watch it, kitties. Hey! Pack it in! Those claws are sharp." There were several thumps and a loud thud as something, most likely Fire Fang, hit the floor.

I waited for Binky and her pal to work their cat magic. "Have you got him?"

There were two high-pitched squeaks, which I guessed were cat versions of yes. I opened the door and peered out. The mortal version of Fire Fang was splayed out on the floor, fortunately on his front, since he was naked again. Binky sat on his head, while the ginger cat was stretched out across his butt.

"Is this really necessary?" Fire Fang grumbled. "I said I didn't want to kill you."

"It's completely necessary. You have more powerful magic than me, which means I'm at a disadvantage if you go rogue hellhound again. I'm covering the bases. And fortunately, the ginger cat is covering your bare butt." I grabbed a clean sweatshirt from the top of my hamper and tugged it over my head, being careful not to touch my injuries. I headed out of the bathroom and nudged Fire Fang with my foot. "What happened to your clothes?"

"I didn't think I'd change so easily, so I wasn't prepared. They ripped when I turned back into a hellhound."

I rolled my eyes. "Anyone would think you like getting naked around me."

He chuckled. "Is that so bad?"

"It definitely is. I have nothing else that'll fit you. And although the ginger cat is doing a great job of hiding your modesty, you can hardly walk around covered in cats all day."

"Why not? I love cats, even the ones who shred me with their claws."

"Stay there. I might have an oversized T-shirt somewhere." After hunting in my bedroom for a few minutes, I discovered an off-white T-shirt with a pumpkin on the front. It was most likely a gift from Odessa. I headed out and slung it next to Fire Fang. "We need to take you shopping if you keep going all hellhound hulk on me."

"I'll work it out. I won't keep ruining your clothes."

I grabbed the coffee he'd made off the counter and took a sip, keeping my gaze on the sink to give him time to dress.

"I'm decent now."

I turned to find Fire Fang on the couch, a blanket over his knees and an amused look on his face. He made the pumpkin T-shirt look good.

After giving him a hard stare to make sure the hellhound wasn't waiting to pounce, I returned to the couch. "If you can keep your murderous urges for me under control, your ability to change from mortal into hellhound in the blink of an eye could come in handy."

"It's definitely a neat trick. It needs finessing, though. I don't want to change when I'm not supposed to. I'll end up giving little old ladies heart attacks."

"Not just the old ladies," I muttered, my heart still a little too fast for comfort.

He patted the seat beside him. "I didn't mean to scare you. I'll have to practice that some more. But there's a lot we need to talk about."

I ignored the space beside him. The furthest corner of the couch worked fine for me. "Like what you'll do now you're back in your true form?"

"Among other things. But it's more than that. Come join me."

"I'm good here."

His brow furrowed. "I feel like you don't trust me."

"I don't know you!"

"Storm, you do. We've been hanging out together for a while. We've got a great connection." He patted the seat again.

I remained perched on the edge of the couch, keeping my distance. "We had a great connection when you had paws and fur. But for me, this is like meeting a stranger. I really don't know this version of Fire Fang."

Hurt flashed across his face, but there was a steely determination in his dark eyes, and that worried me. "You do. I'm the same whether or not I have fur. My personality didn't change because I lost my tail."

"Are you forgetting you tried to kill me repeatedly? Is that a usual character trait?"

"No." He sipped his coffee. "I see you have your usual character trait of stubbornness firmly in place."

I shrugged. "It's not done me any harm so far."

"Really? Is that why your friends have abandoned you?"

"Cheap shot."

"Accurate shot."

"They've abandoned me because they're idiots, and they won't listen to anything I have to say. It's their loss if they don't want to be friends anymore." Did I sound petty and more than a little wounded by his blunt words? Yep, but I had a right to be. I should never have wasted my time on those irritating witches.

"You're not going to try with them again?"

"Nope."

"Even though you messed them around so many times? Are you really surprised they're being aloof?"

"Nothing surprises me much about Witch Haven anymore." I was too exhausted to argue over this. I'd examine my feelings about being ditched by my friends when I was old, gray, bitter, and my only visitors were the postal service and the food truck for decrepit witches. Until then, those feelings stayed locked in the well of despair inside me. "Maybe it's time I moved on."

"From Witch Haven? And leave everything you love?"

"What's here for me? No family, no friends, no sort of hellhound familiar who now walks on two legs. Tell me what I'd be missing out on?"

Binky and the ginger cat yelped a protest. They were perched on the couch behind Fire Fang.

"Stop complaining. It'll be easy to re-home both of you. A vet or a doctor will scoop up a cat with healing powers. And you're a cute little thing, whatever your name is." I pointed at the ginger cat. "You've got a home out there somewhere. Cats don't put collars on themselves. Someone is looking for you. They just haven't put the lost cat poster showing your cute face in the right place, so I know how to get you back safely."

Neither of them looked thrilled at those comments, but Binky knew this wasn't her permanent home. So did Fire Fang, despite how settled he looked on my couch, wearing my T-shirt and drinking my coffee.

"Just because things have gotten tough around here and there have been changes, you want to abandon it all?" he said.

"They're not insignificant changes. And if I'm on the road, it'll be easier to find Eden."

"What if she comes here to find you? This is the only place she knows you'd definitely be."

"Don't guilt trip me into staying somewhere that no longer works. I need a fresh start. Witch Haven has gotten too weird." Maybe this was what I'd been missing. I'd been hanging onto a past that no longer fit me. With my friends abandoning me, there was nothing keeping me here. My business could operate from anywhere in the world. Why not get out and start afresh? I could reinvent myself or at least hide my baggage under a giant rug and pretend it didn't exist. That would work out fine.

Whoops and cheers in the street below my apartment had me hopping up and heading to the window. I was grateful for the interruption. My thoughts had gotten too maudlin to be helpful. There were twelve people running along the street, tossing things in the air and catching them in their mouths.

"What's going on?" Fire Fang joined me, fortunately, keeping the blanket wrapped around his waist.

"Not sure. It looks like they're eating something."

Fire Fang cracked open the window and took a deep breath. "It smells sweet. Like candy."

"I bet some idiot is hosting a dumb candy party. People are still being so weird about that candy store. The whole of Witch Haven is obsessed with it. It's all people have been talking about for weeks. I don't get it. It's just a store."

"Maybe in a sleepy place like Witch Haven, it's the only thing to talk about."

"You don't think people should be interested in the murder that happened in the candy store, rather than getting their next sugar hit? Even Olympus doesn't care about it, and he's in charge of the investigation." I shut the window but remained watching the people. They all had bulging bags over their arms and kept reaching into them and taking more candy. "There's something unnatural about that store. Despite Sherry being so helpful, I still don't trust her."

"It didn't seem odd when I was in there. And Sherry was nice to me. She gave me a ton of free samples. I think growling at her helped her be generous."

I looked at him and then at the marauding crowd outside. "You started behaving aggressively after your first visit to the candy store, didn't you?"

He tilted his head. "That sounds right. We'd just solved the case of the Grimlows and Pepin Flowerbottom killing all those people. We missed the opening of the candy store, so I went a few days later."

"And it was around that time Indigo, Odessa, and Luna started being weird with me. I showed up at Luna's sanctuary to talk about your test results and the case, and they snubbed me. They acted like they didn't know me all that well."

"You find that strange after you gave them the cold shoulder?"

I paced the apartment. "If it was just one thing, the obsessed crowd at the store, you trying to kill me, my best friends snubbing me, or no one caring a guy choked to death on a piece of cursed candy, I'd pass it off as just one of those odd things. Weird stuff happens. But there are too many coincidences. And they take us back to the same place."

"The candy store?" Fire Fang watched me marching back and forth.

"Yes!" I paced some more. "It's the candy. Whatever Sherry is putting in those candies she's selling, it's changing people. And Sherry said you visited her store regularly. You've been eating more candy in between attempts to kill me?"

"Every day until I changed." He didn't look too convinced. "If it's the candy, why do I not still want to kill you?"

I paused. "We were unconscious in that alley for over ten hours. Your body got a break from whatever made you think dark thoughts, and the magic left your system."

Fire Fang scrubbed his chin. "It's possible. My stomach has been grumbling as if I'm missing something, but food and drink don't make a difference. You're sure it's the candy that's the problem?"

"Almost. But we need proof. We have to find out what Sherry's doing with her dodgy candy and stop her from cursing or enchanting anyone else."

Chapter 13

It was two-thirty in the morning, and I was back in the alleyway where I'd been attacked by Fire Fang. He was with me, in his mortal form, dressed in a too tight pair of leggings and the oversized T-shirt with the pumpkin.

After making the connection between the candy store and people's strange behavior, I had to get a better look at the place and figure out what was going on.

Despite the weirdness of the situation, I felt reassured my friends didn't hate me. All this time, it had been tainted candy making them act like jerks. Me, I had no excuse.

I glanced at Fire Fang, who was hunched down, his dark gaze intent on the store. He sensed I was watching and flashed me a smile.

I didn't respond. I wasn't comfortable having him walking around on two legs, but how could I tell him I preferred him with paws and fur? It was much less complicated that way.

"Is something on your mind?" he muttered, his voice pitched low.

I didn't know how to voice my concerns. "I'm adjusting."

"To the new me? Or should that be the old me?"

"Something like that. It was different when you were a hellhound. But now you're mortal…"

"A mortal with enhancements. Enhancements I'm not sure I have complete control over yet."

"Yeah, even with those enhancements. I've never worked with a partner. I prefer to work alone."

He slid me a glance. "You don't want me here?"

"I don't need you here. I can deal with this on my own."

"No, you can't, and you do need me. You'd have been dead several times over if I hadn't formed a bond with you."

"A partial bond, which I never agreed to, so it doesn't count. And I'd never have kept it if I'd known who you truly were."

That comment earned me a sigh. "I'm the same old me. The hellhound you were happy to snuggle with in bed every night. The hellhound you complained about the doom laden news with and fed too many treats while watching terrible movies and rubbing my belly. Which I loved, by the way."

"Sure, but that was before… before the whole mortal thing came out." I sighed this time. "I'm not explaining myself well."

"I may look different, but I still have the same feelings I've always had for you. And even though you protest, we've bonded. And that means where you go, I go."

The intense look on Fire Fang's face unsettled me, so I turned away from him. "What should I call you? Do you have a mortal name?"

"If I do, I don't remember it."

"It's weird calling you Fire Fang, though. But shortening it to Fire or Fang also doesn't work."

"Fang makes me sound like a dodgy biker from an eighties movie." He tilted his head from side to side. "How about Flame?"

"It's also a bit leather-clad biker on a mission to bring down the world."

He chuckled. "Fine. Call me what you like."

"We'll stick with Fire Fang for now. At least when it's just the two of us. But the sooner we find out who you are, the sooner we can learn your name and who's been missing you." And the sooner I could get him out of my life.

Did I want that? No, but I wanted simple, and any kind of relationship with the mortal version of Fire Fang would be anything but that.

"I know who I am. I'm your Fire Fang."

"You're not mine." I spoke through gritted teeth.

His large, warm hand clamping around mine made me jump. "Storm, we've been through amazing times together, solved mysteries no one else could, and dragged ourselves out of the roughest situations. I've seen you at your lowest and when you were raging at the world and overwhelmed."

"I never get overwhelmed." I tried to tug my hand free, but he wouldn't let go.

"What I'm saying is, I've seen all sides of you. And even the terrible, grumpy, curmudgeonly sides don't put me off. I'm still here. I plan to be here for a long time. And that's because—"

"Shush. Someone's coming to the store. I think it's Sherry."

Fire Fang huffed out a breath. "We can talk about this later."

There was nothing to talk about. I was terrified of the direction that conversation had been going. Sure, I'd hidden nothing from Fire Fang, or Flame, or whatever I was supposed to call him when he was a mortal. I wanted my hellhound. Like all faithful hounds, he never judged me, and he was uncomplicated. He didn't mind my bad habits, inability to cook or keep regular hours. He'd accepted me as me. Now he was a mortal, with the expectations and hang-ups that came with that whole weirdness. Everything was different. It was too difficult. The relationship would get messy, and I never handled messy well.

I yanked myself out of my ponderings and focused on Sherry. She opened the store door, slipped inside, and a single light went on.

"What's she doing here at this time of night?" Fire Fang said.

"I reckon it's got something to do with why everyone is behaving so strangely after they've taken a bite out of her candy." I was about to step out from the alleyway and confront Sherry when footsteps approaching made me pause.

Three women stopped by the store, and one of them tapped on the window. Sherry hurried over and opened the door, ushering them in. From this distance, I couldn't see their faces. The cloaks with raised hoods they wore also didn't help.

A moment later, a truck pulled up outside the store, and the women spent ten minutes unloading boxes. The truck disappeared, and a second later, there was a bright flare of magic inside the store.

"They're doing something to the candy," I whispered. "That's how Sherry is getting people to behave so strangely. She's getting them hooked on the candy and... and I don't know the reason. It's making people aggressive, but they're not doing anything else. What's the reason for her to give people candy that makes them obsessed only with her store?"

"To make money?" Fire Fang said. "People are going there several times a day and bulk buying candy."

"There are easier ways to get rich quick. When I was in the store with her, she was run off her feet. She even asked me to help serve. Why would she work herself into the ground just to get people obsessed with her candy? There must be more to it."

"They're leaving," Fire Fang said.

The four women came out, spoke to each other for a moment, and then walked away.

We waited a moment to make sure Sherry and the others weren't coming back, then I shuffled out of the alleyway.

"It's time to find out what the secret ingredient is in Sherry's candy. Let's move."

We dashed to the store, but rather than going through the front door, we snuck down the side alleyway and through the back entrance. There was a super sweet, cloying scent lingering in the air, but mingled in with it was the stench of rot.

"Can you smell that?" I whispered to Fire Fang.

"Whatever it is, it's gross."

"Let's find those boxes." I kept the light off as we made our way to the front of the store. Stacked against one wall were all the boxes, and they were the source of the odd smell.

Fire Fang paced around them, a low growl in the back of his throat.

"Here's the delivery note." I picked it up and checked it. "It's described as promo public candy. This must be what Sherry's planning to sell at the upcoming event in Witch Haven."

Fire Fang was sniffing the boxes. "I don't know what magic they used, but I don't like the smell or the energy. It feels weird. Unnatural. They haven't been doing taste enhancement magic on this stuff."

"No kidding. Do you think it's cursed like the Orange Surprise that killed Galaan?" I set down the delivery note and opened a box. I pulled out a bag of chocolate cream truffles.

"I'm not getting any sense of dark magic or curses, but we should stay away from it until we know more."

I opened the bag and pulled out a cocoa dusted truffle. "I was thinking the opposite. We can't figure out what's wrong with it by looking at it. I should try some."

"That's a terrible idea," Fire Fang said. "Remember how I behaved after eating Sherry's candy?"

"I'll do my best not to kill you. But I haven't tried any, and I'm probably one of the few people in Witch Haven who hasn't been exposed to whatever is in this stuff."

"It should stay that way. What if it turns you rogue?"

I arched an eyebrow. "Knock me out if I get too wild."

"Storm, don't do it."

But I'd already stuffed the truffle in my mouth and chewed. My world spun, stars filled my vision, and an explosion of heat flooded through me.

***

I rolled over and hit a solid wall of warm fur. It tickled my nose, so I backed up an inch and opened my eyes. I was in my bed, Fire Fang asleep next to me in hellhound form, along with Binky and the ginger cat.

I blinked several times, trying to work out if last night's break-and-enter into the candy store had been a dream. Had it *all* been a dream? Fire Fang had never attacked me and then turned into a mortal?

He grumbled a few times before lifting his head off the pillow and looking at me. "Evening."

"Is it? I've lost track of time. And days. Did we go to Sherry's candy store earlier?"

He stretched and yawned. "Yep. At two-thirty in the morning. You thought it was a smart idea to eat the candy."

I dropped back onto my pillow. "It did happen. And you turned into a mortal? And then back into a hellhound?"

"Yes, and yes."

"What happened after I ate the candy? And how did we get back here? How long have you been a hellhound again?"

He chuffed out a doggy laugh. "You might want something stiff to drink before I fill in the gaps. It's a shocker."

I grimaced and shuffled up the bed, plumping my pillows behind my head. "I can't have been that bad. I don't remember doing anything bad. Although I remember nothing. It's one huge blank."

"I'll start with the easy stuff. First, what do you remember?"

"Pretty much all I told you. We figured out the connection between Sherry's candy and people's weird behavior. We checked out the store and saw Sherry and those other magic users bringing in a load of candy and casting a spell on it. Once they'd left, we went inside, checked the boxes, and I ate a chocolate truffle. That's about it."

"Nothing else?"

"No. Did I do something I shouldn't?" I smacked my lips together. "I don't feel so good. I've got a gross taste in my mouth and a raging thirst."

"That'll be from the candy. And as for your question about my hellhound form, while you've been sleeping it off, I've figured out how to flip back and forth between mortal and hellhound. I assumed you'd be more comfortable waking up with the hellhound version of me beside you rather than the mortal version."

"I appreciate that. I expect you sleep in the nude."

He grinned, doggy style. "You know me so well. Anyway, here's what happened. You lost the plot. You ate the truffle and started blasting magic. We got lucky you had little magic juice left, or there wouldn't be much of Witch Haven to speak of."

I blinked slowly. "I didn't do that. I don't remember doing that."

"After you'd had that truffle, you tried to conjure lightning bolts. You said you'd make everyone who'd wronged you pay. Fortunately, the worst you could offer were a few sharp snaps of magic. They were easy enough to dodge, although a couple got me."

"I was trying to hurt you with my magic?"

He lifted his back leg to reveal a healing burn.

"I did that?" I grabbed his leg and examined it. The skin was smooth and pink and healing.

"Don't worry. Being a hellhound has its advantages. I'll be fully healed by the end of the day."

"I didn't know what I was doing. I'm so sorry."

"Let's call it even, since I've been trying to rip your throat out for weeks."

I glared at him. "That hardly makes us even." I lowered his leg and pressed my fingers to the bridge of my nose. "Why am I not remembering any of this?"

"It could be the amount of candy you ate."

"I had one truffle."

His muzzle wrinkled. "You had thirty truffles. Well, I lost count after thirty."

"Thirty!"

"Yep. Stuffed them down one after the other."

"Why didn't you stop me?"

He pointed his nose at his leg. "I couldn't get near enough to clamp your mouth shut. Every time I did, you burned me, you crazy buttoned witch."

I grimaced. "Sorry. I wasn't myself."

"No apology needed, since I've been there, too."

"It's no wonder I feel so lousy. I never eat that much candy. Even Odessa would struggle with so much sugar in one hit, and she mainlines those pumpkin treats she's always chewing on."

"You even fought me for a bag when I took it off you. Then you started singing."

"I never sing!"

"You do in the shower. You're always amazingly off key. It's a talent."

"Not funny. I didn't hurt anyone else, did I?"

"I kept you inside the candy store. Every time you tried to leave, I'd entice you back with truffles. It was the only way I could get you to stay. That and the kisses."

"Whoa! Hold up. Kisses. We kissed?"

He grinned. "I didn't take advantage, but you lunged a few times and got me in a headlock. You said I was just your type."

I hid my face in my hands. "It was the candy."

Fire Fang was quiet for a few seconds. "Sure, it was. Anyway, you kept saying you wanted to visit your old friends and get payback. I was worried you might hurt them, so I had to keep you contained."

I couldn't dwell on kissing Fire Fang. It was too strange. Although he was the most attractive guy I'd seen in Witch Haven for years. But no! He was my hellhound. I wasn't getting the hots for him. "This is what the candy does? It brings people's fears and hatred to the front of their mind."

"Why do you think that?"

I glanced his way, still embarrassed I'd jumped him when high on magic laced sugar. "I always knew my friends would realize I wasn't worth hanging out with. They'd see I was a fraud and wouldn't want anything to do with me. Once they ate the candy, they didn't want me around, because I wasn't part of the sugar gang."

He seemed to turn the idea over in his head a few times. "It could be that, or it could be the candy is addictive. It's become their focus. Indigo, Odessa, and Luna wouldn't be friends with each other if they didn't share their love of candy. You got lucky by not eating some. If you had, you'd still be hanging out together, gossiping about candy."

I wrinkled my nose. "Maybe you're right. So they don't think I'm a loser?"

His tongue rolled out. "They don't. And that theory doesn't explain why I wanted to kill you."

"Maybe you've always secretly wanted me dead. The candy brought out your hatred for me."

He rested a paw on my thigh. "Storm, I could never hate you, you crazy buttoned witch."

I eased my leg out from under his warm paw. "That candy makes people lose interest in everything but getting their next fix. That must have been what happened with Galaan. His ex-girlfriend said they visited Sherry's store when it opened. He was never into sweet things but was hungry and ate Sherry's free samples. After that, he ditched the relationship, quit his job, and moved to Witch Haven to be closer to the addictive candy. It became his only love. He gave up everything for tainted sugar."

"And those people queuing outside the candy store every day must have jobs they should be in or people they're supposed to take care of. They're giving up everything else to get another fix of Sherry's candy," Fire Fang said.

"You're right. Even Olympus has stopped caring about his work, and until he met Indigo, that was his focus. But now, all he wants to do is stuff his face with candy. He's lost interest in investigating Galaan's murder, and he was even mean to Monty. Everyone likes Monty."

"And now you know what people feel like once they've had that candy. It's impossible to break free of."

"And it'll only get worse, since she's the exclusive candy distributor at the next event in the village. If that candy gets passed to everyone, Witch Haven will be destroyed. People will stop working, looking after their families, taking care of themselves. All they'll want is Sherry's candy. And I bet they'd be driven to kill if the supply gets shut off."

"You think that's what Sherry is attempting? She wants to control Witch Haven?"

"It could just be the start. Twisted magic users have targeted this village for hundreds of years. They want the villagers' power. If Sherry controlled the magic in this place, she'd be unstoppable."

"Which means we need to take her down," Fire Fang said. "That goblin nobble can't hand out tainted candy at the event."

I nodded, my stomach growling and a headache beginning. "I knew her sweetness was an act, but that candied apple is rotten to the core, and we need to dig her out."

Chapter 14

Walking was proving tricky as I left the apartment with Fire Fang still in his hellhound form.

After I'd learned how obnoxious I'd been thanks to that tainted candy, I felt even more uncomfortable around him. We'd kissed? Was that me acting out some secret desire? After all, you'd have to be wearing blinkers, standing in a darkened room with your back turned, not to notice how attractive Fire Fang was when he was a mortal. And frustratingly, he was just my type, just like I'd admitted to him.

But I wasn't thinking about his pirate-esque physique, nor the tattoos, nor his messy dark hair. I had no interest in running my fingers through it.

At least, when he was back on all four paws, there was no temptation. Maybe he'd get stuck in his hellhound form again. I had no idea how long he'd be able to flip back and forth between mortal and hellhound. Was that even safe to do?

Having a hellhound partner came with advantages, but now I knew who he was, there couldn't be a partnership going forward. I had to do the right thing by Fire Fang, even if that meant casting him out of Witch Haven and making sure he forgot me.

I stumbled, still woozy from the tainted candy I'd gorged on yesterday.

Fire Fang leaned against my leg to keep me steady. "We don't have to do this now. We can visit Sherry later. It'll take a while for that candy to get out of your system, so you could be tempted if you're near more of it. I'm still getting faint urges, and it's been out of my system longer than yours."

"As much as I'd like to put my feet up and not worry about Sherry blowing apart the magical community with her miscreant candy, we don't have the luxury of taking a day off. We have to stop her right away."

He huffed out his frustration. "Just don't be surprised if you're tempted when you get to her store."

"Sherry's candy won't stop me. And neither will she. It's no surprise the villagers are so obsessed with what she's giving out if it makes them feel like this, though. I keep getting vivid images of bags of candy. It's a struggle to think about anything else."

"I was the same," Fire Fang said. "It's dangerous stuff."

"Which is why we can't put this off a second longer. Sherry should be shutting the store around this time, so there won't be many customers to worry about. We'll confront her about the candy, tell her we know everything, and see what she lets slip out. There's a dark witch hiding under that pink fluffy exterior, and we have to expose her."

"We'll get her to talk, even if I have to shake her a few times to make it happen. That witch isn't destroying our home."

I glanced at him. Fire Fang seemed so certain his place was with me, but I wasn't sure. And I was even less certain now I knew how complicated his life was. He'd be better off getting away and finding help for his condition. He had to figure out if he wanted to stay as a hellhound or a mortal. Maybe he couldn't have both. At the very least, Fire Fang needed to find out how he got transformed in the first place and see if it was safe to be exposed to magic for so long.

"I can hear you thinking," he grumbled. "I know we've got a lot to work through, but we have time. I'm not going anywhere."

"That's just it. We may not have much time left. For all we know, the magic holding you together could vanish at any point."

"Then I'd be back to being a plain old mortal. You definitely wouldn't want a boring donkey helmet like me around then." His furry head lowered, as did his tail.

"I... It's something to discuss later, when we don't have a candy cursing witch to defeat."

He grumbled and growled but said no more as we approached the candy store.

Sherry was at the front door and had just flipped the sign to closed. She raised a hand when she saw us, unlocked the door, and poked her head out. "Is this business or pleasure?"

"Always business. We need to talk." I barged past her and entered the store with Fire Fang.

Sherry left the door open and turned to me. "What is it? You don't look happy. Actually, if you don't mind me saying, you look ill."

"I've felt better. No thanks to you."

"Oh! Me? I'm sorry to hear that. Perhaps some candy would help. It always cheers me up."

"I'd rather swallow warm frog spawn." My mouth wasn't watering at all from the chocolatey scents drifting up my nose.

Sherry's eyes widened. "Not a candy fan?"

"Not any of this candy." My nostrils flared, and an enticing whiff of dark chocolate drifted up them.

She pressed her lips together then smiled. "Good evening, Fire Fang. How's my favorite pup? Being a good boy, as usual?"

He made an embarrassed grumble.

"Fire Fang no longer wants me dead. Any idea why he stopped trying to kill me?" I said.

Her face was a blank canvas. "Kill you! But he's always been a good dog around me."

"How do you know that? You've only been here a month."

"I know good from bad." She made kissy sounds at Fire Fang. "And while I appreciate a visit, it's getting late. Has there been a development with the case?"

"There has. And it led us back to you."

Her black lashes, sparkling with blue glitter, fluttered. "To me! I don't understand. I've been nothing but helpful. I've answered your questions and even let you take away the candy. Did you find anything on the rest of the Orange Surprises?"

"No, but then you knew I wouldn't. You most likely cleared the tainted candy so it wouldn't lead us to you."

Sherry's gaze grew concerned. "Storm, I had nothing to do with Galaan's death. I was shocked when I learned the candy was cursed. If nothing else, it would be terrible for business if word got around."

"That's a lie. Even if your customers hated what you were selling, they'd have no choice but to keep buying it from you."

She stepped away from the open door and headed to the counter. "You've lost me again. I must admit, I've been surprised at how successful the store has been. As soon as it opened, word traveled quickly about how good the candy was, and the queue kept getting bigger. I'm considering hiring an assistant if this keeps up."

"You'd be wasting time hiring help. This store is closed for good. What you're selling, Witch Haven doesn't want."

Those tipped lashes fluttered again. "I don't like to argue, but you're wrong. This store has been a huge success. I can't simply close. What would my devoted customers think?"

"I'm not giving you an option. No one touches any candy from the store. And the stuff you and your friends tampered with last night won't be handed out at the Witch Haven event."

"My... friends? I didn't have visitors last night. Are you getting your dates confused?"

"Even though I've been exposed to whatever toxic magic you use in your candy, my memory is clear. Last night, we watched you take in a delivery. It was an odd time to get candy delivered and outside the usual routine. I've been hearing from your customers that you have deliveries twice a day, early in the morning and a late afternoon slot. So why did a truck show up at two-thirty in the morning to drop off a load of boxes?"

She stared at me as though I was speaking a language she didn't understand. "That never happened."

"We saw you. You arrived just before the delivery, then three cloak wearing friends showed up, took in the boxes, and you blasted them with magic. Is it some kind of control spell or obsession spell to make sure people keep coming back?"

"I... I want to help you, but there was no late night candy delivery. I had a delivery at four o'clock today, like I normally do, but it's been sold. Customers were clamoring to open the boxes and help themselves as I brought it in. If I had more, I'd have sold it to them."

"You're messing with me, and that's a stupid idea. I love this village. I've spent most of my life here, and you're not destroying it."

"I like Witch Haven, too. I don't want to destroy it. I just want to make people happy. My dream has always been to sell happiness in candy form."

"Let's go out the back and look at your delivery, shall we?"

Fire Fang was already padding toward the storeroom.

"You're welcome to look back there, but you'll be disappointed. And it's messy. Don't trip over anything and hurt yourself." Sherry hurried after Fire Fang. "I want to learn what happened to Galaan as much as you do."

"Of course you do. What did Galaan do to you? Was your date with him really so bad?"

Sherry hurriedly shook her head. "I wouldn't hurt someone because we had an unsuccessful date. And as I've already told you, most of the time, he was a gentleman. A little socially awkward, but I had no ill feelings toward him. I don't know what you think you saw last night, but we'll figure this out. I just want everyone to be happy."

I stopped by a huge pile of boxes. "What you actually want is to control this village and all the magic users in it. Explain these."

Her mouth dropped open, and she gaped at the boxes. "I've never seen these before. How did they get here?"

"You and your friends brought them in last night." There was no way Sherry could talk her way out of this.

She inspected a box. "They've been opened."

"That was me. And I'm not apologizing for breaking into your store. I had to know what you were up to. I sampled the candy, and what do you think happened to me?"

Sherry's tongue traced across her bottom lip. "You had a delicious taste sensation?"

"I don't remember. Apparently, I wasn't behaving like myself." I glanced at Fire Fang.

"Your memory loss has nothing to do with my candy. Maybe this is all you." Her lip jutted out. "You're clearly unwell, and you've been suspicious of me ever since we met."

"Because a guy choked to death in front of me on a piece of cursed candy you gave him."

"No! I didn't do that." She jabbed a finger at the boxes. "And you've just confessed to breaking into my store. Did you bring these candy boxes with you? Are you jealous of my success?"

"Sherry, cut the dumb act. Fire Fang and I saw you. The game's up."

She rubbed her forehead with her fingers. "Sorry. I didn't mean to raise my voice and accuse you. I hate confrontation. It makes me blurt out silly things. Of course, why would you be jealous? But I didn't order these, and there's nothing wrong with my candy."

"Maybe it was your friends. The magic I saw blasting out of this store suggests you're all powerful magic users. Are you controlling them, or is someone else in charge?"

"No. I mean, no one is controlling anyone. I've never seen these boxes before, and I know nothing about the people you're talking about. One of us is making a mistake."

"It's not me."

"And it's not me."

Neither of us spoke. We simply stared at each other. Sherry was a hard nougat with a brazil nut center, and she had no plan to break.

She reached into a box and grabbed a truffle. "I should sample this candy. Would that prove to you it's not dangerous?"

I knocked it out of her hand. "Don't. It won't be good for your health. And it won't be good for mine when you lose control."

Sherry looked offended that one of her truffles was on the floor. "Whatever you think best. I really am trying to be helpful, though."

She was excellent at playing Little Miss Innocent, but I wasn't fooled. "No more candy games. When people eat this junk, they do dumb things. That candy made me..." I looked at Fire Fang, and my cheeks flushed. "It doesn't matter. This store stays closed. There'll be no candy at the event, and you're going to jail for Galaan's murder."

"But I'm innocent!"

"Tell that to the Magic Council."

Sherry looked at me, then Fire Fang, then the boxes. She lunged at the open box of candy. Her head disappeared inside before I could stop her, and she grabbed a mouthful of truffles.

I yanked her back by the hair, but she shoved me away, chewing fiercely, an evil glint in her eyes. She backed away, clapping as she chewed. "Congratulations, witch. You figured it out. Too bad you're too late to stop us."

Chapter 15

Sherry's words were barely distinguishable as she munched on the truffles, but I got her meaning. She was evil, just as I suspected, and she had to be stopped.

"You're using candy to bewitch people." I kept my hands poised to fire magic if needed.

She lunged for the box again, but I shoved her away.

Sherry shoved me back twice as hard, and I staggered into Fire Fang. "Leave this alone. Our plans have come too far to let one interfering witch stop us." She blasted out a swirl of gray and pink magic.

I ducked the magic, but it curled around me like a boomerang and slammed into my back. Only Fire Fang standing in my way stopped me from face planting on the concrete floor.

He propelled me back to my feet, but a second later, another powerful blast from Sherry hit us both, and Fire Fang staggered away.

"Since you've already tried my candy, I know you'll want more," Sherry taunted. "Have another truffle, Storm. Forget your cares, your fears about your missing family, and join me. We'll have fun together. I promise an endless supply of treats. All the candy you desire." She grabbed a handful of truffles and threw them at me.

I couldn't believe it, but I was tempted. My hand hovered over a truffle that had hit my head and bounced off.

Fire Fang stomped on it before I could grab it. "If you eat that, you'll be under Sherry's control."

I shook myself from my candy stupor and ignored the treats, even though their enticing smell made me want to drop to my knees and gorge. "Who are you really? You're not sweet little Sherry Brown. Is that a fake name, like Mary Smith?"

"It doesn't matter who I am. It's what I want. And I want Witch Haven. You're not stopping me from getting it."

She kept throwing truffles, bouncing them off my head. I didn't want to be distracted, but I could smell the sweetness, and my stomach grumbled with longing. My head was throbbing, and the taste of just one truffle would take away the pain. Just a tiny bite. That was all I needed.

I inched out a shaking hand and placed it over a truffle on the floor.

"That's it. Become one of Sherry's Sweeties. You'll never have to worry about anything again. So long as you behave yourself, you can even stay in Witch Haven. We need some people around who'll be useful to us."

"What about everyone else? The ones who aren't useful?"

"The rest will go out in a sugary blaze of glory. Don't worry, they'll have smiles on their faces. Maybe they'll feel a small amount of pain, but we only want people who add value to our cause. And I have a feeling, with your control over the weather, I'll want to keep you around for a while. Maybe even forever. How does that sound?"

I was fighting myself, not wanting my hand to raise to my mouth, but it had a will of its own. The truffle crept closer to my lips.

Fire Fang jumped at me, but Sherry's spell knocked him back.

He growled and roared at her. "You goblin nobble sour slug. Leave my witch alone."

Sherry simply laughed as she kept him entwined in a powerful spell that stopped him from getting closer to me.

I should help him, but I couldn't focus on anything but the truffle that was only an inch from my lips. If I ate it, my cares would disappear. I wouldn't have to worry about what to do with Fire Fang, my friends abandoning me, Olympus not bothering to investigate a murder, and how to find Eden. None of that would be important. I could put myself first and forget my troubles.

My teeth grazed the chocolate around the truffle, and then it was gone. I was left with a mouthful of fur and a feeling I'd been deeply cheated out of something incredible. "What the—"

Sherry shrieked and fired spells at Binky's fluffy black butt as she raced away with my truffle hanging off one fang.

I shook myself. That was a near miss. If Binky hadn't stopped me... but there was no time to consider that. "Fire Fang! Protect Binky."

He hesitated, his gaze sweeping from me to Binky. "What about you?"

"I'll deal with Sherry. No one tries to hurt my fuzz balls and gets away with it."

Sherry was laughing as she zapped spells at Binky. "And no one will ruin my plans."

Binky gave a tortured yelp as a spell made contact and she spun across the room. The truffle flew from her mouth.

Fire Fang tore free from Sherry's magic as I slashed my hands through the air. My magic still wasn't at full strength, but it was enough to draw down a lightning bolt, and it slammed Sherry off her feet.

I wanted her dead. She was responsible for all of this. She'd messed with me, ruined my friendships, turned my hellhound against me, and hurt Binky. Sherry was about to see my rage-filled side. A side that bubbled over like a rancid cauldron of destructive magic.

I slammed several more lightning bolts down around her until Sherry was cowering and holding her hands up in defeat.

"Enough! You win. You must understand, I had to protect myself. I thought you were going to kill me."

"Maybe I will," I growled out as I stalked toward her.

"Please, I had no choice. I don't want to hurt anyone in Witch Haven, but they ordered me to do this. If I didn't follow their orders, I'd be dead. I was terrified. There's nothing special about me. I just got mixed up with the wrong crowd."

"Get up." I caught hold of Sherry's shoulder and pulled her to her feet. "Fire Fang, how's Binky doing?"

"She's injured, but she'll be okay," he grumbled. "I'm looking after her."

I focused on Sherry. "Who are you working with?"

Her body trembled. "The worst witches. Dangerous, dreadful creatures who live to destroy. They want to take everything good and twist it into a dark ruin. They want to spoil Witch Haven with their darkness and take control of it."

"Are they here in Witch Haven?"

"No, but they're not far away. They exploited my ability to create the perfect candy." Sherry was sobbing and wringing her hands. "I've been so scared, too scared to tell anyone. I kept hoping someone would see how terribly wrong things were. And there were clues. People buying all that candy, the queues, the fights to get the last bag of bonbons. I got worried when I didn't get help from the Magic Council. Then you showed up, and I wished on all the stars you'd figure things out. And you did. Save me from those dreadful witches."

"How do I know you're not one of those dreadful witches? You fooled everyone in Witch Haven with your candy." I kept a tight hold on Sherry.

Her quivering hands lifted to her face. "I'm not. I'm a good witch who got mixed up with terrible people. I begged them not to do this to Witch Haven, but they wouldn't listen to me."

I didn't believe her. "I'm done untangling your lies. Explain it to the Magic Council once you're behind bars."

Sherry dropped the act, grabbed several truffles off the floor and slammed them against my mouth, shoving hard to get them through my gritted teeth. "Bend to my will. Why must you be so difficult? If only you'd eaten candy like everyone else, you'd have never poked around."

I thrust against her chest and shot out a powerful knock back spell, sending her spinning away with a startled shriek. I swiped as much truffle off my mouth as I could, so I wasn't tempted to lick the chocolate.

Sherry hit a pile of boxes and vanished beneath them as they collapsed around her. As I approached to see if she was injured, I heard her laugh.

"Something funny about going to jail?" I hiss-whispered.

"Storm Winter, you're nothing. Nobody in this village wants you. I've watched your friends abandon you and was happy to see Olympus throw you out of his office. Even if you told the Magic Council what I was doing with my sisters, they wouldn't believe you. They'd listen to Olympus, and I've got him under my chocolate-coated thumb. That fool would do anything for me. Then there's his witch girlfriend, Indigo. She's a firecracker, one that'll go off when I light her fuse. She comes in several times a day, practically begging for candy. I have so much power at my fingertips."

"You're impressing no one." I'd get through to Olympus and Indigo when I revealed the truth.

"All I'd have to do is whisper in Indigo's ear about how awful you've been to me, and she'd make you pay." Sherry blasted the boxes off her and shot up, hovering several inches off the floor. "Witch Haven will soon be ours, and there's no one here to stop us."

I ignored her harsh words. The Magic Council had its inept moments, but they wouldn't turn their back when a murder had been committed. And my friends hadn't abandoned me. It was the candy magic influencing them. They'd soon be back to normal.

"Storm, this is your final chance to join the winning side. Unite with me and my sisters. We'll rule Witch Haven together. Once we've obtained all the power from this place, the world will be ours. We'll have the most powerful magic users at our disposal. Think what we could do with Odessa's army of scarecrows. She's sold those monstrosities in every corner of the planet. We can use them as our army. We will sit back and collect the spoils."

"It sounds like you're making a play for control over the entire magic community."

"Why not? We're done with the ruling elite and their snobbishness. It's time for a change at the top."

"You want to be that change? You'll be telling me next you're doing this for the greater good."

Sherry shrugged. "No, I'm doing it for my own good. I want power and influence. I want to be in charge. I don't want a stuffy, out-of-date council telling me what I can and cannot do with my powers. They have no control anymore. It's been so easy to manipulate them that I'm almost embarrassed."

"I won't disagree that the Magic Council can be easy to humiliate, but that doesn't mean they're always wrong."

"We demand better. And you're the same as us. You want more. This is your time. Forget your past and the problems that keep you stuck in this half existence. You could have it all."

"You don't know about my problems."

She smirked. "I know more than you realize." Her gaze went to Fire Fang and back to me. "I know everything."

That thought left a taste in my mouth worse than Sherry's candy. "Who else are you working with? You keep mentioning sisters. Is it your coven?"

"We're bonded by blood magic. There are dozens of us, ready to take over this power base. Witch Haven was always our initial focus because of the vast source of strength here. Powerful magic users come here for the quiet, but there are so many sleeping giants, getting lazy and not using their power."

"That's the point of Witch Haven. Magic users don't want to be hassled. Look up the word 'haven' if you're struggling with the concept."

"My sisters and I will awaken their strength and encourage them to join us. If they don't, we'll control them, anyway. And so, I ask you, Storm Winter, will you become one of the new rulers?"

There was no way I was joining this insane plan. She could have a hundred powerful dark witches working with her to unseat the current power base, but there was no chance I'd let them win. No matter what I had to do, this power crazed sugar witch was going down.

But before I took her out, I had questions. "Before I answer that, I want to know about Galaan. Did he find out what you were doing and try to stop you? Was that why you killed him with the candy?"

She waved a hand in the air. "He was an irrelevance."

"Galaan didn't know what you were doing?"

"He was clueless. A simple fool."

"So why kill him?"

"To divert. For a long time, longer than you can imagine, we've monitored Witch Haven. Over the decades, things have been tried and tests applied while we've grown our numbers. We've been waiting for the perfect opportunity to strike. This is the closest we've ever gotten. Success is within our sights."

"You killed Galaan to cause a distraction, so we were looking the other way while you gained a foothold in the village?"

"Galaan was a greedy, foolish man who was simply in the right place when I needed him to be."

Anger trickled through me like a splash of acid. Drip, drip, drip. Every drop increased the disgust I felt for this witch. "He wasn't in the right place. You killed Galaan for your own selfish gains."

Her shrug only made me madder. "Galaan was a pitiful man. I could tell he wasn't happy. He had a whining girlfriend with him the first time he visited the store. He needed an escape. So I chose him and gave him freedom with a dose of enchanted candy."

"Galaan's life may not have seemed exciting, but he didn't deserve to be cursed and killed."

"I was surprised how well it worked. When he told me that not only had he left his job and his girlfriend, but he'd rented a room in the village so he could come to the store all the time, I realized my magic had reached its pinnacle. Now was the perfect time to strike. So I gifted him an exclusive piece of Orange Surprise as his final reward, and the greedy piglet snuffled it down." Sherry made pig-like noises and wrinkled her nose.

"You're a disgrace to the magic community. You'll pay for killing Galaan and messing with everyone in Witch Haven." I shot out a bolt of hazy lightning. It slammed into the tainted candy, blasting it apart and causing a shower of chocolate, boiling sugar, and icing to rain down.

Sherry screamed and lunged clumsily at me.

But I was faster and stronger. I grabbed her in a restraining spell and flipped her onto the floor, pinning her in place with my knee and a jagged lightning bolt. "Got you."

Chapter 16

"Let me go. You could have it all. Why do you insist on protecting this pitiful place?" Sherry writhed under my spell.

I was sweating with the effort of keeping her contained, but now I had her, she wasn't getting away. "Stop fighting. I'm not letting you get your hands on Witch Haven. It's home to hundreds of incredible magic users. It's my home. Where I grew up, found my best friends, had my first kiss. It means everything to me. It's not for the sugar witch gang and their dark plans."

Her laugh was strangled and pitchy. "You have nothing here. You've been abandoned, and your only family is gone. You could have joined us and found a new family."

"I want nothing to do with your twisted version of family. And I do have people here who love me, and I love them back just as hard. This is over, Sherry. I'm taking you to the Magic Council to pay for your crimes." I looked at Fire Fang, who stood over an injured Binky. "Keep her safe. Get her to the vet if she needs expert attention. I'm taking Sherry to Olympus's cells. She can wait there until I get sense out of Olympus and we figure out what to do with her."

Fire Fang nodded, and I translocated Sherry into a cell in Olympus's office. It was a struggle to get through the magic. The cells had draining wards surrounding them to prevent criminals from escaping. Getting through those draining wards was, well, as you can imagine, hard on my magic. And I still wasn't operating at full steam, thanks to the suppression potion and summoning a series of lightning bolts one after the other.

It felt like wading through warm toffee as the wards clung to me like sticky-fingered children, but we finally arrived inside a locked cell.

Sherry still fought my restraining magic, and her gorgon-like glare latched onto me. "I'll make you sorry you turned us down."

"Put a sock in it. I can live with not hanging out with a bunch of twisted witches who think they're better than anyone else."

"I'm not finished yet. You don't realize how much power I have over this place. Prepare to be amazed. I've already won."

"I don't see any medal hanging around your neck, so you prepare to be disappointed." I peered through the bars. "Olympus! You need to get in here right now."

Footsteps hurried to the cells, and a few seconds later, Olympus appeared. He stared at us in disbelief. As he approached, I noticed smears of chocolate around his mouth. That was a bad sign. I didn't need a candy-tainted Olympus.

"Sherry, Storm." He rubbed the back of his hand across his mouth. "What are you doing inside that cell?"

"Sherry is behind all of this," I said. "She killed Galaan with cursed candy to distract us from what's really going on."

A glance at Sherry showed her looking like icing sugar wouldn't melt in her mouth. Her eyes were cast down and her hands neatly clasped in front of her. She looked nothing like the murderous dark magic user I'd just fought.

"What is going on? Storm, you're making no sense." Olympus approached the cell, his expression cautious. "Is this a joke?"

"I saw Sherry with three other magic users. They used something on the candy Sherry plans to give out at the event. It'll do something bad to the villagers."

"Like what?"

"When I tried it, I lost control. I wasn't aware of what I was doing. Fire Fang had to stop me. We can't let that candy get to the public. You must keep Sherry locked up. She's dangerous. Interrogate her, so she tells you who her accomplices are."

"We never interrogate. We carefully question when required." Olympus's brow was furrowed as he took a few seconds to consider my words. "Sherry, is any of this true?"

She gently touched my arm, although her nails pressed down for the briefest of time. "Forgive Storm. She's been under a lot of pressure. And I don't like to break a confidence, but she's been telling me about her troubles with her sister and her friends abandoning her. I know she's struggling.

And, well, in my humble opinion, it's made her unstable. I've even been afraid of her a few times."

"I confided in you about nothing. Olympus, she's lying. Sherry has been lying ever since she got here."

Olympus glanced over his shoulder before turning back to me. "It's no secret you have been under immense pressure. I was just talking to Indigo about your issues."

"You can't believe Sherry! Make the connection yourself. Ever since that candy store opened, things have been different. People have stopped caring about anything other than when they'll get their next hit of candy."

"We've been over this. You can't punish Sherry because she opened a popular store."

"I'm not punishing her for that. I couldn't care less about what Sherry sells. It's what she's hidden inside the candy that's the problem. It's messing with people's heads."

Olympus put his hand in his pocket and pulled out a wrapped piece of candy. "I've been eating this for days, and it's done nothing to me."

"Are you sure? You don't care about Galaan's murder. You gave the evidence a cursory inspection and wrote it off as an accident, even after the results came back revealing a curse was involved."

"Well, it could still be an accident."

Sherry hummed an agreeing note under her breath.

"A curse accidentally got into the candy Galaan ate? Is that how curses operate?"

His expression grew grim. "I'm having the tests run again. I'm not convinced it was a curse. And laboratories make mistakes."

Sherry turned to me, so only I could see her expression. It was full of wicked delight. She thought she was winning. "I'm sure you're right, Olympus. And I'm so glad you acted on my recommendation to run those tests again. I was as shocked as you when I learned an unknown person cursed a piece of my candy. So much so, I even had Storm test for more cursed candy. And what did you find?"

I resisted the urge to slam her against the wall. "Nothing. Because you knew I wouldn't. And when did you start giving Olympus orders?"

"Oh, you poor overworked creature. I didn't give any orders. I simply suggested how bizarre it would be to have a piece of cursed candy in my wonderful store. It made no sense."

"I'm surprised I didn't think about it before," Olympus said. "It's a more logical option than the route I was going down. Cursed candy! Impossible."

"It's the route that implicates Sherry in all of this, you mean? Because if she gets locked away, your addictive supply vanishes." I glowered at Olympus while he licked the corners of his mouth to remove chocolate.

"Addictive supply of what?" he said.

"Candy! Have you seen yourself? You're covered in the stuff, and you've put on weight. Sherry's candy is ruining you."

He patted his belly. "It's Indigo's fault. She keeps bringing me treats."

"You're as bad as each other. Forget the candy and focus on Sherry. Lock her up before she destroys this village."

"Storm, you must stop spreading lies. It's important we don't have a scandal in Witch Haven so close to the Magic Council ceremony."

"And of course, we have the big event to think about, too," Sherry said. "It'll bring in so many magic users from outside the village. I'll tempt them in, give them free candy, and they can join in the fun." She winked at me. "They might have so much fun, they never leave. Won't that be wonderful?"

"You're right," Olympus said. "Everyone deserves a taste of Sherry's candy."

Sherry giggled. "Olympus! You tease."

They both laughed while I grew nauseous.

"I'm glad we're on the same page," Sherry said. "Apart from one person, Witch Haven has been so welcoming. I'm glad to call it my home."

"As am I," Olympus said.

"You're controlling him," I hissed at her.

"I told you this wasn't over," she whispered back.

I shoved Sherry away and marched to the cell door.

Olympus dashed to meet me. "Storm! There's no need for violence. Sherry's been nothing but sweet and obliging. She's helped every time I had a question about Galaan's investigation—"

"How many questions did you actually ask about his murder? Or was it an excuse to visit and grab more candy?" I said. "Don't trust her. And lock yourself in a cell with no candy for twenty-four hours. You'll feel different. You won't be under her influence. Snap out of this, or Witch Haven will be lost for good."

"You're talking nonsense. And why would I lock myself up?"

"To break the cycle. Every time you eat a piece of candy, you stay entranced by Sherry. It's the same with nearly everyone in Witch Haven. It even affected Fire Fang. He's been trying to kill me, and it wasn't until I figured out it was the candy that influenced him that we made a breakthrough."

"Perhaps if you looked after your adorable hellhound better, he wouldn't want to hurt you. You fed him the wrong food. And he mentioned you're terrible with regular feeding routines when he was getting candy from me."

"Stop lying," I growled out.

"Oh, Storm, I hate to see you in a mess, but from everything I've learned about you, that's your life. One big disaster and tragedy after the other. Starting with your poor sister and your inability to keep her safe from whoever took her from her bed."

I whirled on her. "How do you know that's what happened to Eden?"

"I asked around. I wanted to know why you were so miserable."

"Storm can be grumpy," Olympus said unhelpfully. "And she's a terrible communicator. Indigo always complains about her bottling things up."

"I can imagine. And then your parents dying so soon after Eden went missing. I wondered if it was because of you." Sherry wisely kept away from me after making that comment.

"What are you suggesting? I killed my parents?"

"Now, there's a thought! Olympus, was that considered when Storm's parents died?"

He tapped his chin with a chocolate stained finger. "No. Storm was only a child when they died."

"She must have been a powerful child, even before her full powers emerged. And bad luck follows her around."

"Stop talking if you want to keep breathing." I marched toward her. My heart raced, and my breath panted out of me. "How do you know all this about me?"

"When you're a real friend to people, they don't keep secrets. And everyone knows about your tragic past. I was hoping I might help you. I always find a high quality box of my favorite candy puts me in a good mood. I may even have some in my pocket if you'd like to try more. It'll take away your cares. Can I tempt you?"

I grabbed her arms and pinned them to her sides. "Keep your cursed candy and your vicious tongue to yourself. Never speak about Eden or my parents again."

"Storm, stop threatening Sherry. Get your hands off her and step away," Olympus ordered.

"She is so intimidating." Sherry's voice had a false wobble to it. "I've been nice to her every time we meet, but she's so abrupt. I never know whether she's going to smile at me or snarl. I don't know how you put up with her, Olympus."

"Neither do I. And you shouldn't have to either." He pulled out a key.

"Sherry must stay in here," I said. "At least keep her in a cell overnight. See the change in people when they can't get their candy. Although, I should warn you, it won't be pretty. People could break into the store to get their next fix."

Olympus unlocked the door. "There is nothing wrong with Sherry's candy. You just don't like her, and that's unfair. She's new to the village and should be welcomed, not subjected to your sharp scrutiny."

"You should be the one scrutinizing her. She's messing with the whole village. And she's not alone. If you don't put a stop to it, it'll be too late for all of us."

Olympus sparked magic in his hand and pointed a finger at me. "Step back."

I folded my arms over my chest. "Or what?" I had little magic left thanks to the wards, but I still had a speedy right hook.

"Keep your distance. Sherry, you're free to go."

I gaped at him. "You can't let her out. She's dangerous."

Sherry's smile was sugary smug as she slipped out the door. "Thank you so much, Olympus. I'll have to reward you with an enormous box of candy. I'll go to the store and bring it straight back while you deal with Storm."

"I wouldn't mind more cocoa dusted truffles. I was dreaming about them last night." The sappy smile on his face made me want to test how hard I could punch. Maybe I could knock sense into him, since nothing else worked.

"I'm your sugar angel, making your sweet wishes come true." Sherry giggled. "I won't be long. Oh, and leave Storm in the cell."

"Of course. Whatever you think best," he said.

I charged to the door but was a second too late. Olympus flicked the key in the lock, and I was trapped. I slammed my fist against the door. "You idiot! You've got it all wrong." I fired up my magic, but the draining wards meant it barely flickered to life.

"Sherry, go wait in the office. I have something to say to Storm," Olympus said.

Sherry looked at me, a stark, flat expression in her eyes. "Feel better soon. Before you know it, this will be over. You don't like me, but I'm sure we'll find a way to bond."

"I'd rather bond with a rotting corpse than spend time with you."

"Oh, dear. You poor, deluded witch. She really is unwell," Sherry said to Olympus. "You don't think she'll come after me again, do you?"

Olympus's expression grew pensive. "She might."

"Is there any way you can charge Storm with an offence so she remains behind bars? I won't be able to sleep, knowing she could be skulking outside my home."

He pursed his lips. "Well, technically, Storm shouldn't have used my cell. But I'm not sure I could call that a crime."

I thumped my hand against the door. "I've done nothing wrong. I'm trying to keep Witch Haven safe."

"What if I told you Storm broke into my store?" Sherry said. "She tampered with the candy for the event. She even ate some. That's stealing, isn't it?"

"I can hold her for that. Would you like me to?"

"Don't you dare," I said through gritted teeth.

Sherry cast her eyes down for a second. "It's for the best. And perhaps Storm needs a medical assessment, too. I'm worrying about her mental health. All this stress is making her imagine things. And she's isolating herself. Weren't you saying she used to be friendly with your girlfriend?"

"She was, but they argued. It was all Storm's fault," Olympus said.

"Stop! There's nothing wrong with me." I was so angry, tears were in my eyes. I wasn't upset, but there was a deep, biting frustration inside me. No one was listening. No one believed me. Deep down, I knew it was because of Sherry's twisted magic, but that didn't mean her words weren't stinging.

And I felt broken. No matter how hard I pushed away the doubts, I felt like Eden's disappearance and my parents' deaths were my fault. I hadn't been good enough to protect my younger sister or worthy enough that my parents stayed so we could search for Eden together.

"What's going on back there?" Indigo appeared in the doorway. "Storm! What have you done this time?"

"Maybe you'll listen to me. Sherry's got everyone under her influence. Olympus believes every word she tells him," I said.

Indigo rolled her eyes. "Being your usual negative self, I see. Stop wasting your time with her, Olympus. That one will never change. She's always telling us that. Sherry, I'm so glad you're here. Although, how are you here? I didn't see you come in through the door."

"Let me fill you in over a peppermint tea. And I've got orange creams in my pocket. You must try them. And I promised to get Olympus more truffles. I'll get you some, too." Sherry tucked a hand through Indigo's elbow and guided her away.

"No! Don't touch that candy." I yanked on the door, but it didn't budge.

Indigo ignored me and left with Sherry, their heads together.

I looked at Olympus, but there was only cold indifference and disappointment radiating back at me. There was no use arguing with him. All he cared about was Sherry and her candy.

He approached the cell door again. "I don't want to charge you with anything, but what you're mixed up in is serious. Sherry is right, you've not been yourself for a long time. You never tell me what you're doing when you investigate a case, and you assume you have to do everything on your own. Look where it's gotten you."

"Not under the influence of a dark witch?"

"You're making things worse for yourself by bullying Sherry. It's time you sorted yourself out. Or maybe even left Witch Haven. No one wants you here, anyway."

I lifted my chin. "I know I'm not perfect, but I'm right about Sherry."

Olympus held up a hand. "I don't want to hear any more. Once you've calmed down, I'll interview you about breaking and entering Sherry's store and stealing from her."

I kicked the door. "It'll be too late by then. She'll have moved the cursed candy, and there'll be no evidence. Go to her store now. I destroyed most of it, but—"

"You're admitting to vandalism and willful property destruction as well as theft?"

"I... no."

"Enough! Sherry is a decent person and has only done good things for this village since she arrived. You're not ruining this. I'll be back in a couple of hours." He turned, left the room, and shut the main door behind him.

I covered my face with my hands and screamed. I screamed and screamed. Nothing I could say would convince Olympus, Indigo, or anyone that Sherry was the bad person here. She'd charmed them all, and I was powerless. And trapped in a cell. For all I knew, Sherry would convince Olympus to leave me here forever.

After pacing for several minutes, I sank to the floor. I didn't want to admit defeat, but it was tempting. Maybe I should let Witch Haven be ravaged by Sherry and her goons. If I could find a way out, I could grab Fire Fang, Binky, and the ginger cat, and we would leave.

That idea sat on me about as well as a feathered bonnet with a pink lace trim. I grimaced and swiped unwanted tears off my cheeks. Just like Sherry, I wasn't finished yet. I'd find a way out of this.

※ ※ ※

I'd been in the cell a couple of hours when there was a soft scratching at the main door. A few seconds later, the handle moved, and the door was shoved open. Monty appeared, his furry head peeking in at me.

I nodded a greeting. "Hey, Monty. I suppose you're here to tell me how useless I am, too."

He snuck in on his toes, his belly low to the floor, and his tail down. "No, but there's someone to see you. We must be quiet, though. I snuck in, and

Olympus doesn't know I left my bed. He'll yell again if he finds out I'm helping you."

I scrambled to the door. "Have you eaten any of the candy from that new store?"

Monty shook his head, his whiskers twitching. "No, I only like meat. And I saw how weird it was making Olympus behave. Plus, he smells strange. Kind of like rotting meat mixed with honey."

"Monty, I could kiss you."

His tail flipped up. "I'd like that. I love nose kisses."

"Who's here to see me?"

Monty hurried back to the door. "It's safe. Come in. Hurry."

The little ginger cat crept in behind Monty and over to the cell.

"Hey, puss. What are you doing here?" I said.

"She's not good at communicating," Monty whispered. "While Olympus and Indigo were eating the candies that pink, lace covered witch left them, I heard something scratching at the door. While they were distracted feeding each other and smooching, I let her in. She kept saying something about Fire Fang but also kept looking at Olympus really hard, like she wanted him to see her. Whatever magic is surrounding her, it makes it almost impossible to understand her. I'm an excellent linguist, but it's impossible to get sense out of her."

"Are you here to help me?" I said to the ginger cat.

She nodded and poked one paw through the bars.

"From what I figured out, she wants you to share her power," Monty said. "You must be quick. The draining wards will affect her if she's here for longer than a couple of minutes."

"You're sure about this?" I had no idea how much power this little cat had.

She nodded again and wiggled her paw.

I gently touched her paw, and a warm flood of gentle magic trickled through me. It felt oddly familiar, as if I knew her power. "Have we met before?"

She flicked her ears, and her eyes narrowed.

The magic felt young and underdeveloped, as if the ginger cat had never learned to use her ability. Although it wasn't powerful, it would give me enough juice to create an unlock spell.

I pulled back my hand and tried the spell. The door opened, and I slid out. "Thanks for getting me out, but we still need to get past Olympus and Indigo. I don't have the energy to use a translocation spell."

"I'll help." Monty puffed up his fur. "I'll cause a distraction, and you and the cat can run out."

"That'll get you in trouble with Olympus, and he's already unhappy with you."

"He's been awful for days. He's always looking for excuses to scold me. At least now I can give him one."

"Come with us," I said. "I need all the help I can to defeat Sherry."

"I don't like her. She smells of old, burned sugar and giggles too much," Monty said.

"I'm also not a fan. Whatever you do, don't eat her candy. It's tainted with something. The second you do, you'll be under Sherry's influence, and that's a terrible place to be. I'm not sure what her plan is, but it won't be good for Witch Haven."

"I'd never touch that stuff. I wouldn't even eat her candy if she made a steak flavored truffle." Monty glanced at the door. "We'd better go."

I scooped up the ginger cat and nestled her against my chest. "We're ready when you are."

Monty poked his head out the door. "The second you hear yelling, run as fast as you can."

"And you'll be right behind us?"

He nodded then crept out the door.

I ran my fingers over the ginger cat, more to reassure myself than her. I didn't have to worry about Olympus's power, but if Indigo saw us escaping, she wouldn't hesitate in taking me out with a spell.

Monty had vanished from sight, and I inched out of the door, holding my breath as I stood poised to run.

There was a crash in the office, and Olympus yelped.

That was my cue, and I was off and running. I didn't hesitate as I shoved through the door and flew to the exit.

"Monty! You furry freak. What are you doing?" Olympus yelled.

I pulled open the door, glancing over my shoulder as I did so. One of Olympus's huge filing cabinets had been knocked on its side and the papers scattered everywhere. Monty was on top of Olympus, who was flat on his back on the floor.

Indigo was holding a tray with a huge mound of candy on it. Her gaze met mine, and she bared her teeth. "Hey! You're supposed to be locked up."

Olympus had a firm grip on Monty, and as much as he struggled to get free, he wasn't getting away.

"Go!" Monty yelled. "Save yourselves. I've got this."

I couldn't leave him, not now Indigo and Olympus knew he'd helped me escape. But Indigo was firing up a spell, and if she caught me, that would be it. I'd have no way out and no opportunity to save Witch Haven from Sherry.

"I'll come back for you." I raced out of the door and slammed it shut a second before Indigo's spell slammed into the wood with a splintering shudder.

I clutched the ginger cat so tightly she squeaked as we raced away. I was free, but for how long? And what could I do to stop Sherry and her devious plan?

Chapter 17

As much as I wanted to, I couldn't afford to hide and wait out this problem. I had to find Sherry and stop her.

I raced to her store, slammed through the back door, and hurried inside. I stopped after I'd taken a few steps and set down the ginger cat. The place was empty. There was nothing in the storeroom.

I hurried through to the front of the store. There was still candy on the shelves, but all traces of our fight were gone, along with the candy I'd destroyed. Sherry must have come back and moved it as soon as she could to hide any incriminating evidence.

More worryingly, there was also no sign of Fire Fang or Binky. I looked at the ginger cat, who followed me around the store as I investigated. "Do you know what happened to Fire Fang and Binky?"

She nodded.

"Are they safe?"

She tilted her head from side to side.

"Sherry hasn't got them, has she?"

The ginger cat shook her head.

"Did Fire Fang take Binky to the vet? Sherry really whacked her with her magic. I didn't get a look at her injuries, though. Fire Fang said Binky was okay, but in the chaos, he might have missed something."

The ginger cat shook her head again.

"I wish you could talk. Is that a no to the vet or a no to serious injury?"

She chirruped.

"Good try, but not that kind of talk. The talk where everything makes sense. But then nothing about this place makes sense anymore, so I guess you fit right in with your chirps."

She swished her tail at that comment.

I pulled out my phone, and my finger hovered over Odessa's number. Then I remembered I'd been blocked from the group chat, so they'd have blocked me on everything, which meant I had no way of contacting them. Even if I found a way to reach them, my friends were on the opposite side. They'd support Indigo and Sherry. They'd be more likely to take me back to the cell than help me.

"Let's look around. Maybe there's something in this place to show us what Sherry's planning. You look on the lower shelves, see if you can find anything down there. I'll search the rest," I said.

The ginger cat set to work, sniffing around and rootling about on the lower shelves.

I scooped the bagged candy off the shelves, not caring if it shattered on the floor. Maybe if I destroyed all the candy, I could put Sherry out of business for a few days. If no one could get their hands on her candy, it would break the thrall and get them to see sense. But knowing Sherry, she probably had an endless supply of the stuff. She'd open tomorrow, and the shelves would be just as they always were. Full of addictive, toxic candy.

I kept looking, sweeping aside bags and opening drawers. All I found was more candy. And at the back of my mind was a tiny voice telling me to try some. But I had to resist. One taste, and I'd want more and forget what really mattered.

A sharp pain raking down my calf made me yelp. I jumped and whirled around. The ginger cat stood behind me, a paw raised as if she was about to scratch me again.

"What was that for?"

She nodded her head at my right hand.

I was holding a truffle. I dropped it and backed away. "Whoa! Was I about to eat that?"

The ginger cat nodded.

I bit my bottom lip. Maybe my control around this stuff wasn't so good. "Ginge, I need you to be candy monitor. If I'm about to sample anything, you let me know. But no more scratches. Hop on my shoulder, so you can keep a closer eye on me."

The ginger cat considered the option for a second before scrambling up my leg and onto my shoulder. When she finally settled, she curled her tail around my neck.

"Let's be quick about this. Sherry could come back, and I don't want to deal with that smug sugar witch until I've got more people on my side."

We spent another half an hour searching the candy store. I'd gone through the drawers, checked every shelf, and looked behind the counter. There was nothing to suggest Sherry was up to no good. Although, I wasn't certain what I'd expected to find. An evil spell book, a list of dark deeds she planned to get done that week, the secret recipe to her addictive candy.

If what Sherry said was true, this plan to take over Witch Haven wasn't new. Sherry and her accomplices had been working up to this for a long time. Maybe they'd tried before and failed, and this was their latest attempt. They were using a candy store as cover to infiltrate the village and take over by stealth.

And it was working, so far.

I leaned against the counter and looked around. I'd searched everywhere. Had this been a waste of time?

The ginger cat made that funny chirruping sound again. She hopped off my shoulder and landed on the counter. She placed a paw on the cash register.

I studied it. It was old, mechanical, and had a handle you pressed to ring up the order. "You think there could be something inside?"

She nodded and tapped it with her paw again.

I'd never worked a cash register, so I pressed a few buttons to get it to open. Nothing worked.

I jiggled the cash drawer, but it stuck. I pulled harder, and it shot out, the metal edge scratching my arm. I hissed in a breath and wrapped my fingers around the cut. Blood oozed out of the wound and dripped onto the floor.

There was nothing on hand to stop the blood, but it wasn't deep and would heal on its own. I was about to look in the cash drawer when light flickered under my feet and radiated across the floor.

Ginge gave another chirrup and watched the light with wide eyes.

I peered around the side of the counter and saw an illuminated map of Witch Haven coming to life.

"What have we got here?" I walked around the counter, and another drop of my blood fell on the floor. It intensified the light, and the map spread out across the entire floor. "Oh, of course. Sherry would use something as nasty as blood magic to hide her grubby secrets. Her plan has been beneath our feet this whole time."

Ginge looked over the edge of the counter, her whiskers twitching as the map flickered to life.

I walked around the map several times. It showed every street, house, and business. But there were differences. Unwelcome, disturbing ones.

"That shouldn't be here." I kneeled over the map to examine a large, dark shape. It was marked as a body pit.

Ginge gave a soft hiss.

"Neither should that. We don't have a prison in Witch Haven. Other than the holding cells Olympus has in the back of his office, we've never had a need for a prison that size." There was an enormous black blob described as a prison camp. Next to it was something called a drone camp. This just kept getting worse.

I tipped back on my heels. "This is what Sherry has planned for Witch Haven residents. She'll imprison, kill, or enslave everyone."

Ginge did an unhappy sounding meow, and I felt like joining her.

I shook my head, still not believing what I saw. Sherry would dispose of magic users who were no good to her, trap those who wouldn't help her, and use the ones she could while subduing them with her candy.

"Look at this. She's mapped out the ancient ley lines beneath the village, too. Sherry must be planning on exploiting them. Maybe she's been using the old power to juice her candy." Ley line magic was as old as time. If Sherry mixed it with something dark, it would have a powerful effect over anyone who was exposed to it.

Ginge squeaked and hid her nose under one paw.

I stood, my gaze sweeping over the rest of the map. I pulled out my phone and took several pictures. "Sherry's been using murder and candy to hide the bigger picture. By the time people come to their senses, if they ever do, it'll be too late. She'll have killed them, trapped them, or used them for her own purposes." I looked over at the ginger cat, who was still hiding her nose, although she gave me a small nod of support.

While Sherry had been plotting, she'd been learning about me. She knew my weaknesses and my failure to find Eden, and she acted like Fire Fang was her neighbor's dog, cooing over him and smirking. All this time, she'd been getting information to exploit.

Did she dig up people's vulnerabilities to bend them even further to her will? Why bother, when she had the candy to do that for her? Had she targeted me for a reason? It didn't make sense.

I looked at Ginge. "Sherry has more secrets. I just know it."

I was bone weary and tempted to vanish into my bed for a week and forget this nightmare. Everything felt too difficult and tangled together. A complicated, dark web had been hanging over Witch Haven for a long time, and I'd been so caught up in my own issues, I hadn't noticed. But no one had.

Dark powers had been trying to take over Witch Haven and test its limits for decades, maybe even hundreds of years. It could even stretch back further.

But I knew the truth, and I wasn't giving up on Witch Haven, my dumb, candy obsessed friends, or my annoying hellhound, who'd just made life twice as complicated by revealing his mortality.

"Come on, Ginge. Let's head to the apartment. Fire Fang could have taken Binky there. I have to make sure they're safe."

The ginger cat hopped back on my shoulder, and I dashed out of the store and raced to my apartment. I hurried inside and was relieved to see Fire Fang in his mortal form, waiting by my bedroom door.

I jogged over to him. "How's Binky?"

"She's... different." He glanced over his shoulder at the closed bedroom door.

"Was she badly hurt by Sherry's magic? Did you take her to the vet?" I dumped my phone and keys on the table. "You won't believe what I found in the candy store."

Ginge jumped off my shoulder and sniffed the gap under my bedroom door. She looked up and meowed at Fire Fang.

"Forget the candy store for a second. I didn't take Binky to the vet. She got a couple of nasty hits from Sherry, but she's healing. I used healing spells to speed things up."

I huffed out a breath. "That's one good thing. But I can't forget the candy store. I've got a lot to tell you."

"And I've got something to tell you, too. It's about Binky. I mean, not only Binky, but it starts with her. It involves her. It's... complicated."

I tensed. "You said she was okay. Where is she?"

"I said she was different. And also okay. But focus on the different thing. I... I don't know how to explain this."

Worry shone from Fire Fang's eyes. I'd never seen that expression before, but then I was still getting used to his mortal face. His very handsome, very worried looking mortal face.

"You're not making sense. Is she in the bedroom?" I tried to get to the door, but Fire Fang blocked my way. I glared up at him. "What are you doing? Is Binky in there or not?"

"Yes." He let out a slow sigh, his hand on my arm. "I don't know how to prepare you for this, so I'm just going to show you."

"Prepare me for what? Binky's not dead. She's healing. What did I miss?"

Fire Fang caught hold of my hand and squeezed tight.

Tension made my spine vibrate. "You're freaking me out. What will I find behind this door?"

To answer that question, he opened the door.

Eden was lying unconscious on my bed.

Chapter 18

I stared at my sister and then back at Fire Fang. "Is this real?" The words came out in a strangled whisper.

He nodded and tugged on my hand. "She's real. I mean, I only know her from the pictures around your apartment, but—"

"It's Eden." I scrubbed my eyes even though I didn't want to stop looking at her for fear she'd disappear.

"Yeah, it is. I saw the family resemblance straightaway," Fire Fang said.

"I... I don't understand. How did she get here? Was she here when you came back with Binky?" I finally got my feet to move and staggered to the bed to look down at Eden. I brushed aside the tangled mess of hair partially covering her face. My heart felt like it was in my throat, beating an unnaturally fast rhythm as I kept staring.

I leaned forward slowly, worried about making any sudden movements, and gently touched Eden's shoulder. I looked over at Fire Fang. "Was she like this when you found her?"

"In a way. And I didn't exactly find her here." He walked over and joined me by the bed.

"Then what happened? Did she walk in? Was she waiting outside? Fire Fang, what aren't you telling me?"

He gripped my shoulder tight. "After you left with Sherry to take her to the cells, I checked Binky. She wasn't waking, but her injuries didn't seem bad. I brought her here to watch her for a while. I'd just put her on the bed when she started flickering."

"Flickering? How? Explain."

He ran a hand through his hair. "I'm trying, but it doesn't even make sense to me, and I was right here. Binky was pulsing with magic. The pulses got brighter, and she vibrated. And then... Binky turned into Eden."

A laugh shot out of me. It was tinged with hysteria and disbelief.

His hand tightened on my shoulder. "I was as shocked as you. But she just appeared."

I slumped onto the bed. "All this time, Eden's been right here? Disguised as a cat?"

"Just like I was a hellhound."

I took a moment to process that information. There was a worrying similarity to their change from person to animal. "Talk me through what happened again. We were in the store, fighting Sherry. Binky came out of nowhere and took the truffle to stop me from eating it. Then as she escaped, Sherry hit her with some kind of spell."

"That's about it. I protected Binky while you fought Sherry. Binky must have followed us to the store and raced in to stop you from eating that truffle."

"Yeah, she must have. How did Binky seem after she'd been injured? Or should I call her Eden? Binky really was Eden?" I kept stroking my fingers through my sister's tangled hair. She was restless, shifting in the bed every few seconds as if she couldn't relax. I noticed several old scars on her arms.

"She was out cold for a few minutes, but her eyes were fluttering, and I figured she was coming around. That's why I brought her here rather than go to the vet. I'm glad I didn't take her there now. I wouldn't have been able to explain how a cat morphed into your sister in the blink of an eye."

"It happened that quickly?"

Fire Fang nodded. "I was standing at the bottom of the bed, figuring out what to do, when she changed. Binky was gone."

"And Eden was back," I whispered.

Ginge dashed into the room with a piece of paper. She hopped onto the bed and set it down before running out.

"It must have been the magic Sherry hit Binky with, or rather, Eden. Somehow, Eden got trapped as a cat, and whatever power Sherry used, it disrupted the spell." I shook my head. "There must be more to it than that. Why would Sherry's magic do that? Binky's been hit with magic before. I've even whacked her a few times when I've tried to capture her. She never changed. Not even a flicker."

Ginge ran back in with another piece of paper. She placed it on the bed before leaving the room.

"What do you think is going on?" Fire Fang said.

"I need to know the spell Sherry used. Did she even know what she was doing or was it a fluke? Maybe Binky's magic was unstable, and it took a hit of a certain spell to release Eden from Binky's form.

Although they're the same person, so I'm confusing myself."

"Let's call her Eden, shall we? That was her name before she became Binky," Fire Fang said.

I let out a breath, only then realizing I'd barely been breathing since I'd seen my baby sister on my bed. "I can't believe it. She's here." Letting out that exhale released a flood of emotions I'd been holding in ever since Eden vanished. I tried to hold back the tears, but there were so many, it was a waste of time. They raced down my cheeks and landed on the bed covers.

Fire Fang didn't speak for a minute. He left the room and returned with wadded up tissue paper, which he handed to me.

I sniffed a thank you and dabbed my eyes and nose. I couldn't stop looking at my sister. It was wonderful but also extremely weird. She was grown up, but it was clearly her. How long had she been trapped inside a cat's body? Ever since she went missing?

"I've been such an idiot," I said after the tears dried up. "Eden's been around for months, telling me who she was. I thought she was a nuisance, but her constant howling and meowing outside the apartment was her way of getting my attention. I assumed she was just a stray cat forcing her way in and claiming a home of her own."

"You weren't to know Eden was hiding inside a cat," Fire Fang said. "I had no idea. Although she does smell like you."

"She's my sister. I should have known. I should have done more for her."

Fire Fang perched next to me. "Why? And what would you have done? This is a unique situation."

I glanced at him. "Not unique. After all, you're not exactly an average hellhound."

"Okay. It's not unique but almost."

I studied my sister's face. Her forehead was wrinkled, and her eyes fluttered behind closed lids, as if she was having a bad dream. "Do you think she's in pain?"

"She hasn't been settled since she's been here. It's not a physical injury causing her distress."

"You're sure your healing magic did the job? Maybe Eden needs to see a specialist."

"She had a couple of burn marks, but they were already healing by the time we got here."

I worked through the possibilities about how this could have happened. "Sherry's magic messed with the spell that trapped Eden as a cat. It disrupted when those spells met. It caused the malfunction and broke the entrapment."

"That's possible," Fire Fang said. "But that usually only happens when the same spell caster hits a person with a conflicting spell they've cast themselves. Some spells just don't work together, so one cancels out the other. Eden hasn't met Sherry before, has she?"

I tucked the covers in around my sister. "No. But the way Sherry talked about Eden going missing, it was like she knew her. She was so smug and seemed to know a secret she wasn't willing to share."

"That was Sherry behaving like a dark magic douchebag. She was distracting you, so you made a mistake."

"I think I'm the one who made the mistake." It felt like a lightning bolt had slammed into my spine. "What if this is part of the dark witches' plan? Sherry said they'd been testing and exploiting us for a long time."

Fire Fang tilted his head, considering the idea. "You think Sherry took your sister and turned her into a cat to further her ambitions? Why do that?"

I stroked the back of my sister's hand. "Sherry was talking about gathering an army. She needs powerful witches on her side to control Witch Haven. What if they've been taking magic users when they were young? They steal them and manipulate them into thinking dark magic is the right path and control them by turning them into animals. Or maybe it's some kind of punishment. I don't know. Eden wouldn't bend to their will, so they trapped her as a cat?"

"But she escaped and found you?" Fire Fang huffed out a breath.

"And Eden's not the only child to go missing in Witch Haven. I know of at least one other, and there could be more."

"Who? You've never mentioned that."

"Olympus Duke's daughter, Bloom, went missing. He's never forgiven himself for losing her. He took her on an investigation and left her outside with his colleagues. She vanished, and no one saw anything. Just like Eden, there was no trace of what happened." I looked over at him, and his stark expression mirrored my shock.

Fire Fang rubbed his forehead. "We need something strong to drink."

My breath came out shaky as I nodded. "All I can offer is coffee. I'm not much of a drinker."

"Stay with Eden. I'll get the drinks." Fire Fang left the room, shaking his head.

I gripped Eden's hand in both of mine. "You need to wake up and tell me where you've been. Is Sherry behind this?"

My sister stirred but didn't wake.

Fire Fang returned a few moments later with two mugs of coffee. He handed me one before joining me back on the bed.

I took a sip, welcoming the warmth into my chilled, shocked body.

"It's weird, but as soon as Eden appeared in cat form, it was like I knew her. And she smelled so familiar," Fire Fang said.

"I remember you saying that. I thought it was strange."

"Not to me. It was a similar scent to you. It smelled like home. And although I couldn't explain it, I knew she was a part of our family. Now, I know why."

I shifted on the bed and glanced at him. The intense look in his eyes had me dropping my gaze. "You're not thinking straight. You probably still have candy in your system. We aren't a proper family."

He slowly set down his mug and tilted my chin up with his finger. "We are. You need to accept that. We've been through a lot together. It matters. And we've always been there for each other. Now we have Eden to take care of, too."

"I've not always been there for you. I tried to get you adopted plenty of times."

His mouth lifted at the corner. "You made a few half-hearted attempts to get me adopted. I remember that adorable older couple who were interested in me, then you told them I chewed the furniture. I've never chewed any of your furniture. Even when I've been tempted."

My cheeks heated. "I don't remember that. You really have been messed up by all that candy."

Fire Fang chuckled, his thumb swiping over my chin. "I remember everything. And I remember how loyal you are and how focused you are on making sure no one around you gets hurt. Even if that puts you in danger. You've always done that. For me, your friends, and your family." He looked at Eden. "It's how you show you care. You never talk about your feelings, but you show them through your actions."

I gently eased his hand away from my face. "I can only think about Eden right now."

"Of course. I understand that, but when she's awake and talking, we need to have this chat. I don't want to go anywhere if you're not with me. I'll do anything for you, including dealing with Sherry and stopping her plans for Witch Haven. Storm, you must know, I—"

I cut him off by pressing a finger against his lips. "You're right. We will talk. But not now. And I know you see me as family, but we have a lot to work through before we make any moves. Anywhere, about anything. Got it?"

A flare of pain shot through my leg, and I yelped and jumped off the bed. The ginger cat was hanging off my calf, her teeth and claws embedded in my skin.

She hopped off, sat on the floor, and glared at me.

"You have got to stop doing that." I grabbed my throbbing leg.

She jumped on the bed and pointed at the paper she'd laid out. I'd been so distracted by Eden, I'd barely noticed she'd put six pieces of paper side-by-side.

"What is wrong with this cat? I don't want this becoming her new bad habit." My hand came away bloody as I inspected my calf.

"She must be trying to tell you something," Fire Fang said. "There are letters on these pieces of paper."

"Binky, I mean Eden, must have been teaching her. She's been learning to spell for a while." I checked my leg one more time then looked at the paper. There was a large loopy, wobbly letter on each one. S I T S R E.

Fire Fang huffed out a laugh. "Let's switch those around." He moved the T, the R, and second S.

"Oh! Sister. Ginge was telling me who Eden was. And Eden did that, too. She'd get so frustrated scribbling things on paper, and then I couldn't make out what they were. All this time, she was letting me know who she was, but I've been too distracted to see."

"No one can blame you for that. How were you to know your sister was trapped in a cat's body? None of us figured it out."

Ginge tapped the back of my hand with her paw and dabbed her nose on the image of a wonky flower. She kept jabbing and pointing and flicking her tail.

I looked at the flower and then at the cat. My heart lurched. "Fire Fang, I don't think Eden was the only one turned into a cat."

Chapter 19

Fire Fang stared at the ginger cat. "Who is she?"

"Look at the drawing!" I grabbed the paper. "It's a flower. A bloom! This is Bloom Duke."

Ginge chirped and stood on her back legs before dropping down onto the bed.

"Am I right?" I stared at the little cat. "You're Olympus's missing daughter?"

She twirled in a circle and nodded.

My mouth hung open, and I gave a snort of surprise. "Wow! This day has turned from weird to insanely weird."

"How do we turn her back into Bloom the person?" Fire Fang looked as stunned as me.

"I don't know. But I have to tell Olympus about this."

"Wait a second. How will you get him to believe you? You two haven't been on friendly terms recently."

"We need to get Olympus here and purge him of candy. Once he has a clear head, I've explained everything to him, and shown him Eden, he'll have to believe me."

Fire Fang looked doubtful, but I was already dialing Olympus's number.

He picked up after the fifth ring. "You've got a nerve calling me. Unless you're telling me you're turning yourself in, we have nothing to say to each other."

"Olympus, don't talk. Just listen."

"You don't tell me what to do. Not only did you break into one of my cells with an innocent person and accuse her of all sorts of unpleasant things, you then escaped using my familiar against me. Monty's locked up because of you. I'm considering having him vanquished. And I plan to—"

"I've found Bloom. She's alive, and she's in Witch Haven." I needed a shock tactic to knock him out of his candy stupor.

There was silence. "You have Bloom? How?"

"I know this is unexpected, but your daughter needs you. She's mixed up in what Sherry's doing to the village."

There was more silence then a heavy sigh. "Storm, you'd better not be messing with me. You know how long I've searched for Bloom." Olympus's voice was sharp and clear for the first time in days. Finally, something had cut through the candy chaos.

"I've got a lot to tell you, and when you see Bloom, she'll look different. But it's her. Trust me."

"Where are you?"

"I'm at my apartment."

"And Bloom is with you?"

"She's here. But she's—"

The line went dead. A few seconds later, there was a flash of magic in my lounge. I hurried to the bedroom door to see Olympus had arrived using a translocation spell.

His gaze locked with mine. Coldness mingled with worry and a dash of hope. "Where is she?"

"In the bedroom. But you need to let me finish explaining."

"I have to see her." He marched toward me.

I held up a hand. "Give me a minute. Things aren't as simple as that. Bloom has been transformed into an animal."

His eyes widened then narrowed, and a scowl appeared. "I knew this was a trick. It's another one of your games. I'm done with you. Storm Winter, I'm arresting you—"

"Storm is telling the truth." Fire Fang appeared behind me. "And you need to listen if you want to see your daughter again."

"Who are you? Are you involved in this, too? Did you take Bloom?" Magic flared on Olympus's fingers, the sparks jagged and as unfocused as he was.

Fire Fang growled. "Listen to Storm. If you care about your daughter, you need to know what's going on. The whole story, not just the bits that fit your view of Sherry and her candy."

"Of course I care about Bloom," Olympus said. "But I need to see her to know Storm isn't lying. And I have no idea how Sherry could be involved."

"When was the last time you ate candy from Sherry's store?" I said.

His fingers flexed, the magic still simmering. "What does that have to do with seeing Bloom?"

"Answer the question. How far gone are you?"

His scowl deepened. "I finished a box of her dark chocolate curls twenty minutes ago."

"Thanks. I needed to know how strong to make this." I focused the energy I had left and slammed a purging spell into Olympus's mouth and down his throat.

He staggered back and began retching.

I pointed at the bathroom. "Head that way and stay there until all the candy has left your system. Then we'll talk about Bloom, Sherry, her tainted candy, and her plans to take over Witch Haven."

"What have you done to me?" Olympus gasped out between retches as he staggered toward the bathroom.

"The next half an hour won't be pleasant, but you'll thank me afterward. Then you can meet Bloom."

Olympus fell to his knees, so I helped him into the bathroom, got him settled over the toilet, and left him, closing the door behind me as he made a noise like a distressed whale using a fog horn.

Fire Fang chuckled as he shook his head. "You could have given the guy a warning."

"And have him dodge the purging magic? I needed to take him unawares. I figured, make him as sick as a dog, get that gross candy out of his system, then we can have a proper conversation without him arresting me every thirty seconds." I grimaced as sounds of violent throwing up drifted from the bathroom. "Olympus won't listen if he's under Sherry's influence. Once his stomach is empty and he's downed a couple of coffees, we'll figure things out. He can meet Eden, spend time with Bloom, and we'll get him to believe. Without the Magic Council on our side, we won't be able to defeat Sherry and her dark witches."

Fire Fang grimaced as more gross retching filtered out of the bathroom. "I'll get the coffee brewing. You spend time with Eden."

I headed back into the bedroom. Bloom sat across Eden's feet, looking remarkably chilled for a kid who was an enchanted cat and about to let her dad in on a big secret.

"So, you're Bloom Duke?" I scratched behind her ears. "Nice work, kitty. Although ease up on the biting. Those fangs are sharp."

She twitched her whiskers.

"Did you know who Binky really was?"

Bloom nodded.

"And did Binky, or rather Eden, know who you were? Was that why she brought you here?"

Bloom nodded again.

"This is a lot to take in. Were you the only ones changed into cats?"

Her nose crinkled, and she shook her head.

I sighed as I settled on the edge of the bed. "That's what I figured. Sherry and her gang have been kidnapping young witches, haven't they? Growing their army in any way they can." I took hold of Eden's hand again, my heart kicking with sadness. "She's had you for a long time, but we'll make things right. Whatever you've learned from her, you can unlearn. You always were the good witch. The perfect daughter. If only our parents could see you and know you got back safe."

There was a thump from the bathroom, and the door opened. Olympus staggered in a moment later. He looked gray and was sweating. "I'll make you pay for this. That was assault."

"Tell me what you think of Sherry Brown?"

"Sherry! She's an incredible woman. Attractive, funny, smart, and makes the best—"

He got another whack of purging magic. "You're not done yet. Back you go." I hopped off the bed and led a protesting Olympus to the bathroom.

He fell to his knees and clutched the porcelain. "I'll make sure you get life imprisonment for attacking a high up member of the Magic Council. I have clout. I can make you disappear."

"Sure you can. You just focus on the fact your daughter is in my bedroom. Get that candy out of you, and then come meet her. But stay here until you've finished puking. I don't want any more mess to clear up."

He glowered at me but focused on the unpleasant job of being violently ill again.

I left him to it, the smell of recycled candy and sweat curdling my stomach.

Fire Fang walked to the bathroom door and tapped on it. "Olympus, I'll leave a coffee outside for when you're done."

He got a fog horn groan in response.

"How's Eden doing?" Fire Fang asked me.

"Still out of it. But I've been talking to Bloom, and they weren't the only children taken."

A scowl crossed Fire Fang's face, and he grumbled a growl in his chest.

Even though the sound wasn't as impressive as when he was in hellhound form, it sent a tingle down my spine. "We'll get them back. We'll make sure every child taken is safe."

"Yes, we will. But we need to focus on the two we've got here," I said.

We headed into the bedroom, and I dashed to the bed when Eden's eyes flickered open.

"Hey, there's nothing to be scared about. It's me, Storm. You're safe and in my apartment. No one will hurt you."

Her eyes flickered again, and she finally opened them fully, not focusing on anything. She gave a small moan.

"Take your time. Whenever you're ready, we're right here." Tears hit my cheeks, but I barely noticed them.

Bloom jumped onto Eden's chest and licked her face.

Eden gave her a weak smile. "Bloom! So happy you made it."

A lump in my throat almost stopped me from talking. "We know who this ginger cat is. You saved Bloom Duke, didn't you? You're a hero."

"Only one. Could only help one." Eden's voice sounded scratchy from lack of use.

"Where is Bloom?" Olympus appeared and leaned against the doorframe of the bedroom, still looking gray but less like he wanted me in chains.

Bloom chirruped at him, but he paid her no attention.

Eden's gaze shifted into focus, and her eyes settled on me. "Storm! It's you! I thought... I thought I imagined your voice."

"I'm here. And so are you. I'm so happy to see you again." I wrapped my sister in a hug, both of us crying and laughing.

"I'm so tired," she whispered in my ear. "I've been fighting and hiding for such a long time."

"Where is Bloom?" Olympus's tone was demanding. "You told me she was here."

I forced myself to stop looking at my sister and turned to him. "Answer me a question first. What do you think of Sherry Brown?"

"The candy store owner? She seems like a nice lady. I haven't had much to do with her."

"Is that all? You wouldn't lay down your life to protect her?"

"What are you talking about? All I'm interested in is where my daughter is."

"Let me explain this to him," Eden whispered. "It might sound better coming from me. Less blunt."

I stood from the bed. "Olympus, this is Eden Winter, my younger sister. She has something important to tell you, so keep it zipped and listen." I stepped away, giving Eden space, even though I wanted to do the opposite. Now she was back, I'd never let her out of my sight. She may have grown up and turned into a striking teenager, but she was still a kid to me, and I was planning on going full-on protective older sister. Eden would hate it, but she'd get used to it.

As if she knew what I was thinking, her eyes narrowed, and she shooed me away. "I've got this. You work for the Magic Council, right? So you know what happened to me?" Her tired eyes focused on Olympus.

"I do. And I remember the investigation into Eden Winter's disappearance, but I wasn't that involved in the case. I have no idea if Storm is telling me the truth about you, although you appear to have seen hard times." His gaze was on an old scar running across Eden's forehead.

Eden shuffled in the bed, so she was almost sitting. "Storm may be a lot of things. Stubborn, quick to anger, holds a grudge, always puts back empty cookie cartons in the cabinet, and thinks she's the best witch in the world—"

I couldn't keep quiet. "Hey, I'm working on myself. Things have changed. And I'm an adult now."

Eden pointed at the old packing case I used as a bedside table. "Sure they have. I have been here for a while, so I know how you still operate. The fridge isn't full of fresh food, and there's a gross pizza box under the couch, growing a new kind of fungus."

"Um... maybe."

"Things aren't that different. You can still be dumb." Eden focused back on Olympus. "As I was about to say before my big sister stomped over my words, Storm is also the most loyal and committed person I know. Sure, I have little life experience, since I've spent the last decade under the control of evil witches who stink like a jello factory gone wrong, but I remember my family."

I got another pesky lump in my throat. I'd forgotten how awesome my kid sister was.

She glanced at me. "I know our parents are dead. I heard you mention it to the hound. And they haven't been around since I moved in."

My heart sank. It must have sucked to learn about their deaths that way. "I would have told you all about it if I'd known who you were."

She lifted a hand to stop me from speaking. "I know. And you can fill me in later. It's just you and Fire Fang?"

"That's it."

Her lips pursed. "I figured you'd be married by now. You're not getting any younger."

I snort laughed. "Really?"

"No! Not really." Eden rolled her eyes. "Guys were scared of you, even when we were kids."

Olympus cleared his throat. "Shall we focus on Bloom?"

Bloom meowed sharply, but Olympus still ignored her. He needed to be careful, or he'd feel her clawed wrath.

"Sorry, sure. It's just I have a ton of catching up to do with Storm." Eden grinned at me then looked at Olympus.

"I'm yet to be convinced of your identity," he said. "Anyone who spent time with Storm would know those things about her. The awful attitude, her parents dying, the issues with men."

"I don't have issues with men," I snarled at him.

Fire Fang chuckled, which quickly died when my glare shifted his way.

Eden shrugged. "Storm has a scar on the back of her right knee. She got it helping me when I got stuck down a cliff. I lost my footing and fell. She grabbed me but got stones lodged in her knee as she skidded. One went really deep. Magic couldn't even get rid of it."

"I have that scar. I suppose you want to see it," I said to Olympus.

"I've seen it," Fire Fang said.

"Oh! I had no clue. You two dated?" Eden's eyes brightened. "He's your type, although I like him better with fur. Is the dating still going on? Wait. The change thing is new, so you dated him as a furry? Has my big sister gone kinky?"

"Stop! Nothing like that! We don't need to talk about... that." My cheeks flamed. Eden had always been notoriously nosy about relationships that didn't concern her.

"A furry?" Olympus's face scrunched in confusion, his gaze moving over Fire Fang. "What do you have to do with this? I don't know you. Why are you even here?"

"I'm a friend. And you know me. That's all that matters," Fire Fang said.

That answer didn't please Olympus, and the men glared at each other.

"Err... sorry. I didn't mean to blow up an issue." Eden looked at me and bit her lip. "I just thought—"

"Stop with the thinking and keep on explaining." I clicked my fingers to get Olympus's attention. "Bloom is here."

He finally grunted and pulled his glare from Fire Fang. "How do I know you're not working with Storm and making this up?" Olympus said to Eden. "I came here to see my daughter, and all I'm getting is the runaround. If Bloom's not here—"

"She's that cat," I said. "The ginger cat who's looking at you with adoring eyes and who's been trying to get your attention ever since you walked into the bedroom."

His eyebrows flashed up. He looked at the cat, disbelief written over his face. "Storm—"

"I was also a cat," Eden said. "It's what they do. The witches who took me tried to break me. They spent years training me and making me like them. I've never had an interest in dark magic, though. But they wanted me because I was already powerful.

They made a mistake. My power doesn't relate to destroying people and hurting them. I'm a healer."

"A cat?" Olympus's nostrils flared. "You want me to believe this cat is Bloom?"

Bloom meowed, hopped off the bed, and rubbed against his leg.

"Yep. We were both cats." Eden grinned at me. "It was weird. It took time to adjust to having four legs and a tail."

Olympus moved away from Bloom. "You're lying. Winter witches control the elements. You don't heal."

"You're wrong. When I was younger, I was jealous of Storm because I didn't have her awesome weather witch powers, but some of our ancestors were healers, and that ability passed to me. Which means I'd never use my power to hurt. The witches were raging when I wouldn't break. And they tried. Plenty of times." Eden's hand went to the scar on her forehead.

I kept a grip on the rage thrumming through me as my brain worked overtime on the awful ways she'd gotten that scar. "You held out against Sherry and the other witches?"

"Sherry! Yes, that was the name one of them used. Although it wasn't her real name. They used fake names like Sherry, Lucy, and Mary. There were four of them, and they'd meet once a week. If I could, I'd listen to their conversations." Eden shook her head, her expression growing stark. "Their plans are terrifying. They want Witch Haven as a power base before taking over every magic community."

"Eden, if that really is your name, do you have evidence to support these claims?" Olympus looked skeptical, and his tone told me he didn't believe my sister.

"What about Sherry's candy?" I said. "You and nearly everyone else in the village have been gorging on it. That's not natural. There's your evidence."

His hand went to his stomach. "I'll admit, I'm not sure what that was about. My memories are hazy. I seem to have eaten a lot of candy recently, though."

"And why would any of us lie about this?" Eden said.

Bloom pressed a paw against Olympus's leg.

He looked down at her, doubt in his eyes. "If this cat is Bloom, change her. Do whatever you did to Eden so I can see her for myself."

"I don't know how. Eden changed because she was blasted with Sherry's magic. The spell she got hit with affected the enchantment that trapped Eden in cat form. We need Sherry to tell us how she did it," I said.

Olympus was still looking at Bloom, who stared back at him with big, innocent eyes.

He wanted to believe, but doubt lingered. And I wasn't surprised. I'd been the same with Eden. It was a huge leap of faith to take that your missing daughter suddenly shows up as a cat.

"That's what they did to magic users who won't obey them," Eden said. "They turned us into animals, usually cats, and forced a familiar connection on us so they could trap us that way. It worked for a few, but not many. Those they considered failures were put in cages."

My hand settled on her shoulder. "How long were you in a cage?"

"Four years. I was there when Bloom came in. She's a fighter. You should be proud of her, Olympus. She fought every time they tried to influence her. The witches soon tired of her feistiness and transformed her."

A smile flickered across Olympus's face. "That sounds like my Bloom. She always dug in her heels if she didn't want to do something."

Bloom meowed and leaned against him.

"Those witches hated her. Eventually, they turned her into a cat and put her in the cage next to me. That's when we made a plan. We figured out how to damage the lock on my cage, and I got out one night. I got Bloom's cage door open too, but then we were almost caught. We had to run and got separated."

"You left her behind?" Olympus held a hand out for Bloom to sniff.

"Hey, less of that. Eden had no choice." My hand tightened on her shoulder, but she shrugged me off.

"I would have gone back for Bloom if I could, but they kept us below ground in a cave system, and I didn't know where to search. I figured if I got back to Storm, she'd help me. And when I wasn't trying to convince my stubborn-headed sister who I was, I looked for Bloom. I knew she'd find her way out on her own. She's so smart."

"Yes, she is," Olympus whispered. It looked like he was too scared to touch Bloom in case he broke her.

"Eventually, I found her, but she was weak. I used my healing magic until she was strong enough to come back to Witch Haven with me." Eden sucked in a breath and glanced at me. I encouraged her to go on with a nod. "Olympus, I know this is hard to believe, but that's what happened. And there are hundreds more trapped magic users."

Olympus bent at the waist and picked up Bloom. She purred and snuggled against his chest. He petted her a few times. "I want to believe you. If this cat is my daughter..." He swallowed and looked away. "If she is, it'll change everything. I'll finally have my family back."

Eden's eyes were closing, but she jerked awake. "Bloom had a purple bear when she arrived. She called it Mr. Fuzz Ball. She wanted to keep it, but the witches took it. They burned it in front of her."

Tears filled Olympus's eyes. "That was her bear. I gave it to her. But... but you could have seen her with that bear in Witch Haven."

"Not possible. Bloom's younger than me, so we never hung out together. The first time I saw that bear was when the witches brought her in. She didn't cry about losing it until weeks later and only when she was alone. I could tell she loved that bear."

Bloom meowed sadly and hid her face in Olympus's shoulder.

A single tear trickled down his cheek as he held the cat against him.

"I know this is weird, but trust me," I said. "I wouldn't lie about something as important as Eden or Bloom. I know you've struggled since your daughter went missing, because I've gone through the same thing. I was devastated when Eden went missing. I blamed myself for years—"

"No, it wasn't your fault. And you wouldn't have been able to stop those witches," Eden said. "Two of them came into my room and took me. They were powerful. I fought back, but my magic made no impact."

I still felt the weight of failure on me. "I'd have tried to stop them."

"And been taken, too? Such a typical answer from you." Eden smiled as she shook her head. "You always thought you were better than everyone else."

"I still do." I gave her a teary smile.

Olympus sniffed. "Can you get Bloom back? As a child, not a cat?"

"If we capture Sherry, we can learn what magic she used on Eden and Bloom. Then we can figure out how to reverse it," I said.

Olympus was quiet, just petting Bloom and holding back tears. "I'm willing to believe you. Storm, you've always been upfront with me, sometimes painfully so. If you believe there's something wrong with Sherry and the candy she's giving out, I'll support you. What do you need from me?"

I was so relieved I could have hugged Olympus. "We must stop those witches. But I also have a theory we need to look into before we do that."

"What is it?" Olympus said.

"These witches have been taking children to turn them to their cause for a long time. Sherry said this battle has been going on for years. Have you got access to records about missing children in Witch Haven and the surrounding areas?"

Olympus nodded. "Of course."

"We need to access those. We have to see who else they took."

Olympus kept hold of Bloom. "What about my daughter?"

"Leave her with me," Fire Fang said. "I'll protect her. And Eden."

"I don't know you," Olympus said. "Why would you protect my daughter?"

"He's a good guy. I'll vouch for him. He's never let me down." I flashed Fire Fang a smile.

Bloom struggled out of Olympus's arms and jumped on Fire Fang's shoulder. She rubbed against his face.

"It looks like my... daughter vouches for you, too." Olympus still looked full of doubt.

"I promise, I'll look after them," Fire Fang said.

With some reluctance, Olympus nodded. "Let's go see about those missing children."

My gaze was on Fire Fang. He was proof of another idea I was working through about how far the dark witches had pushed things. But that was a theory to test later.

Chapter 20

An hour later, and after Olympus had searched the Magic Council records, my worst fears were realized.

Olympus sat in his office seat, his head resting on his hands, his elbows on his desk. "Why was this connection never made? Fifteen children missing from Witch Haven. And when you widen the search map, even more show up. Hundreds."

I nodded, my eyes gritty with tiredness. It was the early hours of the morning, but I couldn't afford to sleep. Not until we'd located Sherry and stopped her.

"Why would you have noticed a pattern? These witches are clever and hid what they were doing. And people come and go in the Magic Council, so these cases got handed on and no one made the link."

"Six children taken every five years," Olympus said. "And because they targeted different areas, no one tied it together."

"And the only connection between the young magic users taken was their potential to become powerful," I said. "There was no similarity in terms of age, gender, or appearance. Sherry and her friends focused on how powerful these magic users would grow up to be. They figured if they got them young, they'd manipulate them easily."

"Giving themselves an army of twisted, dark magic users."

I opened a page I'd been looking at on the laptop Olympus lent me. "There's another connection that was overlooked. They've been hiding what they were doing by staging public events and using murder as a distraction. Every time a child went missing, someone was killed, and there was an event held to distract people. There was the carnival in Spoiled Oak fifty years ago. A guy called Boris Paige was found dead in his car. Although traces of unusual magic were found on him, they ruled it an accident. At the same time, there was a carnival in the village."

"Two distractions, to hide the truth." Olympus scanned through his records. "And a young girl named Darlene Firefly vanished."

"And a hundred years ago, in Misty Brook, Ruby Sparkle died after drinking a tainted hot chocolate. Again, the case was never solved. It was believed to be a suspicious death, but they found no evidence to charge anyone. While that was going on, a traveling circus arrived and put on a week of events."

"While this child, Cedric Oleander, vanished." Olympus pushed back in his seat. "And it'll happen again in Witch Haven. The witches have already killed someone, so our attention should be on that—"

"And getting more of Sherry's candy."

He grimaced. "Of course. That's something I wish I could forget. Do you think this candy is an extra layer in their plan? They're trying something new by including it."

"This is their next phase. An addictive candy store, a death, and the event means children going missing could go unnoticed for hours. It gives them time to escape. Or start imprisoning residents in their camp if they're ready to make their next move."

Olympus sighed. "Eden said they want Witch Haven as a power base. The candy store could be their cover while they get everything in place."

"Makes sense. And they have that creepy blood activated map in there showing their plans. You need to look at that."

"It's on the list. Do you think they're planning to take more children today?"

"The timing fits. It happens every five years. Sherry will want to keep growing her army."

Olympus closed his eyes and pressed the bridge of his nose. "Sherry didn't fool you. You saw straight through her. She completely drew me in."

"Don't be too hard on yourself. I'd have been the same if I'd eaten her candy like everyone else did. I just got lucky. I wasn't in the mood for candy when she opened."

Olympus's desk phone rang. He cut it off by lifting it and slamming it down. "It'll be someone complaining about the ceremony. I can't think about that. Although, this discovery will throw the Magic Council into disarray. Heads will roll because the connection wasn't made between the missing children, the murders, and the surprise events."

"So long as it's not your head, I don't mind. You have a less than terrible head when it isn't clouded by candy."

One corner of his mouth lifted. "I appreciate you not holding a grudge over what I did to you."

"I sort of do, but you were under the influence of Sherry's magic, and that feels gross. Once was enough for me. I may even steer away from candy forever after this experience."

Olympus's expression became grim. "I'm still experiencing withdrawal symptoms, but I won't waver. I want Bloom back more than I want candy." His mouth wobbled. "It really is her, isn't it?"

"I think so. And I'm still getting over the shock of my sister being a cat. A cat I chased away dozens of times. Eden was trying to tell me who she was. She even wrote it down, and I couldn't see the hints, so I get why you're struggling." I leaned forward and patted his arm. "We'll figure it out once we have Sherry in custody. But we'll need help to capture her."

Exhaustion and gratitude tinged his smile. "We have specialists at the Magic Council. Operatives permitted to use kill spells."

"As tempting as it is, Sherry can't die. We have to take her in alive so we can reverse the magic on Bloom and make sure we get the rest of the trapped children out."

"Agreed. Who are you thinking of using?"

"Magic users willing to bend rules to capture Sherry and her witchy friends. They need to be fast and efficient. And we should keep anyone else from the Magic Council out of this."

"They have to know what we're doing."

"You can tell them when we succeed. If more people from the Magic Council get involved, it'll slow things down. Too many questions will be asked, and we'll lose our opportunity. Sherry can't figure out what we're doing, or she could make a run for it."

He didn't look convinced but nodded. "The event starts this afternoon. We don't have time to bring outsiders up to speed."

"I'm not thinking about outsiders." Although I wasn't sure what I had in mind would work, I had to try. "Get Indigo to invite Luna and Odessa for breakfast this morning. You get them in the same room, and I'll do the rest."

Olympus pressed his lips together. "Like you did with me, you mean? You want to purge them?"

"It worked. Once you got the candy out of your system, you were willing to listen. I have to do the same for my friends. They're the most powerful witches in the village. If we work together, we'll be strong enough to stop this takeover."

"This'll get messy, won't it?"

"You should put down plastic sheeting, just in case. There will be a lot of recycled candy making an appearance."

There was a clunk of metal, and a soft, forlorn whine drifted from out the back of the office, where the cells were.

I tilted my head. "If that's Monty I can hear, you need to set him free."

Olympus's eyes widened, and he shot from his seat. "Monty! Of course, I remember now. I was angry when he helped you escape from the cell, so I locked him up."

"If it weren't for him, I'd still be in there. Sherry would still have you under her thumb, and Witch Haven would be about to go down in a blaze of candy infused glory. Let him out."

Olympus dashed to the cells and returned a moment later with Monty beside him. He was bouncing up and down and kept jumping and licking Olympus's face.

"That's enough. You know licking isn't allowed." He laughed as Monty put his huge paws on Olympus's shoulders and gave him a hearty lick.

"I knew you wouldn't forget me." Monty looked my way.

"You helped me, so I'm returning the favor."

"I'm happy Olympus no longer smells gross. All that weird rotting honey scent has gone." Monty kept licking Olympus.

"With help from Storm, I'm back to my old self." Olympus dislodged Monty and set his paws on the floor.

"Monty, we need your help," I said. "In fact, we need all paws on board. We're about to deal with dangerous witches, and we can't afford to fail."

He wagged his tail. "Point me in the right direction, and I'll be a hero again. What's the plan?"

***

Six hours later, and after still having had no sleep, I was tucked in a coat closet in Indigo's house. Olympus had snuck me in before Indigo had woken up, and I was waiting in there with Monty and Indigo's three familiars, Nugget, Russell, and Hilda.

"We've been so worried about her," Hilda whispered. For a small spider, she was surprisingly heavy as she perched on my shoulder. "Indigo has been behaving so strangely. She almost trod on me the other day. I'm sure it was deliberate."

"I always said it was that candy," Nugget said. The cat sat on my feet, ears twitching.

Russell the crow cawed softly.

"Russell says you're lying," Hilda said. "You had no idea it was the candy causing these problems."

"Indigo had that strange smell," Nugget said. "Sweet but nasty. And she threw me outside, even though I told her it was cold. She always lets me sleep on the bed, even though Olympus complains about my fur on his pillow."

"That weird smell is something everyone gives off when they're under Sherry's thrall," I whispered. "It's something toxic in the candy that makes them obsessed with it. None of you were tempted to try it, were you?"

"I tried to grab some candy a couple of times, but Indigo got weird about it. She's usually good at sharing, but she kept bringing huge bags of it inside then would hide in her room and eat it." Nugget's tail thrashed from side to side. "I should have known then something was wrong."

"You said she was greedy," Hilda muttered.

"I'm glad she didn't share any with you," I said. "Otherwise, I'd have to deal with magically tainted familiars, too. And I've seen you when you're mad, Hilda."

The plump little spider tap danced on my shoulder. "We've been staying away from Indigo. She's barely noticed. Her only interest has been the candy. The same with Olympus. He was fine for a while, then they started gorging on it together."

"Indigo and the others will be back to normal soon, providing we pull off this plan." I'd told them about the purging magic I'd used on Olympus, and they agreed the same thing had to happen to Indigo.

She was my first target because her magic was so deadly. Odessa had her scarecrows, but she'd need time to call them, and Luna I could handle if I had to fight her. I hoped it wouldn't come to that.

Olympus had arranged a surprise breakfast for my three candy enthralled friends, and I'd laced the food with purging magic. Once they ate it, they'd get ill. Gross, but there was no other option. We had to get the toxic candy magic out of them, or they'd be no use in the fight against Sherry. And I needed my friends' support.

"Someone's coming to the front door," Nugget whispered.

"It must be Luna and Odessa." A knock on the front door had me tensing, and I crouched so I could peer through the gap between the door and the frame.

Footsteps hurried along the hallway. "Good morning, ladies. You're in for a treat today," Olympus said.

"How exciting. What have we done to deserve this?" Odessa said. "Is it an anniversary? I know it's no one's birthday. I never miss birthdays."

"No anniversary, but you've all been working hard, so I thought you'd like a break. Come in, both of you," Olympus said.

"Are you sure that's all this is about?" Luna said. "Or have you annoyed Indigo and have some making up to do? You know we always side with her."

Olympus chuckled. "Not that I know of. She'll be down in a few minutes. The table's laid, so help yourselves. I'm just brewing fresh coffee."

Coffee that also had an unpleasant purging treat added to it for maximum effect.

No one spoke for several minutes, and all I could hear was chairs scraping and cutlery being moved around.

"Olympus, this looks nice, but aren't we having candy?" Odessa said. "That's all I'm interested in eating."

"Why not start with a muffin?" he said.

"I'm not in the mood. I want candy."

I grimaced. I'd feared this might happen, but we had a backup plan.

"If candy is what you desire, then that's what you shall have. It'll be out soon," Olympus said. "Indigo, are you coming down? Your friends are here."

There was a note of tension in Olympus's voice, and I could understand why. If this went wrong, he'd be first in the firing line. If those three turned against him, Olympus would be dead in seconds.

Footsteps thumped down the stairs. "Hey. Glad you could make it at such short notice. Olympus surprised me with this breakfast idea. I think he's up to something." Indigo's tone sounded sharper than usual.

"He's just being sweet. And I was happy to get the call," Odessa said. "I'm sorry I couldn't bring Sol, but he's away on business. We have a new client for the pumpkins, and you know what a sweet talker my Sol is."

"It's better when it's just us girls," Indigo said. "And of course, Olympus. He can be our waiter."

"It's always a pleasure to serve you." There was a false note of happiness in his voice.

Come on, Olympus, hold it together. As I peered through the gap, I could see him making the coffee. My friends shifted in their seats, none of them touching the food and constantly looking around. I knew exactly what they were waiting for.

"Olympus, I thought this was supposed to be a nice surprise." Indigo rapped the table with her knuckles.

"Is something wrong?" His back was facing me, so I couldn't see his expression, but I could see how tight his shoulders were. Don't blow this, Olympus. Stay calm. One false step, and you're dead.

"Where's my candy?" There was a whine in Indigo's voice I'd never heard before.

"Try a croissant. They have an almond and chocolate filling."

Indigo picked up a croissant and lobbed it at him. "I don't want a stupid pastry. I have a craving for triple chocolate truffles dusted in cocoa."

"Oooooh! Perfect. I could go for some of them, too," Odessa said.

Olympus picked up the thrown croissant and set it on the side. "Are you sure you don't want any food? I spent ages getting it together."

"You spent ten minutes walking to my uncle's bakery," Luna said. "I'd recognize his croissants anywhere."

He laughed. "Guilty as charged. But at least you know where they're from, so you know they taste amazing."

"Olympus, stop being a loser and go get us candy. I'm sure we've got some around here, but if it's gone, walk to the store. Sherry will open early for you," Indigo said.

"There's no need for me to go anywhere." Olympus hurried to the table with a large box of candy he'd pulled from a cupboard. "I thought we'd have these later, but we can open them now."

"Great. Hand them over." Indigo ripped off the lid of the box.

I'd crept back to Sherry's store, grabbed a box of three layer mixed truffles, and laced each candy with purging magic. I wasn't sure what the effect would be when combining my magic with Sherry's tainted candy, but if this was the only way to get purging magic into my friends, then so be it. Whoever was the stronger witch would win this battle. It was me against Sherry.

No one spoke as candy was shoved into mouths. The food Olympus had laid out was abandoned as my friends gobbled down truffle after truffle.

"Olympus, you've been such a good boy," Indigo purred. "I'm giving you a treat." She lifted a truffle and held it out to him.

He shook his head. "They're all yours. I don't want to deprive you ladies of a second of enjoyment."

"You should take it," Odessa said, her mouth so full I could barely understand her. "Indigo rarely shares."

"I do. You're the one that's greedy with the candy. You've already had two more truffles than me."

"I didn't know you were keeping count. And that's a lie. I always share with you." Odessa grabbed another truffle, washing it down with coffee.

"You didn't the last time," Luna said. "You ate that giant family bar of honeycomb crisp candy in under a minute. I asked if I could have some, and you told me to get my own."

"That's different. That was a bar. That's technically one piece of candy."

"Olympus, I insist," Indigo said. "Have a candy. You look stressed. I keep telling you to forget that stupid ceremony for your new boss. No one cares about the Magic Council."

Olympus's hands were behind his back, so only I could see they were in fists. The poor guy. If he ate a candy, he'd fall under Sherry's thrall again and have to go through another purging episode.

"Is there a problem?" Indigo's tone was shrill. "You're being strange. What are you up to?"

"No! There's no problem. I just don't want to deprive you."

"Eat the candy and stop being weird. Once we're done, you can go get more boxes. One for each of us. It's no fun sharing with these pigs." Indigo jammed the candy into his mouth.

I grimaced, and the familiars shuddered. Olympus was about to feel pain.

Odessa hiccupped. "Pardon me. I've never had that happen before when eating Sherry's candy."

Luna wiped her brow. "Maybe this box is off. I'm not feeling so good. Is anyone else hot?"

"You should have more," Olympus said. "I'm sure the candy is fine."

Indigo groaned and pushed away from the table, her hands clamped around her stomach. "Olympus, what have you done to us?"

He was backing away, his hands up. "I just needed you back to your old selves. There's something wrong with Sherry and her candy."

I tensed, ready to spring into action if the spells started sparking. The familiars were crouched too, prepared to pounce.

"What are you talking about?" Indigo growled out. "I'm—" She gave an enormous burp.

"Not feeling so good?" Olympus said. "Sorry, but you're all about to get sick. You know where the bathrooms are."

A spell ignited on Indigo's fingers, but she didn't have time to launch it. She doubled over then raced out of the room and thumped up the stairs.

Odessa was the next to bolt, but she went outside, and the sounds of retching drifted in. Luna only made it to the kitchen sink.

As much as I wanted to stay hidden and plug my ears so I didn't hear the effects of the purging magic, I steeled myself, gave the familiars a nod, and stepped into the kitchen.

Olympus leaned against the table, his face gray. "It worked. Now, if you'll excuse me, I need to go be disgustingly unwell."

Chapter 21

An hour later, Indigo's house smelled like burned sugar, everyone looked queasy, and the shock of the situation was still making Odessa shake.

"Go over this one more time." Indigo sipped water as she held Olympus's hand. He sat beside her with Odessa and Luna at the kitchen table.

I stood in front of them. Indigo's familiars and Monty stood with me, and I appreciated their steadying presence. It was times like this when I missed Fire Fang in hellhound form. I could always lean on him when I needed support.

"What did you miss the first time around? I've told you everything," I said.

"Just the highlights this time. It's too much for my candy fried brain to compute," Indigo said.

"Same here." Luna shook her head. "I keep expecting to wake up. Witch Haven has always been wonderfully odd, but cursed candy and a bid to take over the world with dark magic is insane."

"Insane, but it's happening. This boils down to a sugary sweet mess. Dark witches are setting up a power base in Witch Haven. The candy store is Sherry's cover. She's enthralling people with candy, so they forget everything else in their lives. She wants all magic users biddable so she can control this place with her friends. Good enough?" I said.

"I have embarrassingly hazy memories of gorging on candy," Odessa said. "I even stopped making my famous pumpkin brownies because all I wanted to eat was Sherry's candy." She gave a polite burp behind her hand. "Excuse me, but that purging magic was something else."

"I had to make sure it was effective. Olympus was my guinea pig. When it worked on him, we tried the same on all of you." I looked around at my ashen-faced friends. "Are you all up for this? I can't do it alone. Sherry is already deeply embedded in the village, and most people are obsessed with her candy."

"Does that mean you're asking for our help?" Indigo arched an eyebrow, a smile flickering across her face.

I sucked in a breath. "I am. But I've only ever kept you at arm's length because I never want you getting hurt. Before you protest, I know how powerful you all are. You're incredible witches, and when I thought I'd lost your friendships, it devastated me. I may be a loner, but I don't enjoy being lonely."

"Oh, Storm, we're sorry about the way we treated you." Odessa rose on shaky legs and dashed over to hug me. Her familiar pumpkin scent was back. "We didn't mean any of the things we said. You know how much we love you."

I patted her on the back then stepped away. "I didn't doubt any of you for a second."

They laughed at that. My best and oldest friends knew me too well. Of course, I'd been full of doubt. I never felt good enough to be a part of the group. I used to wonder how it would happen, them realizing I wasn't worthy of their friendship and cutting me out. I'd never expected something like this.

"We'll always be friends." Odessa gripped my hand, seeming to know what was going through my head. "Even though we annoy each other, blunder in and out of each other's lives making unhelpful suggestions, and lurk around when we're not wanted, that's how it is. You've tried to shake us off enough times to know we're going nowhere. Friends for life. Understand?"

My eyes did that annoying hazy thing, and it took me a few seconds before I could see clearly. "Got it. Friends for life."

"I know this is a group hug situation," Luna said, "but I'm still feeling dodgy after that gross purging magic. And I'm never eating candy again."

"Best plan ever. Stay away from the stuff," I said. "It could still tempt you, and as Olympus is experiencing, you don't need to eat much before Sherry's magic influences you again."

His face was grimly determined as he nodded. "The purging magic worked on me again, but I only had one truffle and I was back to believing Sherry was the most incredible thing to happen to Witch Haven."

"We know the truth about her now," I said. "And we also know she has to be stopped."

"All those children she's taken." Odessa shook her head as she settled back in her seat. "It's so shocking."

"It ends today," Indigo said. "No more kids get taken, and we're saving Witch Haven."

"We need to keep Sherry and her friends alive, though," Olympus said. "They have to answer for their crimes."

"Can't we mortally wound them?" Indigo said. "It's no less than they deserve."

"What they deserve is to be dunked into a vat of boiling candy." Anger glinted in Odessa's eyes. "Then deep fried and rolled in shards of glass icing."

"Uh... that sounds a little like burning witches," Luna said.

"I'm with Indigo and Odessa," I said. "They took Eden and Bloom."

"And they will pay for that. Believe me, I'm as angry as you, but justice must be served." Olympus swayed on his feet, but his expression was resolute. "Storm, you taught me that."

I grudgingly agreed with him. But I'd get in a few good blows to teach them a lesson.

Indigo dropped her hold on Olympus's hand. "Do... do you think Bloom will like me? I'm not good mother material. And I have a past. And a sharp tongue. Not everyone approves of me."

Olympus caught hold of her hand again. "It'll be fine. I expect Bloom will have some adjusting to do, and we still need to figure out how to turn her back into a child."

"But I have no parenting skills."

"You look after your familiars."

Nugget strolled over and hopped onto Indigo's lap. "You'll be a great stepparent."

"I'll be the wicked stepmother," Indigo whispered.

"No! You're not wicked. Not anymore. Bloom will like you." Nugget head-butted Indigo's hand.

"I just don't want Bloom to be disappointed in me. Of course, she's got her real mother, but I want to be in her life, too."

Russell landed on Indigo's shoulder and softly cawed in her ear, while Hilda scuttled up her leg, her familiars surrounding her with love. It was times like this when I wondered if having a familiar wouldn't be so rough.

Fire Fang entered my thoughts again. He'd lay down his life for me, and he was protecting the person I loved the most right this second. Yet I'd always shoved him away. And now... now he was different. Should I keep shoving him away or figure out how to make it work? Could I bond with a half-mortal, half-hellhound?

I shook my head. Too many things were in the air, and if I didn't get better at juggling, it was game over.

Olympus kneeled in front of Indigo. "Bloom will adore you as much as I do. Maybe one day, she can call you her mother, too. You know, when we finally get around to making things official."

Odessa squeaked. "That sounded like a proposal. Go on. You two get married as well. Then we'll all be attached. I've got Sol, Luna is marrying Cole soon, and Storm... oh, well, you're not interested in relationships, are you?"

I shrugged. "I've got Fire Fang."

"Exactly. Although, where is he? He rarely leaves your side," Odessa said.

"He stayed at my apartment to look after Eden and Bloom. Eden was shaky after being transformed and needs rest."

"Wait! Fire Fang wasn't at your apartment," Olympus said. "Some guy I'd never met before agreed to watch the girls."

"Um... weird story. Fire Fang is mortal. That was him. Well, he's a mix of magic and mortal. You'd have all known sooner if you hadn't stopped talking to me."

They all gaped at me.

I couldn't help but smile. "I'll fill in the blanks later."

"You need to. I hate missing the gossip," Odessa said.

"I will. But first, Sherry and her candy and figuring out how to get Bloom out of cat form."

"Of course. It must be so good to see Eden again," Indigo said, looking shocked at the suggestion of marriage and becoming a stepmother in the space of a minute.

"It's amazing and terrifying. She's a teenage girl, so I have no clue how to handle her."

"I may have to come to you for advice," Indigo said. "What a turnaround, us having kids to look after. Not so long ago, I could barely take care of myself. Now, I have all this." She gestured around at her friends, Olympus, and her familiars.

Indigo had come a long way. They all had. Thriving businesses, new businesses, strong relationships, happy familiars, and people who adored them. And me, I had Eden and my grungy apartment. My career was decent, but it wasn't without its stress and danger. I had less than my friends, but I was grateful. Although, maybe there was room for more.

Olympus planted a kiss on Indigo's lips. "You were made for the role of amazing stepmother. Bloom has power, so she'll need a witch with experience to guide her along the right path."

Indigo kissed him back. "I'm happy to do that."

I grimaced. "Enough smooching. We have an event to destroy and dark witches to grind into the dirt. Who's with me?"

***

We had little time to prepare. After the unpleasant group purging, we had to scramble to get a plan in place and barely four hours to make sure we had everything we needed.

We spent most of that time recharging our magic. I was operating on mostly adrenaline and caffeine. I still hadn't fit in any sleep. Once this was over, I was sleeping for a week, and no one would disturb me. Well, I'd let my teenage sister wake me a time or two, but that was it. And Fire Fang. Oh, what should I do about him?

Indigo, Odessa, and Luna had spent a couple of hours in deep meditation. Indigo's familiars had surrounded her, and they'd joined their magic to make her extra powerful. Not that she needed the boost.

Everyone else's familiars, Monty, Earl, and Tuffin, were also onboard and would meet us at the park.

I glanced at Indigo as we walked away from her house toward the center of Witch Haven. She was glowing with magical energy.

She caught me watching and winked. "We've got this. Those dark witches won't know what's hit them."

I grabbed Odessa's hand as she pulled a piece of candy from her tunic pocket. "What are you doing? I said no more of Sherry's candy."

She chuckled and held it up. "It's my own candy. Full of pumpkin goodness. Not only is this stuff perfectly legal, perfectly safe, and perfectly delicious, but it'll give me the extra boost I need. I have to be pumpkin powered to win this fight."

"You're sure it's one of yours?" I said.

"Take a sniff. I know you don't like my pumpkin smell." She thrust the candy under my nose.

I grimaced and pulled away. It was one of Odessa's tangy orange concoctions.

She laughed again. "I'm sticking to my own stuff from now on. Although I still plan on dropping by Fandango's for treats now and again. My sweet tooth still needs its fix."

"Uncle Albert would be disappointed if you didn't," Luna said. "And I have some making up to do with him. I abandoned him when Sherry's store opened. The last time I saw him, he was sitting in his armchair, he hadn't washed for days, and empty candy boxes surrounded him. He'd even closed the bakery because customers stopped coming in."

"Once we dig Sherry out of Witch Haven, everyone will be back there," I said. "Come on, we need to hurry." The event Sherry was using to pass out her tainted candy was starting at noon, and we had fifteen minutes to get ourselves in place.

"Uh-oh. This looks bad. They started early." Indigo pointed at the crowd amassing in the park ahead of us.

"Sherry must be worried," I said. "She knows we're going to stop her."

The park was festooned with balloons and streamers. There were pop-up tents and marquees for people to go into, with games and activities inside. Banners said everyone would win a prize, even if they lost. And surprise, surprise, there was free candy. Music was playing, bright trumpet tunes, a bit like a circus big top, and people were dancing along to the beat. The air was thick with the smell of the honeyed rot that accompanied Sherry's candy.

I glanced at my friends and their familiars. "Does everyone know what they have to do?"

"Earl has brought my scarecrows. They're waiting for my command," Odessa said. "I pulled in as many as I could."

"We focus on separating Sherry and her friends from the public. We have to get those witches on their own. I don't know how much control Sherry has over the people who've eaten this new candy, but I don't want her using innocent people to protect herself," I said.

"My scarecrows can do crowd control." Odessa looked slightly worried. "People may end up with a few bruises, but it's a small price to pay to save the village. Earl can help with the scarecrows."

"Earl sticks with that job. What about Tuffin?" I asked Luna.

"Tuffin's with Cole. Don't worry, my hunky werewolf and killer kitty make an excellent team."

"Where do you want us?" Nugget trotted beside Indigo. Russell was perched on Indigo's shoulder, as was Hilda.

"Causing distractions. Get the crowd anxious and moving. They need their attention taken from the candy. Use whatever magic you have. It won't be easy."

"I can go full-out spider," Hilda said, with a little titter. "It always gets people moving. A giant spider with enormous hairy legs isn't popular."

"It's the fangs," Nugget said, "and the venom."

Russell cawed and flapped his wings.

"I'll work with Russell," Nugget said. "I'll spark magic on the ground, and he can do aerial bombardments."

"Perfect. Luna, where are Cole and Tuffin?" I said.

"Close by. We're lucky to have Cole's help. He just got back from a retreat with feuding werewolf packs," Luna said. "I filled him in, and after he stopped threatening to destroy Sherry, he agreed to linger in the crowd. He's ready to go full werewolf if you need him."

"We need him now. The furrier and meaner, the better."

"I'll let him know." Luna turned away and spoke in a low voice, but Cole would hear every word. They were mates, and her voice carried to him no matter where he was. Marrying a werewolf had its problems, but not when you were going into battle with one as an ally.

She looked at me and nodded. "He'll be changing any second."

"And I might need your weather magic as backup," I said.

"I'm sparked up and ready to go," Luna said. "And I know how to handle the elements, thanks to my great teacher."

I grinned at her. Teaching a grown witch a new power she'd suppressed for years hadn't been easy, but Luna could twirl a tornado like an expert.

"Olympus, you're with me," I said. "Sherry has to know we mean business. She thinks she's got the Magic Council on her side."

"I'll be ready to make the arrests," he said.

"There she is," Luna said. "And she's not alone."

I looked to where Luna pointed. Sherry stood with three other witches, and they were handing out candy from large containers on a long wooden table.

"They've resupplied," I muttered. "I blasted the tainted candy in her store so she wouldn't be able to use it. Her friends must have brought new stock with them."

The four witches looked like butter wouldn't melt in their mouths. They were all blonde, doe-eyed, and laughing. They also had on similar outfits of pink, cream, and yellow.

"They're not wasting any time," Odessa said. "They're shoveling candy out as fast as they can."

A group of people almost walked into us, swerving at the last second.

Olympus caught hold of one guy by the shoulder. "Hey, are you okay?"

I joined him. The guy's eyes were unfocused, and he was unsteady on his feet. "Jeez! That's bad. Smell him."

Olympus sniffed the man and recoiled. "Sherry's candy?"

I nodded. "And it's potent."

"Best day ever," the guy slurred out. He stuffed a handful of candy in his mouth and staggered off to join his friends.

"Sherry's made the candy more powerful," I said. "If people eat too much, it could kill them. That guy could hardly stand."

"Maybe that's the plan," Indigo said. "Didn't you say she wanted to dispose of magic users who were no use to her in a body pit? Why not start now? She could have put a spell on the candy to weed out weak magic users. Those who survive get to be a part of her freakish candy cult."

"We've been spotted." Odessa leaned in close. "Sherry and her friends are leaving. They're on to us."

"We need your scarecrows," I said. "Use a pincer movement around those witches. Separate them from the crowd."

Odessa clapped her hands then spread her arms wide and tipped her head back, issuing a silent command to her scarecrows and Earl as they lurked in the shadows among the tall trees surrounding the park.

Ten seconds later, the crowd erupted into chaos as an army of pumpkin-headed beasts and a fire-breathing cat lurched into view. The scarecrows carved their way through the crowd, heading for Sherry and her friends. The crowd scattered, screaming and clutching their candy like it was a new-born baby.

"Let's go. You all know what you need to do," I yelled.

The familiars scattered to add to the chaos, and I raced toward Sherry with Olympus, Indigo, and Luna. Odessa stayed behind to control her marauding scarecrows as they tussled and grabbed the rioting crowd.

"Odessa, we need a way through your scarecrow blockade," I called over my shoulder.

As if by magic, and of course, it was magic, two scarecrows stepped back and gestured us in with grunts and snarls. I whizzed through with the others, and the exit sealed. We were trapped inside a wall of enchanted scarecrows with our mortal enemy.

I bared my teeth as I met Sherry's blank gaze. "Hey, Sherry. It's time we talked about your killer candy."

Chapter 22

Any semblance of the sweet Sherry who'd infiltrated the stomachs and minds of the residents in Witch Haven faded away. Her eyes became coal black, her nails pointed, and her hair a mass of writhing, dark matted curls. The frilly clothing flickered away, and soon she was draped in shimmering black from head to toe. Dark veins crisscrossed her skin, and her teeth were pointed like a wolf.

I didn't hide my disgust at being so close to something so corrupted. Dark magic destroyed everything it touched.

"I'd say it's nice to meet the real Sherry, but I'd be lying," I said.

Her gaze flickered around the group, and she smirked. "Who wants my candy?"

None of us moved, although Olympus's right eye twitched uncontrollably.

Sherry tutted, the sound a dry click on her tongue. "No takers? Sisters, it appears we need to develop their palates."

"You've lost. We've figured out what you've been doing, and your cursed candy caper ends now." I stepped forward, the others right beside me.

"Wrong. I'm tasting victory like it's one of my special truffles. You like those, don't you, Storm?"

"Everything about you disgusts me."

Sherry's smirk hardened. "I should have killed you with that cursed candy rather than Galaan. You've been annoying ever since I opened the store. Sisters, this is the one I told you about. She's always sniffing around and snooping where she's not wanted."

"Because you took my family." My gaze flicked to the three witches standing beside her. Their colorful, frilly outfits were also gone. One of them had silver hair, the other was dirty blonde, and the other was completely bald. Their eyes were the same coal black as Sherry's, and dark magic flickered around them in jagged waves.

"Forget your troubles," the silver-haired one said. "I can promise you candy and fun."

"We're wasting time," the bald one said. "Destroy them. Call forth the crowd. We control Witch Haven now."

The witch with the dirty blonde hair clicked her fingers. "Arise slaves. Destroy these magic users." She pointed at us.

"Odessa, don't let the crowd through," I yelled.

"I'm on it." Her voice came over the top of the scarecrow barrier. "I've also called for reinforcements. And Cole's arrived."

Luna grinned. "My wolf won't let anything bad happen to us."

The scarecrows buckled for a moment but held the line. The odds weren't in their favor, though. The whole of Witch Haven had turned out for this event, and from the number of people already in the park, there were others here from surrounding villages. Odessa's scarecrows were awesome, but even they had their limitations.

There were screams and sparks of magic from the crowd. A loud rasping caw overhead revealed a resplendent Russell sailing past and dropping objects from his claws. The objects scattered magic in all directions.

"My familiars will get the crowd's attention," Indigo said.

A menacing roar that could only be Cole in werewolf form rocked the ground, and there was more screaming.

"And there's my gorgeous werewolf," Luna said. "Right on time. I can always rely on him."

Sherry hissed at us. "It makes no difference that you have a few pitiful helpers. I know you won't kill your fellow villagers."

"We don't have to kill them. We just have to defeat you, and the candy curse will be broken," I said. "We know everything. We know about the children taken, where you're keeping them, and what you've planned. It's all over."

"Nothing's changed." Sherry twirled a strand of her matted hair around a clawed finger. "My offer stands. We can add one more to our group, can't we, sisters?"

The other witches didn't look happy about swelling their ranks with a weather witch.

I spun a finger in the air. "We'll all take a hard pass on that offer. Dark magic has no place in Witch Haven."

"You're wrong. There has always been a delicious undercurrent of darkness in this village. Why do you think so many magic users have tried to take over?" Sherry spread her arms. "We've never taken our eyes off the mission. Unlike others who blundered in and attempted poorly planned takeovers, we bided our time and grew our ranks."

"Not as much as you'd have liked," I said. "I got my sister, Eden, back. We know you turn what you consider failures into animals to keep them under control. How's that going?"

"Eden Winter," the blonde witch growled out. "She's here? That witchling was nothing but trouble."

"Bad luck for you, you took my only sister. What did you expect me to do, give up on her?"

Sherry opened her mouth to argue, but the bald witch silenced her with a wave and shuffled closer. "Storm Winter, you've been the thorn in our side on many occasions."

"I'm always happy to hear that, especially when it comes to interfering with dark magic."

Her black gaze trickled over me as if she was looking for a weakness to slice into. "You came close to discovering what we were doing several times. If it weren't for our quick thinking and distractions, you'd have discovered us a long time ago. I admire your perseverance. Everyone else gave up looking for those we took. Of course, they made an effort to begin with, but time passes, and people move on. The memories of lost loved ones fade."

"Not mine," I said.

"Or mine," Olympus said. "Give me back Bloom. You turned her into a cat, so you can change her back."

The witches looked at each other and cackled.

"I see nothing amusing about this," Olympus spat out, a pulse pounding in his forehead.

"Bloom Duke was also a difficult child." Sherry took over the conversation. "But I had fun enthralling you, Olympus. All the time, I was the witch who had your daughter, and you had no idea. She doesn't take after her father. You were so quick to obey everything I told you to do. I had to stop from laughing when you kept Storm trapped in a cell."

"Tell me how to turn my daughter back," he growled out.

"That little ginger escapee is still ours. They all are, Eden included. This has been our tradition. We take children with potential and shape them in our images."

"Some traditions must die out," I said.

"Not this one. Generations of dark witches have wanted to achieve this. We've finally done it."

"We're bringing this to its rightful end. You can come quietly, but I have the permission of the Magic Council to smash you into the ground if you protest." I gestured at the scarecrows. "As you may have noticed, we've got murderous backup."

The scarecrows' eyes glowed red, and they took a step closer to Sherry and her friends.

Olympus caught hold of my arm, his mouth moving to my ear. "I know how good it would feel to destroy them, but remember what we talked about. I despise them as much as you do, but they must pay for their crimes."

I bit down on my rage. It would be easy to blast Sherry and her goons into oblivion, but I saw the sense in Olympus's words. "Don't go easy on them once they're arrested. They must be locked away for the rest of their lives."

"They'll get the punishment owed them," Olympus said. "And anyone who hurts my daughter will be made to pay."

"Olympus, we grow tired," Sherry said. "Even if you capture us, which you won't, we'll arrange a plea deal. We have many secrets, including the locations of our children. If you want to know where all our precious charges are, you will negotiate."

"No deals," I snapped.

"You'll be the one making deals with us," the silver-haired witch said. "The Magic Council is pitiful, Witch Haven is pitiful, and it is overdue a change. We'll make that happen."

The crowd surged against the scarecrows, and several of them staggered back. One scarecrow caught on fire, but a dousing of rain from me put him out.

"Thanks for the save," Odessa yelled. "You need to speed this up. The crowd is getting bigger, and they're charging this way."

"If you let us go, we'll call off the crowd," Sherry said.

"You're going nowhere," I said.

"Walk away while you can. And if you're quick, I may let you and your friends leave Witch Haven. You could get far enough away that we won't bother you for months. We may even give you a year of reprieve before we take over wherever you move to." Sherry shimmered with hazy gray magic. "Because that's the plan. We're taking over everywhere. We have our power base, perfectly tainted candy, and soon we will have armies to bend to our whims."

Her sisters murmured their agreement.

The surrounding crowd roared and stamped its feet as if in approval of Sherry's words.

A quick look around the perimeter showed the scarecrows were under increasing pressure. Three were missing heads, and four more were on fire.

"Time for talking is over," I said to the others. "Get ready."

We spread out, all sparking magic. I was whisking my hands through the air when there was a crackle of energy in front of me. A dark blast slammed into Sherry and her ghoulish sisters, knocking them back in a splatter of jagged magic and cries of pain.

A gap developed in the scarecrow perimeter and Eden appeared, Bloom on her shoulder.

Horror sideswiped me with a ninja kick, sucking air from my lungs and sending an earthquake of terror through my feet, until my brain rattled.

Eden was alive with dark energy, her eyes black and smoke billowing from her mouth. My sister had gone dark.

Chapter 23

"The rest of you see to the downed witches." I raced over to Eden, my heart a thunderclap of panic in my chest. My sister used dark magic? I didn't want to believe it, but I couldn't doubt my own eyes.

Eden's gaze flashed my way. Her eyes were as coal black and lifeless as Sherry's. She blinked, and the blackness was gone. She staggered forward and caught hold of my arms. "Did I do it? Are they dead?"

Bloom leaped off her shoulder to avoid being crushed. Her fur sparkled with gray, unhealthy magic that swirled around her in a maelstrom of chaotic power.

I looked over to see Olympus, Indigo, and Luna peering at the fallen dark witches. None of them were moving. "I don't know. What did you do? What magic was that? It felt dark." Had these witches turned my sister? It didn't matter. I'd still protect her. I had to make this right. I wasn't losing Eden to darkness, not now I'd gotten her home.

"I had to save you, and I knew you'd go after Sherry. You always put yourself first when we were kids, so I figured nothing had changed." She sagged against me. Her skin was hot, and the occasional flash of dark magic shot out and pinged into the ground, scorching the grass.

"Of course, I'll always do that. But how did you get so strong? You're not old enough to come into your full powers yet." I was trying to stay calm, but there was so much hurtling through my head. Sherry had corrupted Eden. It was painfully unfair. My sister had always been a good witch.

She clung to me, her body shaking. "Those hags care nothing about that. They forced power into me. I'm supposed to be a healer, but they taught me to destroy. The magic is unstable though, and I keep rejecting it, so it never fully takes hold. I wasn't sure if I could do that spell, but it worked." The worry in her eyes hurt my heart.

"You shouldn't be here. Fire Fang was supposed to be looking after you. Let's get you somewhere safe."

Eden shook her head. "They deserved it. I had to make them pay for what they did to me, Bloom, and all the other children. Some of them didn't survive. And don't blame Fire Fang for me being here. I zapped him with magic then snuck out with Bloom."

I held Eden tight and led her and Bloom away from the edge of the circle, so we weren't so vulnerable. "I understand why you feel that way, but there's still so much we need to know from them. If Sherry dies—"

"All you need to know is they're pure evil. They have no right to take over and use their magic on us. That's not how magic works. There has to be balance." Eden's eyes filled with darkness again. She shook her head. "My healing magic is battling with the dark power. I'm worried I'm losing. Storm, help me."

"You know I will. But we need to get out of here alive first. Come with me." I clutched her hand as we headed over to see the damage done to Sherry and her friends. Bloom hurried along beside us, keen to stay close to Eden.

Olympus looked up at me as he administered healing magic over Sherry. "They're alive, but I'm not sure for how long. That was quite a blast, young lady." His gaze went to Bloom, and his eyes widened. "Were you involved in that magic attack too?"

Eden's mouth twisted, and she lifted her chin. "They deserved it."

Bloom meowed her agreement, although her tail was down, suggesting she knew she was in trouble with her dad.

"You'll never take us alive." Sherry's chest rattled as she spoke.

"Even though we all want you dead, you will make it out of this. You have crimes to answer for." I kept an arm around Eden, so she knew I was on her side.

"And I'll do whatever it takes to keep them alive." Olympus's gaze flicked over my shoulder. "But right now, we have more immediate things to worry about."

A hole had appeared in the defensive scarecrow line, and the candy crazed crowd was shoving through, murderous intent shining in their sugar fueled eyes.

I backed away with Eden. "Indigo, Luna, Odessa! I need you all here."

Indigo and Luna joined me and Eden, and we formed a circle. A few seconds later, aided by her scarecrows, Odessa vaulted over their heads and landed beside us.

She sparked with orange magic, her cheeks glowing. "Woo-ee! The crowd is still raging. Sherry's magic has a hold over them, but it's malfunctioning, and they're turning on each other. Oh! And I see why." Her eyes took in the slumped, injured witches.

"The crowd is still coming for us," I said. "We have to hold them back without killing them."

"What about using your purging magic on them?" Luna said.

"There are too many, and it won't be enough to bring them around in time." I dragged my friends back, but the crowd kept approaching, more and more piling through the fighting scarecrows.

"What do we do?" Eden said.

"The purging magic will work if we mix something with it." Indigo grabbed Luna and Odessa's hands, and we formed a larger circle. Bloom hopped onto Eden's shoulder and booped her cheek with her nose.

"You're thinking their anger could be doused with a little positivity?" Odessa said.

"You've just read my mind." Indigo grinned at her.

"We have to speed this up. What's the plan?" I kept yanking my friends away, but it was a matter of seconds before we were set upon.

Indigo whacked my arm. "Haven't you learned yet?"

"I'm certain we're about to die under a writhing body of sugar addicts, if that's what you mean."

Odessa laughed. "It's your least favorite word."

"Moist?"

I got another whack for that.

"Love, you dope! Love defeats hate," Indigo said.

"Oh! Ooohhh! Sure." The fear left me, my gaze going from my incredible friends to my awesome, brave, strong sister, and a steely veil of hope wrapped around me. "We remind them what it feels like to be a part of a real community?"

"Finally! The most stubborn witch I've ever met has seen the light." Indigo nodded, her eyes reflecting her fondness for me. "And you'll be leading by example."

"If positive vibes will fix this crowd, I'll do it." I held a hand out and swirled purging magic in front of me. "Grab this spell and mix it with whatever you need. Then we'll blanket this village with... love."

Indigo laughed. "You said it. Come on, ladies. Let's get to work."

There was a roar from the crowd as I bound our magic together. Bleary-eyed villagers bundled toward us, tripping over their own feet, anger radiating off them in hot, foul smelling waves of honeyed rot.

"You ready?" I yelled above the roar of the crowd.

"We've got this." Eden gripped my hand so hard the bones creaked, but I let her. I was never letting go of her again.

We raised our arms as one, an all-powerful group of incredible witches. None of us were perfect, but we were made stronger and better by being together.

Our combined magic blasted out and blanketed the baying crowd, scarecrows, and Sherry and her friends and spread out in a pale, sparkling green mist toward the village.

"Keep it going," I said. "We can't afford to leave anyone out. This candy magic leaves Witch Haven right now."

The attacking crowd slowed. The ones who'd gotten through the scarecrow blockade stumbled to the ground, shaking their heads and groaning. There was also a gross amount of retching as the tainted candy left their systems.

"It's working." Odessa was ablaze with green and orange magic. "Sherry's influence is fading."

Eden groaned and leaned against me. "I don't feel good. Something is happening to me."

Bloom also looked shaky. Her fur was puffed out and her eyes narrowed. Tiny sparks of black magic shot out of her and exploded in the air.

Eden staggered and sank to the dirt. "Storm! I can't breathe. Am I dying?"

"No! You'll live, but they shoved the wrong kind of magic into you. I have to get it out. Eden, do you trust me?" I kneeled beside her, keeping the circle linked.

"With my life. Always." Her honest declaration made my heart thud with joy and apprehension. Black sparks of magic flitted out of Eden, just like Bloom.

I looked at the crowd. They were under control. My gaze went to Olympus. He had Sherry and her friends in magical chains, and they weren't going anywhere. I could focus on my sister.

"I'm breaking the circle," I said to the others. "Keep blasting out the magic for as long as you can."

My friends let me loose and looped arms with each other, so the magic only broke for a second.

I scooped up Bloom, who was about to fall from Eden's shoulder. I pressed my hand against Eden's chest, the other holding Bloom firmly against me. "You've both got something inside you that must come out. Don't fight this, even though it'll hurt like a stab from a unicorn's horn. Sherry has forced powers into you that don't belong. It's been there for years, so I have to drag it out."

Eden gritted her teeth, but she clamped her hand over mine and dug her nails in. "Do it. Get this dark stuff out of me."

I redirected the magic I'd pulsed out to the crowd and flooded it into Eden, with an extra hit of the intense, pure love I felt for my sister. The rest entered Bloom, making the little cat shake.

Eden screamed, and Bloom howled, but I kept pouring magic into them. It was purging magic and pure love. The love I felt for my family, my friends, and the place I called home. Nothing was stronger. I'd been fighting being a part of this community for such a long time, but I finally let go. I embraced it all, every messy, glorious inch. And Eden and Bloom were on the receiving end of that love. I shouldn't have held back for so long.

My magic faded, and Eden staggered, going to her knees. Bloom pulsated in my arms, white light flashing under her fur. I swiftly set her down. I had a feeling she was about to undergo a big change.

I dashed to Eden just as she retched and coughed up what looked like a chunk of soggy coal. The lump pulsed several times then exploded, leaving tiny black fragments in the air.

I blew them away and engulfed my sister in a hug. "How do you feel?"

"Like I hacked up a serrated saw. And I ache everywhere. I'm exhausted but... also better." She pulled back from our hug. "How did you know how to do that?"

"I didn't, not really. But Sherry's been forcing magic into you that was unnatural. I figured she must have used an anchor to keep it in you. The purging magic and my desire to keep you safe forced it out."

Eden hugged me again. "I love you, Sis."

"Bloom!"

I turned at Olympus's anguished cry as he dashed over. The ginger cat had gone, and a naked, shaking girl was curled on her side in her place, a lump of black toxic magic dissolving beside her.

I destroyed the lump then pulled off my jacket and covered her with it. She lay there gasping. Her gaze met mine, and she gave me a simple nod of thanks.

Olympus also had his jacket off and wrapped Bloom in it before taking her in his arms. "It is you. You're really back."

Bloom's smile wavered as tears ran down her cheeks. "Hey, Dad. Miss me?"

I checked on Eden, who was content to rest, then left Olympus and Bloom to have some much-needed catching up. I walked over to where Sherry and her cronies were trapped.

Indigo, Luna, and Odessa joined me, and the remaining scarecrows flanked us. Some of them were on fire. It made for an impressive sight.

Sherry glowered up at me. "Why couldn't you meddling witches mind your own business?"

"Because Witch Haven is our home. Everything we love is right here." I nudged Sherry with the toe of my boot. "And you're not welcome."

My friends nodded their agreement. We were joined a second later by all the familiars and Cole still in werewolf form. Our army of awesomeness just kept getting bigger.

"I will have my revenge. We will destroy you," Sherry said.

I rolled my eyes. "Odessa, could you get your boys to deal with this noise?"

She giggled. "With pleasure. Scarecrows, if any of these witches make a peep, you may sit on them."

The scarecrows swarmed around Sherry and her goons, growling and glowering at them. The witches squeaked and hung their heads.

So much for them being all-powerful. They were bullies, using magic they didn't understand to achieve an impossible mission. And it would remain impossible, because there were amazing people in this world, unlimited love, and forever friendships. Darkness would always be defeated.

I linked hands with my friends and grinned before taking in the mess around us. "My best witches, we have some clearing up to do."

***

Who'd have thought, three days ago, I was in a stand-off against the population of Witch Haven, almost defeated by a candy cursing witch, and discovered my sister had been turned into a cat. A lot can change in a short space of time.

"I'll take that last croissant if it's going spare." Eden lounged on my couch, a huge mug of coffee balanced on the arm and several newspapers spread across her lap.

"It's all yours." I'd give Eden my last anything, so long as it made her happy. I was still getting used to having my sister back in my life, but it was something I was happy to work on.

Eden grabbed the croissant, dunked it in a pot of cherry preserves, and flicked through the newspapers I'd grabbed when we'd been to the bakery. "I have so much to catch up on. Being trapped by a bunch of dark witches has made me out of touch with the world."

I shrugged. "You didn't miss much."

"Indigo came home, and she's no longer evil."

"True."

"Odessa is married!"

"Yep."

"And Luna is about to get hitched to an influential werewolf and have the wedding of the century."

"Also true."

"And all the murders! Are you sure Witch Haven is a safe place to live?"

"The safest. So long as I'm here taking care of business."

Eden smirked. "Such a show off."

"Not showing off, just stating facts."

She laughed. "I can't believe you're a private detective."

"I never had it as a career choice, but it meant I made useful contacts so I could look for you."

Eden's smile was grateful. "I knew you'd never give up on me. I might be the darker sister now, but you'll keep me on track."

"There's nothing dark about you. We got that out. Now we just need to work on your magic control. I expect Sherry and her evil groupies gave you terrible habits."

"They tried, but I had plenty of bad habits before they caught me. You taught me most of them."

I set aside my plate. "They won't be able to do anything to you ever again. They're behind bars, the candy store has been shut and cleared out, and everything is back to normal."

"They don't bother me, not now you're watching my back. Although, I'm kind of amazed you work so well with the Magic Council. I remember you used to hate those guys."

"Hate is a strong word, but I never loved them. Olympus Duke is one of the good ones, though. He'll tie up the loose ends in this case and make sure Sherry and her crones are out of the way for good."

"That's the guy Indigo's dating?"

"You got it."

"Will Olympus tell that dead guy's family what happened to him?" Eden set down her croissant. "It was horrible for Sherry to kill Galaan to distract you, but I'm not surprised she did. Those witches would have stopped at nothing to get what they wanted."

I reached for her cherry preserve smeared fingers. "Galaan's family has been told. Although they didn't get the full story, since the Magic Council doesn't want people knowing how close we were to being taken over. They were told justice was served, and the person who cursed Galaan will pay for their crime."

Eden stuffed the last of the croissant in her mouth and chewed noisily. She ate like me. "So we'll have to keep this a secret?"

"Would it benefit everyone to know? It would panic people. We've handled things. The Magic Council is clearing up the mess, and Witch Haven is safe once again. That's all that matters."

"I suppose. But what about everyone else? All the families who lost their kids."

"Olympus is working on it. He's drafted Indigo to make things happen quickly. There's a joint working party with the Magic Embassy, and they've dispatched a team to the places Sherry told them about. The children will be set free. And those we weren't able to save... well, we'll do the best for them." It pained me that we hadn't been able to stop Sherry before innocents got hurt. "The Magic Council is talking about a memorial. And of course, all the families will learn what happened. No one will be left not knowing what happened to their children."

Eden's bottom lip jutted out. "It's a shame our parents aren't around to know what happened to me. It sucks they gave up so quickly, and it was unfair on you. They left you to deal with this on your own."

"I wasn't alone. I've always had my friends. Our parents handled their grief in their own way." I glanced at the single photograph of them I had on display. "Maybe they could have done it differently, but they were distraught and not thinking clearly."

Eden was quiet for a few seconds. "And you think they blamed you?"

I looked away, my eyes hazy with tears. "I don't know. Maybe they did, or maybe they blamed themselves. They didn't talk to me much after you vanished, so I'll never know for certain."

She leaned over and caught hold of my other hand. "They were sad and made a mistake. We all do. But don't be like them. If you keep things hidden inside for too long, it festers then explodes. They loved us the same. They were just bad at showing it."

I blinked away the haze in my eyes. My little sister suddenly seemed a lot smarter than me.

Fire Fang strolled through the door of the apartment in his mortal form. He nodded at us.

"Talking of love..." Eden flashed me a grin and hopped off the couch.

"Where are you going?" I jerked upright in my seat, refusing to look at Fire Fang. Since we'd gotten things sorted with Sherry, I hadn't spent much time with him. It was a deliberate move. Every time we were alone, he kept talking about his feelings and us being a family, and basically freaking me out.

"I'm going to take a shower, go through your closet and see if you've got anything decent to wear, which by the way you haven't, and let you two talk. Have fun." Eden finger waved me then pressed a kiss to Fire Fang's cheek.

"You're still not forgiven for knocking me out with that spell and running out of here," he said.

"I am. And I had to keep you safe, or Storm would never have forgiven me." She giggled then disappeared into my bedroom and made a show of closing the door, all the while giving me wide eyes.

"I see your sister is still being weird." Fire Fang settled on the couch next to me.

"No change there. She always was an oddball." I smiled. "And I wouldn't have it any other way."

He returned my smile, reaching for my hand in that easy way of his. It was a behavior I never knew how to respond to.

Rather than pulling away, I kept hold of his hand. "So, what next?"

Fire Fang lifted one shoulder. "We have free time, since Witch Haven is no longer in danger."

"And let me guess. You want to... talk?" I cringed.

Fire Fang chuckled and pulled me closer. "You can avoid me for the rest of your life, but will that make you happy?"

"I don't know. It's been awhile since I've known what happiness is. It's not a default position for me, so I'm sort of used to it."

"That's got to be one of the saddest things I've ever heard. But we can work on that, together. And I know, you keep saying we aren't a real family, I don't know what I'm talking about, and being a hellhound has scrambled my brain. Even so, I'm still saying this to you." Fire Fang drew in a long, steady breath and looked me straight in the eyes. "Storm Winter, I love you."

I made a sound halfway between a snort and a cough. I tried to cover it with a fake sneeze, but it came out as a messy noise, revealing how uncomfortable I was with his declaration.

"And," he stretched out the word, "you love me, too. I know that word sticks in your throat, but everything you've done for me shows what you feel, and that's good enough."

The time for avoidance and deflection was over. I wanted this mortal hellhound mix in my life, and if I was going to keep him, I had to let him know how I felt. I almost wished I had another dark witch to battle. It would be easier.

"Fire Fang, I do care about you. You've been a big part of my life these last few months, and you've made me realize being on my own has its downsides."

"This sounds promising."

"It could be. There is room in my life to do this on a part-time basis. We can feel our way through whatever we have between us."

He wagged a finger at me. "No part time. We've been living together for months, and we know each other backward and forward. We've seen each other be amazing and awful. You've handled me when I tried to kill you, and I've dealt with you when you've been raging at the world because everyone turned against you. We're both still here. And I have a Storm-shaped place in my heart where you fit, and I don't want it to open up. What about you?"

"You're asking if I have a Fire Fang-shaped space in my heart?" This was getting worryingly smooshy.

He tapped a finger against my chest. "I'm asking if you have room for me in your life for good. You're amazing. You're messy, chaotic, unpredictable, too stubborn, but amazing. And that's what I want. I want you."

I wasn't sweating or forgetting how to breathe as the enormity of what Fire Fang said settled around me. "But... but what about your past? What if there's someone waiting for you?"

He shook his head. "I still don't have all my memories back, but I've never remembered anyone special. I think, if I'm being honest, I was a geek. I liked role-playing and reading about fantasy worlds. Maybe that's what led me here, to you. I already believed in magic, and Sherry made my dreams come true."

I poked out my tongue, making him laugh. "What led you here was Sherry and her crones messing around with mortals. She did this to you. You may not remember it, but I'm certain she changed you forever with her spell."

"So am I. And I spoke to Olympus on my way here. Sherry's singing like a phoenix, in the hopes of getting a deal with the Magic Council."

I made a noise of disgust. "Are they giving her what she wants?"

"Amazingly, no. They're holding fast, all thanks to Olympus refusing to budge. If anyone suggests allowances, he reminds them about Bloom and the stolen children, and they stop protesting. Sherry's confessed to gathering dozens of mortals and testing magic on them. I was one of the few who survived."

"And now you're stuck in this weird world. Are you sure you're happy with that?"

He lifted my hand to his lips and kissed the back of it. "Couldn't be happier. I found my perfect family. I found my perfect woman. And I just hope she lets me keep hanging out with her."

I swallowed my fears, lifted my chin, and nodded. "We need a bigger place. With only one bedroom and Eden living here now, we'll have to upgrade."

His eyes sparkled with joy. "Is that a yes?"

"It's a yes, let's see how this goes."

"Good enough for me, because I already know how amazing this relationship will be." Fire Fang leaned forward, his lips about to touch mine, when the apartment door was barged open.

Indigo marched in with a small table in her hands. Olympus and Bloom, who was in her full witchling form and looking healthy, followed her. They also carried random bits of furniture.

I leaned away from Fire Fang, not happy about the interruption. "What's going on?"

"We figured you needed more stuff." Odessa bustled through the door, carrying a huge plate of brownies. "Sol, hurry up with that mattress."

I stood and watched as my friends set down their offerings. "I don't get it. I don't need more things. They won't fit in here."

"You're a family of three now." Luna walked in with a box of crockery. "And you can't keep eating off paper plates and making your guests sleep on the couch. So, we got together some useful things and figured you could keep them until you figure out what you're doing." She set down the box with a thud.

Cole came in a second later, staggering under the weight of five more boxes. "Where do you want these, babe?"

"Set them on the kitchen counter," Luna said.

I glared at Fire Fang. "Did you put them up to this?"

He laughed. "No, but given what we were just talking about, great minds think alike."

"I can figure things out on my own," I said to my friends, not amused by their interference. "I was just doing that with Fire Fang."

"Who is the most handsome mortal I've ever seen." Odessa fluttered her eyelashes. "Someone is a lucky witch."

"He's part mortal, part hellhound," I muttered. "There's a big difference."

"Even more intriguing. You still haven't given us the gory details of when the transformation happened," Odessa said.

"It's true. We're long overdue a girls' night out to catch up," Indigo said. "All this dark magic and evil witches invading our home kills the social life."

"Without the men, though," Luna said.

"We can have a guys' night out," Cole said. "Although I'm always happy to hang out with you." He kissed Luna's forehead.

"No boys allowed," Odessa said. "No offence, sweetie." She kissed Sol.

"None taken. We all want everything to get back to normal. And since there are no more dark witches to battle, I'll be glad not to worry about you every time you leave the farm."

"You know there's never anything to worry about," Odessa said. "I have my scarecrows if I need help. Although having you as my knight in shining armor is always welcome." More smooching ensued.

I loudly cleared my throat, still not comfortable with public displays of affection. Some things really never had to change. "Odessa, how are your scarecrows after the fight?"

She extracted herself from Sol's arms. "Oh, they're amazing. They all pulled through. I've had to patch up a few, but they'll live to fight another day."

There was a crash outside, and a moment later, Indigo's familiars and Luna and Odessa's cat familiars bundled into the apartment. They were followed by Monty, who carried a bag in his mouth.

"You have to get a bigger place if you want all of us to keep coming over." Indigo stepped back to avoid being knocked off her feet by Monty dashing past.

I bit my tongue. None of them had been invited over, but I was glad they were here, even though the timing was terrible.

Fire Fang stood and slung an arm around my shoulders. "We were talking about that and making plans for our future."

Odessa gasped, Luna grinned, and Indigo rolled her eyes.

"You two have made it official?" Odessa said.

"It was so obvious he liked you when I saw you together," Luna said. "You couldn't stop looking at Storm."

Fire Fang shrugged. "I make no apologies for keeping an eye on her. Storm can go wild card without warning."

"I'm right here. Stop gossiping!" I looked at him and couldn't help but smile. "But it's not so bad to have someone around if I ever need help."

Everyone laughed at that comment.

Eden came out of my bedroom. She wore my best white T-shirt and a pair of black jeans I'd never seen before. She strolled over to Bloom and hugged her. "How you doing?"

"Adjusting to not having four paws but so happy to be home." She grinned at her dad. He ruffled her hair, and she shoved him away. "Dad! You know I hate that."

"I can't help myself. My little girl's home," Olympus said.

"I'm not so little anymore," Bloom muttered.

As my friends talked over each other, laughed, bickered, and joked together, I snuggled under Fire Fang's arm. The happiness surrounding me was laced with chaos, and my life would always be messy, but maybe perfection was impossible to find, and that suited me fine.

I looked at my sister and then up at my new... boyfriend. I knew then I'd found the right kind of happiness. I had my forever home, and everyone I needed was right here.

This kind of imperfect, messy love was the best kind. It fit me, my loved ones, and Witch Haven. I wouldn't change a single thing about it.

About Author

K.E. O'Connor (Karen) is a cozy mystery author living in the beautiful British countryside. She loves all things mystery, animals, and cake. When she's not writing about mysteries, murder, and treats, she volunteers at an animal sanctuary, reads a ton of books, binge watches mystery series, and dreams about living somewhere warmer.

Here's how you can stay in touch:

Newsletter:
www.subscribepage.com/cozymysteries

Website:
www.keoconnor.com/writing

Facebook:
www.facebook.com/keoconnorauthor

Also By

Spells and Spooks
Hexes and Haunts
Curses and Corpses
Muffins and Moonlight
Cupcakes and Cauldrons
Pancakes and Potions
Hauntings and High Jinx
Hauntings and Havoc
Hauntings and Hoaxes
The Case of the Screaming Skull
The Case of the Poisoned Pumpkin
The Case of the Cursed Candy
Fire Fang
Silvaria

If you enjoyed

The Case of the Cursed Candy

turn the page to read an extract from the next Witch
Haven mystery (Fire Fang's origin story)

FIRE FANG

Chapter 1

"How does this magic system work?"

I had my hands squashed under my thighs to resist the urge to clench my fists. This was my third therapist in six months, and each of them had reacted in the same way when I'd told them about my intense magical dreams and visions. Mild surprise, amusement, and then resignation. Here we go again, another loser with no life.

"Noah? I'm interested. You need to open up to get any benefit from these sessions." My therapist, Doctor Tom Saunders, please, call me Tom, was about my age, in his mid-thirties, neat hair, tidy suit, red tie, with the top button of his white shirt undone to show he was professional but not uptight.

"You really want to know?" I said.

"It would be useful to both of us. It's good to talk about these things. It's why I'm here."

I shrugged. "The magic isn't infinite. If spells are cast or potions used, they drain the magic user. Magic has a cost. It's basic magical lore." I cringed. Total nerd geek comment.

Tom had the decency not to smirk, but it looked like a struggle. "Of course. We don't want witches and wizards casting their spells with abandon. What would us mere mortals do? Roll the dice and see if our number let us raise a shield spell?"

"It's not Dungeons and Dragons. Not role play. It exists." What I saw wasn't in my head. But if it wasn't a hallucination, where was it coming from, and why could no one else see it? "It would make more sense if I didn't know any of this was real. Imagine the panic if everyone knew magic existed, yet we didn't have it, so we couldn't keep ourselves safe?"

"Which suggests what to you?"

I clenched my teeth. "That magic isn't real?"

"Right." Tom's pen was poised over his pad, hoping something meaningful would come out of my mouth that he could scribble down and dissect. "Tell me more about the magical codes."

I tried to relax. I needed this outlet, or I'd stop functioning. And this was all confidential, so he couldn't joke about me to his wife or friends. Hopefully. "You need rules for any way of living. It would have to be illegal for people who had magic to use it on those who didn't."

"Why do you think that?"

"It's the same as armed police going into a crowd of peaceful protestors. They have an unfair advantage. They could control us with magic. Do what they liked to us."

"Is that something you're interested in? You want someone to have power over you and tell you what to do?"

My fingers flexed under my thighs. Tom was looking for the reason I had these delusions. He was doing his job, but these therapists were all the same. Rather than supporting my imagination and open-mindedness, they squashed it and looked for some deep psychological issue.

I didn't know if I agreed with past trauma making me believe in magic, but something was wrong with me. Otherwise, I wouldn't be here for the fourth time this month.

But just once, it would be amazing to talk to someone who was willing to consider the possibility magic existed, and living in a world where magic was real would be better than the world I lived in.

Silence stretched out for a minute before Tom adjusted his tie and clicked his pen. "How are you getting on with cutting back on your working hours?" He flicked through his notes. "Are you still working seventy-hour weeks?"

"My work isn't the problem. I love my job."

"Designing games for online platforms? Do the games involve magic?"

"It's what I'm known for. My boss, Gideon Masters, poached me because my Enchanted Forests of Avalon game was so popular. It was optioned around the world, and there's a spin-off series being made for TV."

"Congratulations. I've never played it."

"You'd enjoy it. But you need to believe in magic to get the most out of it. It's based on the legend of King Arthur. And there are dragons."

"Like you? Do you really believe in magic? Don't the laws of science make it impossible?"

"The best scientists are the ones working to disprove their own theories."

This earned me a smile. "Perhaps your belief that magic exists suggests there's something missing in your life."

"Such as?"

"You could be using this fantasy to give you a system to operate in. Almost like a belief system or a faith. The magic creates a skeleton to hang everything else on."

"Faith? You're asking me to believe in a higher being?"

"Or simply recognize you're part of something bigger. It doesn't have to be a god."

"It's not that. My games are important to me, and I enjoy my job, but these dreams I have are so intense. And the visions..." I shook my head. It was hard to describe what I'd seen and experienced. It was something other. Something not normal. Something magical.

"Have they changed? You mentioned seeing flashes of light and thought you were being watched, but there's never anyone there."

"It's the same, although they're getting more frequent."

"You've not added any medication or tried natural remedies? Some of the CBD drops they sell are strong. They alter perception if you take enough of them."

"Nothing like that. I've been trying the relaxation techniques you suggested and the meditation, but they make no difference."

"It can take a while. Give it another month. If that doesn't work, I'll suggest a prescription medication."

"I don't want pills to mask the symptoms. I need to know what this is."

"You want the visions and the feeling of being watched to disappear, don't you?"

"Sure. It's creepy thinking someone is following you. The weird light flashes and strange smells I can handle."

"Medication can help if this turns out to be a chemical imbalance. We have excellent on-site doctors who'll make a tailored recommendation. Therapy and the appropriate medication will change everything."

"Sounds great."

Tom smiled. "It's a sensible course of action. But with your intense work schedule, you must factor in time to relax. Overwork is a killer. In Japan, they call it karoshi. It translates into overwork death."

"I have no plans to die at my desk."

Tom tapped his pen on the pad resting on his knee. "If you cut back your hours to a more regular forty or fifty hours a week, your problems could go away. Why don't we focus on that?"

"And do what? My work is my life."

"Remember karoshi."

Maybe Tom thought he was being impressive with his Japanese knowledge, but I was losing patience.

"Will your work be there on your deathbed? Do you think it'll say goodbye and pat you on the head because you did such a good job?" Tom shook his head. "If you left your job for a few months, you wouldn't be missed. I hate to be harsh, but everyone is replaceable, no matter what incredible magical system you dream up."

"You've never played the Forests of Avalon." My games rocked the gaming community. I'd had three in the top ten charts for almost a year.

Tom set down his pen. "Your work has overtaken your life, and you're blurring reality with fantasy. It's not the first time I've seen cases like this. Guys get obsessed with a project, and that's all they think about. We get single-minded. All or nothing. It haunts us day and night."

"You get like this?"

"No, but I focus hard on having a solid balance in my life."

Of course, Tom hadn't gotten into therapy to sort out his own messed up head. Wasn't that why all people became shrinks? "What happens to the guys who don't get their Zen on and find balance?"

"They burn out. Some lose their edge or simply can't get out of bed. We're human beings with an operating system not meant for this twenty-four-hour culture and obsession with screen time. If we work too hard and put ourselves through too much stress for too long, something will break. Maybe not physically, but in here." He tapped the side of his head.

I didn't like to agree with Tom, but I could try harder. "I'll keep trying the meditation."

"Excellent. I'll also send you a link to some cognitive behavioral therapy. It's a proven method to change the way you think about things. It's been effective for all addictions."

"I don't have an addiction."

Tom tapped away on the tablet he'd picked up. "I'm going to disagree with you. You refuse to cut back on your working hours. You dream about something that doesn't exist, and you're having visual hallucinations. All signs you have work to do. Keep up with the meditation, do the cognitive behavioral therapy, and speak to your employer about reducing your hours. If they value you, they'll make it happen. Oh, and cut back on the caffeine." He looked at the empty takeout mug I'd brought in with me.

"I only have a few cups a day."

"Caffeine overstimulates the adrenals. Combine that with stress and long hours, and you could be in real trouble." He checked the time. "That's our hour up. I'll book you in for the same time next week."

"Sure. Thanks. See you then." It was an effort to pull myself out of the chair and walk into the reception area. No amount of talking would help, but I had to find something that would work. Maybe taking a few minutes to myself and clearing my head would help, but it wouldn't stop the visions.

I checked in at the reception desk with Maggie and pulled out my wallet. "What do I owe you?"

"Same as always. All fixed?" Her big smile lit up her dark eyes behind cat's eye glasses.

"Almost. I'll be back next week, though, just to make sure nothing has shaken loose and needs a repair."

"Perfect. I've already had your next appointment through from Doctor Saunders." Maggie pressed my card against the payment screen. "You had a late session. Is Mrs. Drake picking you up?"

"No, I'm walking home. It's near here."

"I'm sure she'll have made you a nice dinner. You can relax together." Maggie studied the card reader.

I rubbed the back of my neck. "There is no Mrs. Drake. I'll pick up takeout. There's a decent Thai place close by."

Maggie's eyes widened, and her fingers brushed mine as she passed me my card. "I don't like to think of you going home alone. Your girlfriend will be there, won't she?"

I stepped away from the desk, shoving my card into my wallet. "Nope."

Her tongue darted out. "This won't sound professional, but do you mind me asking if you're single?"

"I don't mind. And I am. Work keeps me busy." There was something else that kept me from dating, though. Or rather, someone else.

"Oh, I'm the same. Tom is a slave driver. I don't mind, though. I like this job. It's good to help people. I mean, not that you need help. You seem fine."

"I appreciate that, but I wouldn't be coming to therapy if I was fine."

Her cheeks flushed. "Of course. What I meant was we have all kinds of people who come for therapy. And I'm not breaking confidentiality by saying this, but some of them are messed up. They've been coming for years to get their heads right. Others simply need a few sessions to figure things out."

"You think I fit the last category?"

"I hope so. Because when you've finished your treatment, I'd love to take you for a coffee."

"Oh! Um... thanks. Tom told me I can't drink coffee."

She giggled. "Or tea, beer, water. Whatever you like. Dating patients isn't allowed, but once you're done, we could meet anytime. Do anything."

"That's sweet of you, Maggie, but I'm not dating right now. I'm... focusing on myself." It was a lame comment, but I really was making my health a priority.

Her mouth twisted to the side. "Take my number. When you feel ready, let's talk. No pressure."

Maggie was pretty and friendly, but she wasn't what I was looking for, and I didn't want to give her any false hope that I'd call. "You seem like a great lady, but I'm not the guy for you."

"Maybe you are. You just don't know it yet." She held her phone out.

"Do you like role play?"

"What are we talking? A French maid outfit?"

"No! Witches and wizards. Magic. Dragons. Tom believes I prefer fake worlds to real ones."

"Oh! That kind of role play." Her face went scarlet. "Board games?"

"Online games. I don't see you as the kind of girl who'd happily sit by my side for hours while I play Dungeons and Dragons or work on coding for the latest glitch in a game. That's what I do all day, every day. It makes me happy."

"You must go out to eat. Or we could go for a drink. Anything you like. It could get your mind back in the real world."

I arched an eyebrow. "You haven't been reading my file, have you?"

"No! I'd never do that. I'd lose my job. But the way you talk, it made me wonder if you need more fun in your life."

"I have fun. I sometimes even play laser quest."

Her smile faltered, and she lowered her phone. "You know where I am if you change your mind."

"I'm flattered, Maggie. Thanks again, but now's a bad time for me." I dashed out of the office.

Maggie would probably make the perfect girlfriend. She was cute, had a good job, and didn't seem complicated. But there was only one woman I wanted, and she lived in my fantasies. I saw her in my dreams all the time. She smelled like rain and sometimes garlic bread. I couldn't get her out of my thoughts, and the option of dating anyone else wasn't there. I'd met no one in real life who came close to her. Unfortunately, until I did, dating was out of the question.

I welcomed the cool evening air as I stepped outside. It had just gone nine in the evening. Tom usually shut at eight, but this was the only time I could get off work, and I'd paid double for the session, so he could hardly complain.

Tom thought I was just another loser nerd, obsessed with games and nothing else. And maybe that was a problem for some but not me. I got his point about working too hard, though. What else did I have? No wife, no girlfriend, or any family left. Not even a cat. All my friendships were online.

And the gaming community was amazing. No one mocked me when I talked about magic systems or fighting evil with spells and potions. They encouraged me. My tribe of questing geeks welcomed me in.

I didn't have a family waiting for me at home, but when I opened my computer and logged on, I had my perfect found family there. A band of messy, too smart for their own good misfits, who made their own world, one we fit in so much better than this cold, clinical reality.

While I waited at the lights until it was safe to cross the road, my phone buzzed with an incoming message. I pulled it out.

New game starts in thirty minutes. You in?

It was Lord Storm Thrower, a regular gaming buddy. He was loud, obnoxious, and his avatar had an eight-pack and glowing green eyes.

I'll be there. What's the mission?

Usual dark witch scum wanting to take over and destroy the world. Exclusive game, only four of us. Don't be late.

See you soon. I signed off with the initials FF. We all had gaming names, and I'd picked Fire Fang. My avatar was a seven-foot half-man, half-werewolf with huge teeth. I breathed fire and growled so loud the ground shook.

It was a better look than my human form. I worked out and didn't slob out too much on the junk food, but how amazing would it be to breathe actual fire and make the ground tremble under my paws?

I strode across the road. The real world could suck it. There was somewhere else and someone else I much preferred to be.